# The Grasmere Grudge

LA

D1148636

# *The Grasmere Grudge*

## REBECCA TOPE

The paper used for this Allison & Busby publication
has been produced from trees that have been legally sourced
from well-managed and credibly certified forests.

Printed and bound by
CPI Group (UK) Ltd, Croydon, CR0 4YY

Allison & Busby Limited
11 Wardour Mews
London W1F 8AN
*allisonandbusby.com*

First published in Great Britain by Allison & Busby in 2019.
This paperback edition published by Allison & Busby in 2020.

Copyright © 2019 by Rebecca Tope

The moral right of the author is hereby asserted in accordance with
the Copyright, Designs and Patents Act 1988.

*All characters and events in this publication,*
*other than those clearly in the public domain,*
*are fictitious and any resemblance to actual persons,*
*living or dead, is purely coincidental.*

All rights reserved. No part of this publication may be reproduced,
stored in a retrieval system, or transmitted, in any form or by
any means without the prior written permission of the publisher,
nor be otherwise circulated in any form of binding or cover
other than that in which it is published and without a similar
condition being imposed on the subsequent buyer.

A CIP catalogue record for this book is available from
the British Library.

10 9 8 7 6 5 4 3 2 1

ISBN 978-0-7490-2440-6

Typeset in 10.5/15.5 pt Sabon LT Pro by
Allison & Busby Ltd

has                                                              ced

| LANCASHIRE COUNTY LIBRARY | |
|---|---|
| 3011813998636  2 | |
| **Askews & Holts** | 03-Jun-2020 |
| AF   AFC | £8.99 |
| CLE | |

*For Caitlin*
*and with thanks to Jennifer Margrave*
*for help with the legal stuff*

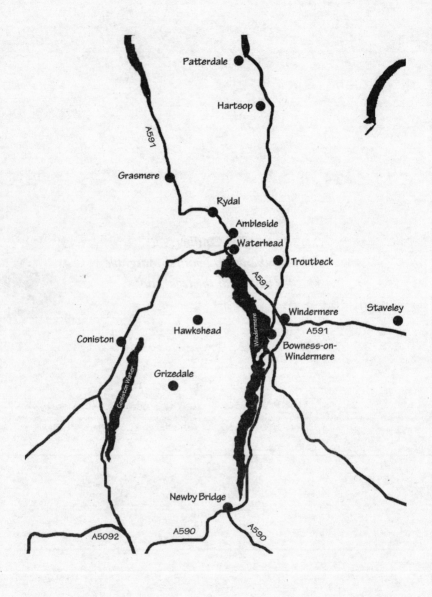

# *Author's Note*

As with all the other titles in this series, the story is set in real places. However, I have slightly expanded Banerigg, and invented a medical facility in Kendal. Also, the auction house in Keswick is entirely imaginary.

# Chapter One

Not even the late arrival at Manchester airport, or the screaming toddler in the next row on the plane, or the pouring rain when they got outside could sully the euphoric mood. Simmy and Christopher had just experienced the best week of their lives in the sunny Canary Islands, and nothing could dampen their spirits.

'And we still have all day tomorrow,' sighed Simmy, when they were in the car. 'Isn't that wonderful!'

'Just make sure I don't fall asleep between here and Troutbeck. It's been a long day. It'll be two in the morning before we get there.'

'I could sing to you,' she suggested.

'Maybe not. Lord – look at that rain! In June! The farmers will be in despair.'

'Aren't they always?' she laughed.

They fell into Simmy's bed in the small hours of Sunday morning, and didn't wake until half past nine. Outside, it was cloudy but dry. Christopher's car was parked crookedly in the road just past Simmy's cottage, there being no space for both his and hers inside the gate. Troutbeck had not evolved with vehicular traffic in mind. Large delivery trucks or lorries transporting animals had to inch between parked cars and stone walls. Drivers unfamiliar with the place were liable to find their wing mirrors cracked and their tempers frayed if they did not quickly adapt.

'Must have rained all week,' said Christopher, looking out of the bedroom window. 'There's mud everywhere.'

'What a ridiculous place to live. Can we emigrate, do you think?'

'Nowhere's perfect,' he told her. 'Although I always think Tangier is close. It's got a lot going for it.'

'Yes, you said.' After a partnership of six months or so, they had reached the point of repetition. Simmy didn't mind that, but now and then she pointed it out.

'Sorry. I know I'm a boring old fart.'

'You are,' she said happily.

'And you love me for it.'

'Fool that I am.'

'And if I'm old, then so are you, remember.' They had been born on the same day, their mothers bonded in the maternity ward; a fact that created a sense, at times, that they were more siblings than lovers.

She rolled out of bed and joined him at the window. 'Bit different from the mountains of Lanzarote,' she said.

'Still mountains, though. Sort of.'

Wansfell rose before their gaze, its detail blurred in the unseasonably poor light. 'Not a flicker of sunshine,' he complained. 'It's a disgrace.'

'Don't take it personally. It'll make it easier to go back to work tomorrow if the weather's bad.'

'Don't mention work,' he groaned, with exaggerated drama.

'We should tell people we're back.' Simmy had parents and Chris had siblings – none of whom would be particularly anxious for news of them. 'And check for messages.' They'd agreed to leave their phones behind for the duration of the holiday, as a boldly unconventional move that would horrify most people they knew. A holiday meant leaving everything behind, Christopher had insisted. He had roamed the world in his twenties, never telling anybody where he was going, and the habit had stuck.

But it had been harder for Simmy. 'What if my father has another stroke?' she'd worried. 'Or the shop burns down? Or my house is burgled?'

'It'll have to wait until you're back,' he replied. 'It's only a week, after all. I used to drop out for *months*.'

'Those were the good old days.' It seemed almost criminal to simply disappear in this brave new world of the twenty-first century.

When they finally checked their phones, Simmy had

no meaningful messages at all, but Chris had several. 'Grasmere again,' he sighed.

'What?'

'That house clearance I told you about. There are complications, evidently. I *knew* there would be. There's been too many people involved, right from the start.'

'Do they need you to do anything?'

'They did, three days ago. With any luck, they've sorted it without me by now.'

Simmy found the whole subject of house clearances profoundly appealing, as well as somewhat melancholy. It seemed there was a burgeoning number of them, as old people – almost always women – died in their nineties, leaving good-sized houses stuffed to the rafters with treasures. Their space-limited descendants closed their eyes, held their noses and called for the professionals to dispose of it all as best they might. Much of the treasure found its way to Christopher Henderson's auction house. 'Not so much treasure as junk,' he'd said more than once.

But now and then there would be something worth fighting over, and the descendants belatedly realised their mistake. The scope for conflict was considerable when a rare Japanese brush pot emerged from the depths of a forgotten cupboard and earned hundreds of pounds for the house clearance men, because nobody in the family had spotted it. For this reason, many clearance specialists travelled to other regions of the country with their well-filled vans, to use salerooms far from the original house. That way, the descendants would never know how much Mum's old rubbish sold for. They might already have taken the grandfather clock and Victorian oil painting that they believed to be the most valued objects in the house. 'Most people are always about ten years out of date when it comes to what's making money,' said Christopher.

But the Grasmere house contents were due to be sold nearby in Keswick, because there were no descendants to cause trouble. An old lady had died, and her friend, left to deal with the aftermath, was a frail old man known to Christopher. 'Leave it to me,' the auctioneer had said. 'Where should the proceeds go? Did she leave a will?'

'Sadly not,' the old man had replied. 'Just a little note to say I was the main person to contact if anything happened. She didn't think she was ever going to die. She was very keen on dogs. There's a local charity she supported. Maybe they should have some of it. In fact, I believe she already donated a few items to them.'

'Poor old Philip,' Christopher had sighed. 'He really doesn't want to be bothered with all this business.'

'Won't there be horrendous legal complications without a will?' asked Simmy, when she heard the story.

'Probably,' said Chris.

He had gone off on holiday, hoping his friend Jonathan could see to everything. The old lady – Kathleen Leeson by name – had died about a year ago, her house untouched since then. Everyone agreed it couldn't stay like that, but there were legal issues that lumbered slowly into action, forcing everyone concerned to wait for the deliberations to be completed. Christopher had elaborated bit by bit during the holiday. 'And on top of all that the old dear wasn't at all keen on Jon. He visited her a time or two, trying to get her to part with a few things, and she took against him.'

'Tricky,' Simmy agreed.

'I expect it'll be okay in the end. Jon really is the most obvious chap for the job. But I'm not sure how the neighbours are going to feel, if they see him loading it all into his van. It's no secret she'd gone off him.'

Simmy's phone suddenly pinged in her hand. 'Oh – it's Ben,' she announced. 'He says "Welcome home. Exams all finished. Driving test tomorrow afternoon." He'll pass, of course.'

'Sheldon didn't,' said Christopher, shaking his head. 'Don't count your chickens.'

Christopher's admiration for *The Big Bang Theory* had at first amused and then irritated Simmy. He would quote from it constantly, focusing particularly on Sheldon. 'That's so *old*,' moaned Bonnie, Simmy's young assistant. 'It must have started when I was about seven.'

'He'll tire of it eventually,' said Simmy. 'He thinks it helps him to understand Ben, because he's so like Sheldon.'

'Except he isn't,' argued Bonnie, who was Ben's beloved. 'He's *totally* nothing like him.'

Simmy had watched enough episodes to judge for herself, in the end. Ben himself favoured the even more superseded series *Bones*, seeing himself as the boy assistant in the forensic laboratory, more than any other TV character. 'None of them are much like real people,' Simmy concluded.

Now she said, 'Ben's not Sheldon, Chris. I keep telling you that.'

'Yeah, well, I've hardly seen him, have I? All I've got to go on is what you've told me.'

'He's free now for the next three months. His dad's quite likely to get him a car. If you're not careful, he'll be bothering you up in Keswick every five minutes, asking you how an auction house works. He'll probably drive you mad,' she finished cheerfully.

'How do auctions link to forensic whatever-it-is that he's doing?'

'I hope it doesn't,' she said with feeling. 'He's just interested. That might be because I've talked about it so much lately. I've whetted his appetite.'

'He'll be bothering you in the flower shop even more with his girlfriend there all day,' Christopher countered. 'Are you going to phone your mum, then?'

The change of subject was the result of their lazy mood, aimlessly taking biscuits to nibble and leaving half-finished mugs of coffee to go cold. Conversation was desultory, neither of them putting much thought into what they were saying. Picking up the threads of normal life was still not urgent. Midday came and went, and still they were half-asleep.

'We should find something to eat,' said Simmy, with very little conviction.

Chris wrinkled his nose. 'Sunday roast in the pub doesn't really appeal,' he said. 'I'm actually not very hungry, anyway.'

'We will be, though. I suppose we could go to Ambleside or somewhere and buy something.'

'Food is such a bore. Haven't you got any baked beans? Eggs? Frozen pizza?'

'All of the above. Sounds a bit depressing, though.' She thought of the exotic meals they'd enjoyed on holiday. Fish done Italian-style. Spanish tapas eaten on the pavement in a tiny village. Salads thrown together at a moment's notice. Everything enhanced by the sunshine and the sense of liberation.

'England *is* depressing. Surely you knew that?'

'No, it's not. Or only when you compare it to somewhere with a better climate. We both love it, most of the time. After all – you came back, didn't you? You saw the world and came right back to where your whole family lives. You *must* love it. Your actions prove it.'

'I took one look at Coniston Water and that was it,' he mocked. 'Trapped for life. Except for when I was nineteen and desperate to get away. I came back because I couldn't afford anywhere else. I was over thirty by then and didn't have a pound coin to my name. Sophie made sure of that.'

'Okay.' Simmy had no great objection to mentions of Christopher's ex-wife, but she had no intention of encouraging a revisit to his marriage. 'Let me rephrase it, then. We both arrived here after we'd failed up to that point. We started again, and so far it's working out pretty well.'

'You're talking about the Lakes, not England. If I have to be an Englishman, I choose Cumbria as the best place to be it in.'

'Good,' she said.

Then she phoned her parents, calculating that they would have finished their midday meal – which was unlikely to be a Sunday roast. They ran a busy bed and breakfast in Windermere, which Simmy feared was making them old before their time. Angie Straw spent her days changing bedding, keeping the dining room clean, buying ingredients in bulk and controlling the diary. Russell, her husband, was of minimal help since the onset of an ill-diagnosed mental condition, which had been exacerbated by a 'TIA' – what most people called a 'mini-stroke'. He required little actual care from his wife, but he had become more of a hindrance to her than the help he had been initially.

'Was it nice?' asked Angie.

'Lovely. Wall-to-wall sunshine. Bit of a shock coming home to all this cloud.'

'Must be. It rained for four days in a row. There's mud everywhere.'

'So I see.'

'You haven't seen my rumpus room. There's been an Old English sheepdog in there, shaking itself dry all over the jigsaws.'

'Do you want me to come over after work tomorrow? Or should I leave it till Wednesday, as usual?'

'Entirely up to you. It's busy here whenever you come.'

'How's Dad?'

'Same as usual. He's been swotting up on the Canary Islands, so he'll be wanting to talk to you about it. And he thinks you're taking him to the auction next weekend. Is that right?'

Simmy hesitated. 'I'll have to be in the shop until two. It's probably not worth going after that. When did I say we could go to Keswick?'

'Don't ask me. He seems pretty sure about it, though. You'll have to let him down gently.'

'I'll come tomorrow, then,' she decided. 'And sort it out.'

'Good. Nice to have you home again.'

'I'm not sure it's nice to be back,' Simmy laughed. 'We could easily have stayed there all summer.'

'You'd get bored,' said Angie, and finished the call without another word.

Christopher was in the living room, thumbing his own phone, when she went to find him. 'Weather all set to improve from tomorrow,' he reported.

'Good news for the farmers. My mother sounds exhausted. I'm going there after work tomorrow. My dad thinks I'm taking him to your auction on Saturday. I don't see how I can. There'll be loads of catching-up to do at the shop.'

'You remember we were supposed to be going to the evening sale near Kirkby Lonsdale, do you? It starts at five on Thursday. You said you might come with me, if you can close the shop a bit early. It's a small two-man enterprise in a village hall. I want to see how they've set it up. It's all quite new.'

'I had completely forgotten about it,' she admitted. 'It does sound like fun, but I'm not sure I ought to take the time off. What time would we have to leave Windermere?'

'Three-thirty or thereabouts. We should try to get there by half past four, to have a look at what they're selling. Bonnie can handle things at the shop for a couple of hours, surely?'

Simmy's head was buzzing. It was unusual for Chris to

18

try to organise her in such a way. He'd gone on playing with his phone as he spoke, and now he showed her what he'd found. 'Here it is, look,' he said.

She read the few lines of information, which said hardly anything more than he had already told her. Sellers should deliver their items by midday and take away anything unsold by ten the next morning. Buyers, likewise, should remove their purchases immediately. Fifteen per cent commission. 'I'll think about it,' she said, with scant enthusiasm.

'Ben could go as well,' he added, which surprised her even more.

There followed five minutes of easy silence, as Chris slumped comfortably into the sofa cushions, and Simmy opened the modest pile of junk mail that had arrived during her absence. She took it out to the recycling bin by her gate, pausing to scan the sky for signs of improvement. Troutbeck was quiet. A scattering of walkers was visible on the slopes of Wansfell and sheep were bleating not far away. From where she stood, she could see into two gardens up the road, both vibrant with colour. Her own little patch at the front needed weeding. She had been experimenting with sweet peas, and their supporting bamboo poles looked somewhat askew. Wind, she supposed, along with the rain of the previous week.

She drifted back indoors, thinking she really should try to produce a meal of some sort. It was well past lunchtime, and they'd had nothing substantial since the previous day. Scrambled eggs and baked beans were about as good as it was going to get, she thought regretfully. The village shop would have closed for the day, so there was no chance of buying milk or bread. What a *bore* it was, she thought irritably, echoing Christopher.

He had got off the sofa and was standing in the little hallway. He didn't move out of her way as she went in. Instead, he reached out and took her right hand. She frowned, wondering what in the world was going on.

'Simmy . . . Persimmon . . . will you marry me?' he asked.

# Chapter Two

Her first thought was that he was tempting fate. The second was that his timing was always going to be reliably bad. Why couldn't he have done this on a foreign beach, as the sun was setting? The third was not so much a thought as a surge of euphoria.

'I will,' she said firmly, suppressing an urge to add, *Although* . . . followed by a string of reservations.

'Good.' He pulled her into a long warm kiss, which she cut short in order to look into his face. His grey eyes were unclouded, shining with high spirits. His skin seemed to glow, and his mouth was still soft and loose from the kiss. He was glorious to look at.

She felt young – sixteen, to be precise. The years of separation melted away, and here was that tanned Christopher from the Prestatyn beach. Her closest friend, summer after summer, with his four younger siblings providing her with all the experience of a big family she would ever have. They had kissed obsessively that last summer, wanting and needing to take things further, but oddly unable to manage it. Lack of privacy and, perhaps, lack of courage both worked against them. Their parents had become aware of the danger, and there had been no more joint summer holidays after that. She saw Chris three or four more times, writing letters and phoning in a decreasing frequency until life got in the way and they almost forgot each other.

Now the wheel had turned, and here they were again. And he wanted to marry her. They were close to forty, with turbulent events in their respective pasts. His parents were dead, but his siblings remained at close quarters. He and Simmy lived twenty miles apart, each with commitments that would be almost impossible to shed. There was no avoiding the practicalities, she realised. Her unspoken *Although* . . . could not be dodged for long.

'But . . . *how*?' she breathed, hating herself for being the one to raise the question.

'We'll find a way. Don't go all unromantic on me,' he begged. 'Not for another few minutes, anyway.'

Romantic? Sweet scents, soft light, moody background music? None of that fitted how she felt. Her momentary lapse into her sixteen-year-old self was already over. Her

22

mind was full of images of her shop, Bonnie, her parents and this much-prized little Troutbeck house. All that would have to be downgraded, if not entirely discarded if – when – she married Chris. 'Sorry,' she said.

'What do you mean, sorry? You're not retracting already, are you?' He hugged her close again. 'I mean it, Sim. It's really going to happen. Once that's settled, everything else'll just fall into place around it. You'll see.'

'Yes,' she said. 'But what about . . . ? I mean, shouldn't we just wait to see . . . ?' Again she shivered at the sense of tempting fate. 'We could just give it a few more months.'

He drew back slightly. 'Oh, I see. What a twit I am. You mean the baby.'

She shivered again at the starkness of the word. 'There *isn't* a baby. That's the whole point. There might never be a baby. Are we sure we can cope with that?' She had watched one husband break down at the non-appearance of his expected child. There was terror in the prospect of that happening again.

'That sounds as if you want a baby more than you want me.' His frown was only very slight, but his eyes were less clear than before.

'Oh!' She hadn't ever thought in those terms. Her worries had all been about him and how he might deal with childlessness. It was astonishingly difficult to examine her own innermost wishes – like turning a massive container ship around and sending it off in the opposite direction. She knew she *did* want a baby. She knew she needed a man as a result of this great desire. It had never crossed her mind to deliberately enter into single parenthood via some sort

23

of fertility clinic that would manufacture a child for her at a price. Neither had she contemplated adopting a child. She knew with an equal certainty that she had a definite fondness for Christopher – but was that fondness born of his apparent willingness to share the parenting with her, and nothing more than that?

It hurt to follow this logic. A real pain took root inside her, born of fear and self-dislike and the extreme difficulty of facing the unvarnished truth.

'I don't know,' she said wretchedly. 'What a horrible person I must be, if that's true.'

'Don't be ridiculous. I'm not accusing you of anything. I was just hoping we could get to the heart of it and see what we might do about it. We're not sixteen any more, Simmy. It's no use pretending we are.'

'I was, though, for a minute.'

'So was I. So were we both all last week. Sunshine, chips, the incoming waves. But we're back on solid ground now, and I want you to marry me. *I* want a baby – or two – almost as much as you do. I want a proper house and a few of the ordinary things that other people want.'

'Only a few?'

'I can do without the garden shed and the designer kitchen. And I'm never going to keep anything tidy. And I'm never going to have as much money as I really want, because I'm incapable of putting in the right sort of effort.'

'Especially not with two children. You'll be expected to change nappies and take them for long walks and be home at six o'clock every evening without fail.'

He tilted his head in a warning look. 'And what if they never happen? What if it's just you and me?'

It was the vital question, taking her back to the core of things. Before she could answer, his phone rang, loud in the painful silence.

To his credit, he made no move to take the call. But the relief they both felt at the timely interruption could not be concealed. 'Answer it,' she said. 'We need a breather.'

'Don't we just,' he laughed. 'Did I forget to mention that I really, really love you?' The insistent device only partly obscured the feeling that these words came wrapped in. 'It's Jonathan,' he reported, having glanced at the screen.

She flipped a hand at him and moved a few steps away.

'Hi, Jon,' he said. 'Something up?'

The one-sided conversation that Simmy could hear gave rise to a wholesale change of mood. Chris was obviously concerned, making his friend repeat himself and asking abrupt questions. Finally, he finished the call and looked at Simmy, his face no longer soft and adoring. 'He's got himself into a right bit of bother,' he said.

Simmy had met Jonathan once, and recognised this as a direct quote. 'So I gathered,' she said. 'But I didn't hear you promise to dash up there and rescue him.'

Christopher did not smile. 'Nothing I can do, as far as either of us can work out. The best thing would be for him to keep his head down and let it all blow over.'

'What, though? What's his problem?'

'It's a long story. And I suddenly feel desperately hungry.' He looked at his phone. 'Not surprising, actually. Do you know what time it is?'

She gave it a moment's reflection. 'Two, or a bit after?'

'It's three-twenty-five. And we haven't eaten more than a couple of biscuits all day.'

'What a weird day! I can do eggs and beans, or I suppose we could go down to Bowness and find something. It's summer – there'll be ice cream or cream teas, or even fish and chips, if we're lucky.'

'I don't want to go anywhere. Just a tin of baked beans is all I ask. There doesn't even have to be any toast.'

With a concerted effort, Simmy found a frozen loaf and a long-forgotten tin of spaghetti hoops to go with scrambled eggs in a meal that would have horrified both their mothers. Within ten minutes, they were eating these remnants of a once well-stocked cupboard as if they were dining at the Belsfield in Bowness – which they had done once or twice over the past half-year. 'I should go shopping one day this week and get something more interesting than this for emergencies,' she said. 'I never was very good at catering.'

'Nobody is any more,' he consoled her. Then his eyes went misty and he added, 'Not like in Mexico, where they can produce a fabulous feast in seconds. Guacamole, beans, ribs. Incredible bread. I never ate so well as I did in Mexico. Not to mention the drink, of course.'

'I might not let you go travelling when we're married,' she said thoughtfully. 'Is that going to upset you?'

'Can't afford it, anyway. I'm too old for all that rough sleeping or bunking up in hostels with smelly Americans.'

'Pardon?'

'They stink of synthetic chemicals. Antiperspirant

26

mostly. And the stuff they wash their clothes in. And extra spray for no reason. And something vile to repel insects. They're like walking pharmacies. Makes me retch to think of it. Give me good old-fashioned sweat any day.'

'My mother would agree with you,' laughed Simmy.

They finished their meal and Simmy went upstairs to unpack her holiday bag. 'Are you staying tonight as well?' she asked him, from the top of the stairs.

'I want to, but that would make tomorrow a real beast – unless I left here at about six.'

'It wouldn't be the first time.'

'True. I'm just trying to be grown-up and sensible. Of course I'll stay. If you'll have me, that is.'

'It'll be a come-down after that fabulous big bed.'

Simmy's bed was a large single, which meant that two people sharing had to remain in close contact all night. She had done her best to get used to it, but it did no favours to the quality of her sleep. 'I should have got a bigger one months ago,' she reproached herself.

'We'll get ourselves a luxury king-size for our new house,' he promised.

'What new house?' She was in the bedroom, calling down the stairs to him, missing some of his words. It was something they did a lot, and she could always hear her mother shouting, 'Come downstairs if you want to talk to me,' as she had done throughout Simmy's childhood.

Now Christopher said almost the same thing. 'I'm not having this conversation until you come down again.'

She was at his side two minutes later. 'What new house?' she repeated.

27

'Well, we can't live here, and we can't live in my little hovel, so we'll have to get somewhere new. Stands to reason.'

It should have been exciting, full of future promise and a whole new beginning. Instead she could only think of money, and her shop and how she would spend her days if she no longer had Persimmon Petals to fill her time. 'Where?' she breathed.

'The logical thing would be halfway between here and Keswick. That's Grasmere, if you look at a map. In fact, there's nowhere else *but* Grasmere that would work. We'd both be about thirty minutes from our places of work. It'd be perfect.'

'We can't afford Grasmere. And, besides, there are hardly any ordinary houses. They're all holiday lets or tea rooms.'

'Who says? What about all those lovely stone cottages clustered around Dove Cottage, for a start?'

'Won't they be a bit pokey, as well as expensive? And there'd be hordes of trippers coming and going all year round.'

'There's a few other side streets with some nice properties. Kathleen Leeson had one of them, I think.'

'Have you ever been to her house?'

He hesitated. 'No, but I know where it is. Are you thinking it might suit us? It'll probably go on the market any time now.'

'I wasn't thinking that, actually. I was just wondering about all the dusty treasures there might be there.'

'Always less exciting than you think. Now – stick to the subject. We want to find somewhere to live, remember. There's a lot of building going on across the road from the main village in Grasmere. Honestly, Sim, I think you should keep an open mind, don't you?'

She shrugged, unable to cite evidence for her pessimism about property prices, and unwilling to drop the subject of forgotten antiques in locked-up houses. 'So, tell me about Jonathan,' she invited. 'What's his problem?'

# Chapter Three

'Mainly, it's the way he makes enemies,' Christopher began.
'He says what he thinks and never lets anybody get away
with anything. But he's got a weird sense of fair play. It
makes people nervous.'

'I think I get it. I quite like the sound of that, actually.
But what's the matter *now*? Why did he phone you? You
were talking to him for quite a while.'

'He wanted me to back him up in a row he's having
with a bloke called Nick. And I'm not sure I should,
even though you could say Jon's officially got right on
his side. Nick's an old-school wheeler-dealer. The sort we

auctioneers love to hate. Turns up in a massive van, and bids for all the job lots – big boxes of junk, with a bit of treasure tucked at the bottom. Then sells it at about a thousand per cent profit. All cash, hardly any paper trails. And he's incredibly clever at it. Jonathan worked with him for a bit and learnt some of his tricks, but they fell out, and it's been war ever since.'

'Nasty,' sighed Simmy, trying to picture it all.

'It happens. It's all a big game, with rules, when you boil it down. But Jon has a way of making his own rules. And now someone's dobbed Nick in to the taxman, and he's convinced it was Jon.'

'And was it?'

'He says not, but it's the sort of thing he might do, on a whim. You can go online anonymously and just give a name and address and leave it to them. Treacherous thing to do. But Nick gets away with so much, it makes a lot of people mad.'

'Does Nick pay *any* tax?'

'I doubt it. I never asked him.'

'Does Jonathan?'

'He does. That's the whole point. He's insanely meticulous with the paperwork, which is odd, I suppose. Registered himself for VAT, which the girls in the office curse him for every time we sell anything for him.'

'I see what you mean about rules,' Simmy commented. 'He sounds a bit obsessive about them.'

'He is a bit, yes. But he doesn't always understand the unspoken ones that have to do with people and how they interact. He's no good at that stuff.'

'On the spectrum,' said Simmy. 'Like most British men, according to my mother.'

'Whatever. Anyway, Jon wants me to talk to Nick, and persuade him that nobody gave him away and it's just a random check. After all, the tax people are obviously interested in our line of business. Everyone uses cash and, even if they've got a docket for their total sales, they'll be doing little deals in the car park without even thinking about it.'

'They'll probably ask you about Nick anyway, then.'

'They probably will,' he agreed. 'And I've got no problem in sticking up for Jon, if Nick plays rough. He's a good bloke, under his grubby exterior. They both are, basically, but Nick can take care of himself. I'm not so sure about Jon.'

'You should be careful,' she said, without thinking.

'What do you mean?'

'Oh – I don't know. I must be channelling my father. It just sounds rather fraught. I mean, Jonathan must be quite worried to phone you on a Sunday afternoon about it. He'd already texted you, hadn't he?'

'That was about something different.' He sighed. 'Which still isn't finally sorted, but it's not going to be long now. He wants me to put pressure on the legal people. I told him that's a long way beyond my pay grade, but he still wants to see me about it all, sometime this week.'

'You're talking about the house clearance in Grasmere?'

'Right. The people who take charge of this sort of thing have kept it all sealed up until somebody got around to ticking all the boxes. Poor old Philip thinks he'll be dead before it's all finished.' He wiped a hand across his brow in a parody of exhaustion. 'It's all too much. I need you to rescue me from it all. Oh – silly me. That's what you've just done, isn't it? A week on a faraway island was supposed to recharge my batteries. Now they're already running down again.'

Simmy laughed. 'All these men in your life! You make it sound so exciting and important. I don't understand a fraction of it. How does it all get decided, for a start?'

'You don't want to know. There's a cruel and unnecessary punishment for people who let their old folks die without making a will. Except the big guns are only brought in when there are no relations, and the friends can't prove their honesty.'

'Seems fair enough to me.'

'It's very fair. But incredibly long-winded. I do my best not to get involved in any of that stuff, but it catches up with me from time to time.'

She knew they were deliberately prolonging this conversation, for fear of having to face difficult personal questions. Or one particular personal question, which was still hanging in the air. It had occurred to her before that absolute frankness in a relationship might sound desirable, but it failed to recognise that most people had a very shaky grasp of their own inner workings. Try as they might, they couldn't capture all the nuances and contradictions that governed their emotions. She had discovered that something that felt true one day might change overnight into something much less dependable. If you put that thing into words on a Monday, you might well be in trouble if it came back to bite you on Tuesday, when your feelings had altered. Safer, then, not to say much in the first place.

But Christopher had other ideas. Having made his proposal and had it accepted, he was eager to take things to the next stage. 'We don't want a big production of a wedding, do we? Do you think September's too soon? What's this house of yours worth?' Before she could say much, he was looking at property websites. 'Hardly anything for sale in Grasmere at the moment. But I don't think it's any more expensive than here.'

'Chris, you're going too fast.' She looked round at her pleasant living room, with favourite pieces of furniture from her home with Tony in Worcestershire. Moving up to the Lake District had been traumatic and exhausting. Another move was not entirely appealing.

'Why? What is there to wait for?' He was genuinely confused. 'Have I missed something?'

'Not really. It's just me. I'm a moral coward. You're making it all sound easy and obvious. And I suppose it is – I just need to get it all clear in my mind. The shop . . .'

'What about the shop? Nothing needs to change where that's concerned.'

And so they went on, with Christopher making strenuous efforts to be patient and understanding in the face of her worries. She could see he wanted reassurance that she really did love him, really wanted to marry him and live with him. And she really did – in theory. But his earlier question – would she love him enough, if there was just him and no baby? – remained unanswered. She needed someone uninvolved to talk it over with, space away from Chris to carefully analyse the answer. And he lacked the patience to let her have that. Eventually, he brought himself back to this core issue.

'I want a baby as well,' he insisted. 'And I get that it's less urgent for me. I've got twenty years to play with – although I don't much fancy changing nappies when I'm sixty. But – God, Sim – here I am, offering you the best chance you're ever going to get of achieving your dearest wish, and you're putting up objections.'

She smiled helplessly. 'I told you – I'm a coward. And a bit of a pessimist at heart. You're right. I'm fantastically lucky to have you. They're not objections, anyway. Just reservations. Maybe not even that. I am going to marry you, okay? I just want you to be clear as to what you're getting.'

He puffed out his cheeks. 'Cliché, my love. That line's from a film, if I'm not mistaken. I know exactly what I'll be getting. I can give you a list of your qualities, and why I love you, if that'll help.'

She laughed. 'No, don't do that. It'd be embarrassing.'

At seven they walked to the nearby village pub and drank beer with sandwiches. At nine, they remembered how short the previous night had been and took themselves to Simmy's narrow bed. 'The holiday officially ends now,' said Chris sleepily. 'Tomorrow is the first day of the rest of our lives.'

'And that's a cliché, if ever there was one,' said Simmy.

\* \* \*

Monday arrived in a flash, birds singing outside at four-thirty, and the sun making itself felt an hour later. 'I'll make you a cup of tea,' said Simmy, without moving.

'No, you won't. We're not starting that game.'

'But I'm your fiancée now. I exist to serve.'

'Shut up, woman. I can recognise a trap when I see one.'

'Good luck with everything, then,' she said. 'Give us a kiss and I'll see you next weekend.'

He moaned. 'We can't go on like this. You know we can't. It's cruel. And don't say we can do FaceTime or whatever it is now. The very idea freaks me out.'

'And me. We could meet halfway one evening for a meal. Or something. I'll phone you after work. Or more likely after I've been to Beck View.'

'Great! We could have a look at properties in Grasmere.'

'Go, Chris. It was a lovely holiday. Really lovely. And it's sunny out there, look. Just like Lanzarote.'

'Bye, then,' he said, and went heavily down the stairs, like a banished schoolboy. It bothered Simmy slightly that she couldn't be sure whether or not he was play-acting.

She was at her Windermere shop twenty minutes earlier than necessary, having been unable to get back to sleep after Chris's departure. It was a forlorn scene with all the cut flowers missing from their usual buckets and pots. She and Bonnie had cleared them all away before closing up for a week. The pot plants looked lonely and neglected, even though Bonnie had been in twice to water them while Simmy was away. The table she used as a counter was bare, because the computer had been removed and all the scattered paperwork tidied up and dealt with.

That at least could be quickly rectified, and she extracted the laptop from the bag on her shoulder and set it up in its rightful place. If everything went according to plan, there would be a large delivery of summer blooms at any moment. June was a time for scent and colour, but ironically these were so freely available in the countless lovely Cumbrian gardens that fewer people felt moved to come to a florist and buy them. The embellishment of house interiors was lower priority when life was mostly conducted outdoors for the few brief months of summer. The business survived mainly on orders for deliveries of flowers for special occasions in this season of the year.

The computer needed close attention. The message that no deliveries could be made for the week she'd been away had to be deleted, for a start. Emails had to be carefully sifted and the point made on various sites that Persimmon Petals was fully operational and eager for custom. She was still working on all this when the doorbell pinged, and Bonnie Lawson came in.

'Hiya!' she chirruped. 'Hard at it already, then? Gosh, you've got a fabulous tan! Was it amazing? Did you get back on time? Are the pot plants okay?' The questions poured out, giving no opportunity for reply.

Simmy looked up at her assistant with a smile. The girl was wearing a thin cotton top and cut-off trousers. Her hair was as wild and fair as ever, forming a silvery halo around her face. Her skin showed no sign whatsoever of having been exposed to sunshine. 'Everything's fine,' Simmy said. 'Did you have a good week?'

'Ben had his last exam on Friday. We were out *all day* on Saturday. First, we did a boat trip on Windermere, then we went over to Hawkshead on the ferry with the bikes. It rained a bit, though.' She sighed. 'It rained nearly every day you were away.'

'So I gathered from my mother and the mud on the roads. Chris and I timed it well.'

'Was it amazing?' Bonnie asked again.

'There's a volcano, and the plants are all succulents and cacti, growing in black soil. Hardly any grass. Whole fields of lava, like the surface of the moon or something. A few really nice beaches. Brilliant food, if you get out into the smaller inland places.'

'And Chris liked it, did he?'

'Chris was very happy,' said Simmy with a secretive smile. 'Everything went perfectly, in fact.'

Bonnie was giving her a searching look when the doorbell pinged again and the first customer of the day arrived.

Five customers later, it was past twelve o'clock. The expected wholesale delivery had given them more work to do than was comfortable, arranging the new flowers for maximum effect. Bonnie tackled the window display and Simmy found two new orders on the computer. 'A birthday in Bowness, and a baby in . . . gosh, somewhere called Banerigg – if that's how you say it. Where on earth's that?'

'I think it's on the edge of Grasmere – the lake, not the town. You'll need the map.'

'Why are they sending me all the way up there?' grumbled

Simmy. 'They should use a closer florist, from Ambleside, if not Grasmere. It's nine miles from here.'

'Reputation,' said Bonnie. 'Did you say "baby"?'

'I did. The message reads, "Welcome to little Lucy May Penrose, from Great-Granny Sarah." And there's to be baby's breath, pink rosebuds and honeysuckle. I guess Great-Granny Sarah just picked me out with a pin on Google. She lives in Bristol, so she probably doesn't know much about the geography up here.'

'I hope she didn't prick her screen,' giggled Bonnie. 'When does she want it?'

'As soon as possible. I'll have to take it this evening, I suppose. But I said I'd call in on my parents.'

'It's really not far,' Bonnie assured her. 'Look – here it is.' She proffered her all-purpose smartphone, showing a map. 'It's on the 591. But there are hardly any houses there.'

'There's a postcode. I expect I'll find it. I'll have to tell my mum I won't be seeing them this evening, after all.'

'It's pretty nice up there,' Bonnie encouraged. 'It'll be a nice little jaunt for you.'

Not for another twenty minutes did Simmy remember that she had suggested to Chris that they meet one evening in Grasmere. Was this too soon in the week? Should she let him know she'd be there and see what he said? It seemed silly, and even a bit tight-lipped, not to say anything. But the prospect of rerunning the same conversations again so soon made her feel pressured and slightly panicked. She needed some time to think before that could be readily faced.

Only three more people came in for flowers during the afternoon, giving Simmy time to assemble the bouquet for little Lucy May. 'Lucky I've got some baby's breath,' she muttered. 'even if it is more than a week old.'

'It lasts for ages,' said Bonnie. 'That's why we didn't throw it out before you went away.'

The girl had been looking at her phone even more than usual in the past hour or so. 'Are you waiting for something?' asked Simmy.

'It's Ben's driving test at two forty-five. He must be finishing any time now.'

'Oh, drat! I forgot all about it. I was going to send him a good luck message.'

'He didn't want to make a thing of it. I'm surprised he told you.'

'I got a text yesterday saying welcome home. He mentioned it then.'

'He's dead scared, you know. It's quite funny, really, when he's been fine all through the A-levels. I can understand, though. This is so much more *physical*. And he's got to take other people into account and keep his eyes open the whole time. I mean – he's got to really *concentrate*.'

'That shouldn't be a problem, surely?'

'He overthinks things. He watches what a lorry's doing a hundred yards up the road and misses the cyclist that's only inches away. And people keep comparing him to Sheldon Cooper, which isn't very helpful.'

Simmy refrained from admitting that Christopher Henderson had been one of those people. 'I'm sure he'll be fine. And if he fails this time, he can do it again in a month or two, can't he?'

'Ben doesn't handle failure very well,' said Bonnie

regretfully. 'Oh! Here it is . . . *Failed*. Just one word. Damn it.' She slumped against the wall at the back of the shop and stared at her screen. 'That's such a downer. What if it's an omen for his exam results? That's what Corinne's going to think. She always says he's got too many big ideas for his own good.'

'It's not an omen. That's ridiculous. Most people fail first time. It was probably some tiny little technicality. You know what they're like, these examiners.'

'Not really. What am I going to say to him?'

'Don't ask me,' said Simmy, who genuinely had no idea what the best response would be.

While she was still thinking about the unprecedented word 'failure' used in conjunction with Ben Harkness, Simmy's own phone tinkled to indicate a text from Chris. *We need to buy a ring. Always nice jewellery at the auction, of course. You should be here on Saturday.*

There was a pleasing subtlety to it that made her smile and feel more confident. *I might close at 12 and get there for 1, if that's any good*, she replied.

*Better than nothing*, he flashed back.

'This must stop,' she ordained, talking to both Bonnie and herself. 'Texting at work is a very bad habit.'

'Better than waffling on and on like some people do,' said Bonnie. 'I was kept waiting well over five minutes in a shop last week, in Bowness, while the girl chatted to some friend on her phone. It was a disgrace. I was just going to walk out when she finally finished.'

'Lucky it wasn't my mum. She'd have started throwing things.'

They both laughed – all the more so because the image was not so very far from reality.

'What did you say to him, then?' Simmy asked a few minutes later.

'I said it wasn't a disaster, and I loved him just the same.' Bonnie and Ben were both delightfully unselfconscious about how they felt towards each other.

Simmy wished she could be like that too, but strongly suspected that it was already too late. 'Perfect,' she said, with a smile.

The bouquet for Lucy May was a work of art, though she said so herself. Delicate, fresh, distinctive – it seemed to symbolise all that was wonderful in a new baby. 'Wow!' said Bonnie. 'You're brilliant at this job, you know. It's absolutely gorgeous.'

They closed up at five and, having made a quick call to her mother, Simmy carried the flowers to her car, parked several streets away. The traffic was heavy between Windermere and Ambleside but thinned out after that. Her satnav directed her to an isolated little house up a short but steep track off the main road where it ran alongside the small lake of Grasmere. Five minutes before arriving, she thought she heard a warble from the phone in her bag, but the focus required for getting to the right place made her instantly forget about it.

She left the car on a small rough patch beside a stone wall and got out with the flowers. She could hear the baby crying through the closed front door. She had to ring three times before anybody came. Then a tear-stained woman in her thirties flung it open, holding a near-naked infant tight against her chest – which did little to stifle the cries. She took in Simmy and the flowers with total lack of comprehension.

'Here,' she said. 'Take her, before I murder the little beast.'

# Chapter Four

The baby was lighter than most dolls that Simmy had handled. The red face was screwed up in distress and the mouth wide open, the tongue vibrating with the screams. But the shock of being handed to somebody new quickly arrested the complaints. The mouth closed and the eyes half-opened. 'Hello,' said Simmy. Something unsettling was being stirred up inside her. 'What's all the fuss about, eh?'

Somehow the flowers had been exchanged for the baby, the mother holding them to her chest in evident pleasure. That at least gave Simmy some reassurance. She had once had her creative effort thrown violently across a farmyard. 'How old is she?' she asked.

'Nearly three weeks. It feels like three years.'

Simmy looked into the little face, searching for signs of a person who could be accessed and engaged in some sort of interaction. 'You must be Lucy May,' she crooned. 'Isn't that a nice name? Why are you being so mean to poor Mummy, then?'

'Listen to you!' scoffed the woman, who seemed to be close to collapse. 'Bring her in, will you? I've got to sit down.'

They went into a long room with a kitchen at one end and big pine table at the other. There was a carry-chair on the table – a heavy-looking thing with a handle and a sort of nest for the baby. Simmy remembered that she and Tony had bought one for their baby, but never had occasion to use it. She couldn't even remember what they were rightly called. What did hit her with a thud was the fact that this was the first baby she had held since her own stillborn Edith. The similarities were outweighing the differences, despite the jerky movements of this one, and the living warmth of her.

'Sorry,' said the woman. 'I'll take her now. You caught us at a bad moment.'

'No problem.' The prospect of having to relinquish the little thing was appalling. 'I'll hold her for a bit, if that helps.'

'You can keep her for all I care. She seems to like you better, anyway.'

Simmy could think of nothing to say. She was totally unequipped to console, advise or even commiserate.

Anything she might have heard about the trials of early parenthood flew out of her head. Babies screamed and kept you awake at night. Your nipples got sore. That was pretty much it. A featherweight scrap of life could turn the world upside down. Could and did, evidently.

'I should have hired a nanny, like my grandmother did,' said the woman. 'Or left her in a nursery after the first week, like American women do. As it is, I can't see how we're going to get through without one of us going mad or being killed. I even thought I could manage a bit of painting while she's asleep. What a joke!'

'Are you on your own?' Simmy asked cautiously.

'What? Oh – no, not exactly. I've got a husband, if that's what you mean. But he had to go back to work last week and doesn't get home till nine or later. That's when everything went wrong, really. At least I could give her to him some of the time. Now I can't even get to the loo without her bawling blue murder.'

'She's not ill, though, is she?'

'Apparently not. She's not growing much, but she's not *losing* weight. The health visitor is obsessed with all that, which makes everything worse. I cried all over her on Friday. Looks very bad in my notes. They've probably got a black mark against me, and next thing I know, Social Services'll be coming round.'

'I imagine crying on them is fairly usual, actually.' Simmy had cried quite a lot herself, but with far greater reason. 'Isn't there somebody who could come and lend a hand – friend or relation or neighbour, or someone? It must be grim doing it all by yourself.'

'I've got a mother, two sisters, a rather batty friend in Ambleside and about twelve others around the country. Not one of them seems to be available. My mother was going to come, but she's got shingles. I thought a summer baby would be so easy – just park her out in the sunshine, or go for walks by the lake, and everything would be idyllic. Instead, she won't ever let me put her down. I can't do *anything*.'

'Have you got one of those sling things, where you tie her onto your front?'

The woman blinked at her. 'No. That never occurred to me. How stupid. She'd probably scream in that as well, but at least I'd have my hands free.'

'You can probably order them on Amazon. It'd arrive in a day or two.' The relief at having found a helpful thing to say was enormous.

'Have you ever used one? They look horribly complicated.'

Simmy shook her head. She laid the baby on her thighs, still watching the little face for signs of protest. Gently, she swung her legs from side to side in an instinctive rhythm.

'I should hate you,' said the woman. 'Look how quiet and happy she is now.'

'She was just reacting to your stress levels, I suppose. She's still pretty much part of you, isn't she?'

The woman sniffed. 'You think?'

'I don't know. It's all very mysterious. Who knows what it's like to be her?'

'I never stopped to wonder. It's all been so . . . chaotic.

47

Nothing's gone to plan, right from the start. She was eight days early, and I was nowhere near ready. Scott's in the middle of something crucial at work. It's really not his fault. He keeps saying their whole reputation is at stake. I was meant to be helping, but that all went out of the window when Madam arrived early. And he's got other kids, so he can't see why I'm in such a meltdown over it. I think I'm basically too old for a first baby. All my instincts have dried up, and I've got no idea what I'm meant to be doing. Even feeding her is painful, and she's obviously not getting enough.'

Simmy was gripped by a crazy notion that here was God trying to tell her to abandon all thought of producing her own baby. The message was all too dreadfully clear: it would lead to disappointment, resentment and a grudge against the man who was failing to provide adequate support.

'At least Great-Granny Sarah is thinking of you,' she said foolishly, indicating the flowers lying forgotten on the table.

Tears filled the woman's eyes. 'She's ninety-two and lives in Bristol. If I had any sense I'd get in the car right now and drive us down there. She'd know what to do. Fancy her sending flowers! Did she phone you? Did you speak to her?'

'No. The order came through on the computer. I don't know how she found me. I'm really not the obvious florist to use. I'm all the way down in Windermere.'

'I'm glad she did. My name's Flo, by the way. Short for Florence. Usual story – they say that's where I was conceived, heaven help me.'

48

'And I'm Simmy, short for Persimmon. You think you've got problems.' They both laughed.

It was nearly seven o'clock when she left, the sun still high in the sky. Lucy May had fallen asleep on her lap, and neither Simmy nor Flo had dared to move her. Flo made coffee and found some bread and cheese for a meagre snack. She also put the flowers in a vase she'd grabbed from a shelf at random, arranging them in an instinctive harmony that Simmy found entirely satisfactory. Sometimes people treated her blooms with a terrible philistinism. Conversation had lapsed, with the new mother more than half-asleep. The wrench when Simmy finally handed the baby back had been every bit as awful as feared.

She sat in the car for two minutes, wrestling with the acute sensations of emptiness and bereavement. Would it never go away, she wondered. Would she find herself avoiding all contact with babies as a result? Restlessly, she got out of the car again, and walked down a path and across the road to the brink of the lake. Flo wouldn't mind or even notice that Simmy left her vehicle outside her house. And the husband wasn't due home for a while yet.

The absent Scott gave Simmy a degree of concern, on top of everything else. On the face of it, he was a typical selfish male, probably at least ten years older than his second wife and already somewhat bored with her. In Simmy's limited experience, such men went on to a third wife in late middle-age and didn't always improve their behaviour even then. So, what did that say about Christopher? She spent a full minute thinking of reasons why nothing in poor Flo's story had any echoes whatsoever for her and Chris. Everything was completely different.

She used the pavement that ran alongside the main road, with the lake immediately to her right. The traffic was moderately busy, but not enough to intrude on her thoughts. The wall that bordered the lake came to an end, opening a way down to the water's edge and a well-made path that encircled the lake. Banerigg was on the eastern edge of Grasmere, comprising woodland and very little else. The evening sun was throwing long shadows onto the water, creating picture-postcard reflections of the trees. Everything was still and sharply-focused, quite unlike the blurred edges of the previous morning. On the other side of the water, in shadow with the setting sun behind them, were crags and fells whose names she didn't know. They seemed impossibly close in the clear light, the line where their tops met the blue sky a vividly defined edge. The entire scene was timelessly beautiful, despite the traffic ceaselessly passing. It made her think of Ben and Bonnie, and their researches into William Wordsworth, who had lived right here at a time when there would not have been all these roads and houses and cars. She thought of her father and his acute grasp of the ironies associated with Wordsworth and the Lakes. The excessively famous poet had been posthumously responsible for much of the increased traffic that threatened to spoil the peace of the region. Not entirely posthumously, either, according to Ben. In his later years, the old man had attracted legions of admirers to Grasmere and Rydal, all wanting accommodation and food.

And yet, it still wasn't really spoilt, if a person could stand here in complete isolation on a long summer's day and see almost nothing but natural beauty. It made it all the more dispiriting that Flo and her new daughter were having such a horrible time, when there was all this on the doorstep. It made Simmy think about something Ben had once said – that human beings were cursed by their intelligence. They had removed themselves from the rest of earthly life, by thinking too much. Technology, psychology – even literature – had all formed impassable barriers between the human species and the immense network of flora and fauna living so brainlessly around them.

She turned to go back to her car, still letting her thoughts drift from one topic to another. Ideas connected without any conscious effort, until landing on the greatest curse of them all, in some people's opinion: the mobile phone. Hadn't hers chirped at her about two hours ago and gone ignored? What message was sitting there, waiting for her attention? Some unwanted junk, or a call to action? An intrusion or a cry for help?

When she finally summoned the text to the screen, it read

*Jonathan has been killed in Grasmere today. I need you!*

# Chapter Five

So why hadn't he phoned her, instead of just sending a text? Was he too distraught to speak? And in what way, exactly, did he need her? Surely not for an alibi? She shook that idea away as being far too melodramatic. He needed her because he wanted reassurance and consolation. His friend was dead – killed somehow – and he was upset.

She was practically in Grasmere, she realised. The little town was barely half a mile away, situated on the northern side of the lake. She definitely couldn't drive home to Troutbeck without checking to see whether Chris was anywhere near. Impatient with texts, she called him for a proper conversation.

It was a long time before he answered, and she was preparing a voicemail message when he was finally in her ear. 'Simmy? Where've you been?'

'Never mind that. What's happening? Where are you? Do you want me to meet you somewhere? I'm right outside Grasmere at the moment.'

'Oh, Lord. I've just got back from there. I'm in Keswick again now, after being questioned for hours by the police. Why are you in Grasmere, anyway?'

'I delivered some flowers. I stopped to admire the view. What *happened*, Chris? With Jonathan?'

'He was throttled. With a leather belt. His own belt. For a bit, they thought it might be suicide, but any fool could see that was impossible.'

'You've seen him?'

He did not answer this directly. 'I told you he wanted to talk to me. He phoned this morning and asked if I'd meet him at the Grasmere house. He'd found a key to it that Philip told him about last year. He said he just wanted a quick look round and I should be with him as a witness that he wasn't nicking anything, and to fend off any suspicious neighbours. I left my car in the first car park you come to – there's never anywhere to park in Grasmere – and walked up to the house. The front door was open, so I went in. He was in the main room on the ground floor. I couldn't believe my eyes. I can't even remember what I did, but in the end a chap out in the road called the police.'

Simmy didn't even try to follow this garbled account. She understood that he was reciting a summary of everything he'd told the police as they interviewed him. Her slender grasp of the sequence of events meant she would have to ask several annoying questions before she could get the full picture. 'So – then what?' she prompted.

'All hell broke loose. They kept me for ages while all sorts of bods came and went. Then I had to give a statement in Penrith, formally identify him, try to make them understand what he did for a living. When I texted you, we were still at it. I thought you could drive me back to collect my car, but in the end, I got hold of Hannah and she did it for me.'

Hannah was his sister, who lived not far outside Keswick. 'Penrith! Why not Windermere? Surely that's much nearer?'

'I don't know,' he said tiredly. 'I didn't like to argue. They probably would have taken me back for the car, but I was sick of the sight of them by then. And I wanted a familiar face.'

'So,' she said slowly. 'You and Hannah were here in Grasmere while I was half a mile down the road, and you've only just got home again. How absolutely maddening.'

'So, where were you?' he asked again.

'At a house down by the lake, delivering flowers. I stayed for a chat.' *There was a baby*, she wanted to add, but resisted. Another element in the conversation now would do no good at all. 'I can come now, if you like. I'm only half an hour away. Is Hannah still there?'

'No, she dropped me and left. Are you sure? I'm in rather a mess, I warn you. His *face*, Simmy. It was all black. One of the police people told me it was the same as hanging – has the same effect. The belt did the same as a noose – the person often dies of heart failure before they asphyxiate. Very quick, apparently. Poor old Jon!'

'You said he was worried, yesterday. He thought this might happen, do you think? He was not so much worried as scared, right?'

'I didn't listen properly,' said Chris wretchedly. 'I just fobbed him off. If I'd done what he wanted, he'd probably still be alive.'

'So . . . was it Nick, then? The one with a grudge against him?'

'Must have been.' The wretchedness level increased. 'I didn't know what to tell the cops. I mean – I haven't got any evidence, have I? It didn't feel right to give them his name without knowing a bit more.'

'How could you *not*, if you think it must have been him? What stopped you?'

'Nick's not such a bad chap. I can't really believe he'd do something like that. What good would it do him? But I did tell them about him, in the end.'

'Why? Did they torture it out of you?'

'Pretty much. Just kept on at me until I cracked. Made a few veiled threats. It could have been Mexico.'

'I don't believe you. But, as Ben would point out, if it was Nick that did it, he'll have left fingerprints and hairs and so forth all over the house – and on the body.'

'Yeah – but I don't see Nick doing it. He wasn't involved in the Grasmere business. I don't understand how he'd have found Jon there.'

'But it's quite possible that he did, surely? Just let me get something clear – we *are* talking about the same house you told me about yesterday, aren't we? The one where the old lady died?'

'Right.'

'So, Jonathan was within his rights to just walk straight in, was he?'

'Not exactly, no. I admit I was surprised. Last I heard, the Leeson lady had told him to sling his hook and never darken her doorstep again, because her dog didn't like him.'

'What?'

'That's where it gets a bit murky, you see.' He stopped, and then said, 'You don't need to know all that. It's not important. Some burglar must have spotted the open door and got into a fight with poor old Jon. Or maybe a Grasmere resident recognised him and saw his chance to get even over some ancient grievance. He left his van right outside the house, with "Woolley's House Clearance" on the side. Anyone would have known he was there.'

'So not a burglar, then,' said Simmy, remembering how Ben Harkness automatically dismissed conveniently homicidal burglars.

'I don't see why not. Everyone would know there was good stuff in there.'

'And everyone would know the neighbours would be keeping a close eye on the place, as well.'

'Maybe.' He groaned softly. 'I've had enough for one day. I can't talk about it any more.'

'Okay, then.' But she found herself unable to let him go for a little while longer. 'I'm so sorry, Chris, that this has happened. And sorry I wasn't there for you. Do you want me to come up to Keswick now? I could, if it would help.'

'I'm not sure, Sim. I don't want to drag you into this

– I don't want *me* to be dragged into it, come to that. It'll be eight before you can get here, and you'd be wanting to leave again before long. Have you been home this evening? Have you seen Angie and Russell today? Things must be busy at the shop.'

'You're my top priority,' she said softly. 'All those other things can wait, if you need me. That's what the text said, remember. "I need you", you said.'

'Did I? That seems ages ago now. Must have been five o'clock. I needed you to drive me.'

'I was in the car and didn't look at the message. It's nice you tried me first.' Again, she felt Ben Harkness at her shoulder. 'What time did you find Jonathan?' Confusedly, she recalled the lengthy police procedures that followed the discovery of a violent death. The body wasn't removed for many hours. Various sorts of officers came and went. If Chris had needed her for a lift at five, didn't that mean the main action had been early in the afternoon? 'Why didn't you call me then? It must have been halfway through the afternoon.'

'Why would I? I told you – I couldn't bear to drag you into another murder. It's only a few months since that business in Staveley. Before that, there was my dad. You've had much more than your share, sweetheart. I think it's best if you keep your distance this time.'

'And it won't be Moxon,' she realised. DI Nolan Moxon was the Windermere detective she had encountered repeatedly, when drawn into a criminal investigation by the simple error of delivering flowers. They had slowly developed a friendship that they both valued highly. She trusted him, and he understood her. 'Who's the SIO this time?' she asked.

'What?'

'Senior investigating officer. Didn't they tell you? Who interviewed you?'

'I don't remember the name. Some bloke my age, Detective Superintendent something-or-other. Seemed a bit of a robot, just going through the standard routine.'

'Mm.' She managed a minimal laugh. 'Well, Ben's exams are over and he's got nothing to do for a while. I very much doubt we'll be able to keep him away from this. And the whole thing sounds so complicated, we could probably do with him, anyway.'

Chris said nothing to that for a moment. Then, 'Did he pass his driving test?'

'Sadly, no.'

'Told you,' said Christopher, with a not entirely pleasant laugh.

Simmy drove back to Troutbeck, bursting with conflicting thoughts and emotions. Whatever ghastly fate had befallen the unfortunate Jonathan, it had done nothing to strengthen the bond between her and Christopher. He had 'needed' her only for the purpose of driving him from one place to another. And place A had apparently been Penrith, which was considerably beyond her comfort zone. She would – she supposed – have flown to his rescue, if she'd seen his message in time. And then there would have been an opportunity for them to talk more intimately about fear and shock and bewilderment. She would have consoled him and offered help and improved his frame of mind. As it was, the phone call had been awkward. He had been traumatised and she was simply confused. The garbled details about the Grasmere house, and the angry Nick and the brutal killing were a long way from forming a coherent picture.

For a few minutes she was tempted to shake it all out of her head and choose not to care about shady antique traders and their problems with the Inland Revenue. It felt like the sort of crime that featured in the tabloids, men killing other men for reasons of money and reputation and ungovernable rage. Nothing subtle or susceptible to sympathy. But her acquaintance with Ben had taught her a lot. There was no way of preventing her efforts to understand what had happened. The timings were odd, even at a casual glance. Christopher should have phoned her several hours earlier than he did. And if he was found at the scene by the police, driven to Penrith in a police car and questioned there, then left to make his own way home – didn't that suggest a central role in the crime, in the minds of the investigators? After all, Jonathan had apparently directly asked him for help.

There were others who needed her, perhaps even more than Chris did. Her parents would be trying to deal with a remorseless stream of B&B guests, with no outside assistance other than Simmy's. She anticipated a mountain of ironing, for one thing, when she finally presented herself. Her father had lost much of his earlier competence, forcing his wife and daughter to watch and worry over him more than was comfortable. But recently it had appeared that he was actually less disordered than before. Much of his old humour had returned. He gave his little dog a better level of attention and was marginally more relaxed about dangerous intruders. When Simmy had been dragged into the murder of a man from Staveley, she had successfully kept her father in ignorance. It had been her fault that he became so frightened in the first place, after a succession of violent episodes in Ambleside, Bowness and other places.

But Russell and Angie would have to wait another day or so before they saw their daughter. She was tired and not very happy. Something had gone awry with Christopher and her, causing internal churnings that could only be labelled as anxiety.

In her Troutbeck house, she made coffee and ate an unwholesome mixture of biscuits and chocolate. It was still light outside but wouldn't be for much longer. Traces of Christopher lingered in every room – the mug he'd used was still unwashed; a paperback he'd been reading on the flight home from Lanzarote had been left on her sofa; the bedding smelt of him. He had *proposed* to her, and she had accepted. He should be at her side at every available moment. Instead, he was miles away in Keswick, grieving for his dead friend, unable to give a lucid account of the events of the day.

She had not told Bonnie about the proposal, she realised. Nor had she told her parents the news when she phoned them. Did that mean she had yet to believe it was real? Or was she apprehensive as to the reactions she would get? Her mother had been friendly with Chris's mother, both women claiming to want their offspring to form a couple. Yet when this had almost happened, over twenty years before, the parents had panicked and taken action to separate them. They were too young and inexperienced. They didn't know their own minds. And neither of the fathers had seemed to approve of the prospect very much at all.

Everything would be better in the morning, she assured herself. A quick check of the weather forecast revealed light cloud but no rain. She would share with Bonnie almost everything that had happened since she got back from the holiday and pay a belated visit to her parents at Beck View. She would commiserate with Ben over his unprecedented encounter with failure.

And she might even ask him to help her understand just what had been going on in Grasmere and Keswick, between men who bought and sold valuable antiques, and harboured serious grudges against each other.

# Chapter Six

Then, on Tuesday, somehow all her resolutions fell to dust. A hotel called and asked for a number of floral displays at short notice. A bride in a hurry wanted a hall decorated for her wedding reception. Two funeral tributes and a golden wedding anniversary added to Simmy's tasks, and completely filled the day. She spent nearly all of it in her small back room, constructing the sprays, making notes for the hotel job and listing all the fresh blooms she would need to order for the rest of the week. Bonnie handled customers and phone calls, and they barely had a moment to speak to each other.

'I've got to go and see my parents,' said Simmy, at four o'clock. 'I can't leave them any longer. We'll be closing on the dot of five today, whatever happens. How's Ben?' she added as an after-thought.

'He was going to come in today, but I texted to say we were too busy. It's not been like this for ages, has it? That hotel's pushing it, wanting everything so quickly.'

'They are, but it's better than not wanting anything at all. If I get it right, it might be a regular order, all through the summer. Like the one last year in Hawkshead, and a lot closer.'

'Should be easier tomorrow,' said Bonnie, ever optimistic. 'I'll tell Ben he can drop in after lunch to see you.'

'There was a murder yesterday in Grasmere,' said Simmy. 'I haven't had a chance to tell you about it. Chris found the body. It's a friend of his.'

But before she could say any more, a customer came in, hoping for a lavish bouquet, made on the spot. 'Give me twenty minutes,' said Simmy, returning to her airless workroom with an armful of lilies, tulips and rosebuds. She could hear Bonnie making idle conversation while the man waited.

Finally, they were alone again and Bonnie exploded with pent-up curiosity. 'Who got killed? Do they know who did it? Is Moxon investigating? Why didn't you tell me sooner?'

'It's all very confusing. I was right there, delivering those baby flowers. Except I still don't understand the timing properly. The woman with the baby was in such a state, I stayed with her for nearly two hours. It's an awful baby – cries all the time. Except, when I held her, she was fine. The poor woman was dreadfully stressed out.'

'Isn't there a father?'

'Yes, but he's busy with work. I got the feeling he can't stand the atmosphere.'

'Selfish pig. It'll be his fault there *is* an atmosphere in the first place.'

'Probably,' said Simmy, impressed for the thousandth time by Bonnie's insight. 'Anyway, Chris sent a text and I didn't see it until it was too late. The police took him to Penrith, leaving his car in Grasmere.'

'That was stupid.'

'I know. His sister Hannah took him back for it, when he couldn't reach me.'

'But who *was* he? The murdered man?'

Simmy looked at the time display on her computer. 'I can't tell you all of it now. After I've been to Beck View, I'll phone Chris and see if he can explain it any better. And then tomorrow I can fill you in.'

Bonnie sighed happily. 'Ben's going to be so thrilled. Let's hope it's *seriously* complicated.'

Angie and Russell were on better form than Simmy had feared. She found her father laying tables for the next morning, humming a tune and wearing a colourful summer shirt. The front door had been unlocked, which was a great improvement over the past several months. 'Hi, Dad,' Simmy called from the doorway. 'Busy, I see.'

'Standing room only,' he returned. 'Your mother's been muttering about making people book a time for their breakfast. Apparently, they're all doing that now.'

'Seems a shame.'

'That's what I said. Liberty Hall – that's us. They can lie in bed as long as they want to, as far as I'm concerned.'

'What about the ones who want to see the sun rise from the top of Wansfell?'

'They don't get their sausages. We give them a packed lunch instead. You know that,' he reproached her.

'I thought you might have changed it.' The truth was that she was rather unsubtly testing him. His mental competence waxed and waned unpredictably, with spells where he scarcely seemed to understand that there were any guests in the house at all.

'No, you didn't. You wanted to check my marbles.' He laughed at her. 'I can see right through you, Simmy Straw.'

'Brown,' she corrected – and then giggled self-consciously. 'Soon to be Henderson, as it happens.'

'Good God!' he stared at her. 'The man's going to marry you, is he?'

'He proposed at the weekend.'

'As the sun was rising over the romantic volcanic coast, with Africa just beyond the horizon,' he sighed. 'I can see the whole thing.'

'Actually, he waited until we'd got home again. It was on a rainy Sunday afternoon in Troutbeck.'

'Disgusting!' he asserted. 'That boy never did have any sense of timing. Always late, or in the wrong place. Are you sure you want to spend a lifetime with a man like that?'

'I am, Dad,' she said softly.

'Oh, well. Nobody's perfect,' said Russell with a shrug.

'Your mother's in for a surprise. She thought it would never happen.'

'It's a pity about Frances. She and Mum would have competed for the credit.'

'Mm,' said Russell. Frances was Christopher's mother, who had died the previous year, in her early sixties. 'I think you might be somewhat out of date on that topic.'

'Oh? What does that mean?'

'Not for me to say.'

'You're not suggesting she isn't going to like it, are you? She thinks Christopher's great, surely? She's never said a word against him to me.'

He put a finger to his lips. 'Hush, girl! Let her speak for herself. Ange!' He raised his voice. 'Where are you, woman?'

*Girl? Woman?* This was a new idiom since she had last seen him. 'She won't like being called "woman",' she warned him.

'She doesn't mind. It's meant fondly.'

Simmy's mother was heard coming down the short passageway to the dining room. 'Here I am, my lord,' she said. 'Oh, P'simmon! How long have you been here?'

'Ten minutes or so.'

'She brings tidings,' said Russell.

Angie looked at her daughter. 'Had a good holiday, then?' she said. 'There was some story about a rare old embroidery fetching a huge amount of money at the Keswick auction, while you were away. Christopher must have heard about it by now. Or was he following it from his phone, on the beach?'

'We left our phones at home.'

'How very sensible. So that's not the news, then. The commission must be substantial. He'll be excited when he hears.'

'That's not the news,' said Russell impatiently.

'He's asked me to marry him,' said Simmy quickly. 'And I said yes.'

'Oh. I see. Can't pretend it's a surprise. That means you'll be moving house, then? What about the shop?'

'All that comes after you offer congratulations and good wishes for my happiness.'

'You'll be happy enough without my wishing it. And the practice of offering congratulations has always struck me as a trifle tactless. Even mildly offensive, when you think about it. Like applauding an angler for landing a big fat fish.'

'So, you don't object?'

'You're nearly forty, for heaven's sake! What difference would my objections make? But no – I think it's quite nice news, actually. Excellent timing, for once. When's the wedding?'

'Are you pregnant?' Russell suddenly asked, his face galvanised with excitement. 'Is that the *real* news?'

Simmy flushed. 'I doubt it,' she said stiffly.

'But you want to be!' he triumphed. 'Hallelujah!'

'We haven't set a date or anything,' Simmy told her mother. 'The idea is to live somewhere halfway between here and Keswick and carry on with work as it is now.'

'The only place that fits that requirement is Grasmere,' said Russell. 'Or some tiny fellside settlement like Rosthwaite, and that's much closer to Keswick.' His knowledge of the Lake District was prodigious, as hundreds of B&B guests had discovered. 'Grasmere's not bad,' he said grudgingly. 'If you like that sort of thing. They've gone overboard on the Great Man, of course, and you never saw so many tea rooms in your life.'

'I was there last night – or very close by,' said Simmy. 'Delivering flowers.'

'Rather outside your usual patch, surely?'

'I know. I think it was a bit of an accident. The person sending them must have just found me at random, on the Internet.'

'It's been frantic here,' said Angie, with a martyred sigh.

'No worse than usual,' her husband argued. 'And I've been helping, haven't I?'

Simmy headed off the predictable rant that this sort of remark always provoked. *Helping* was a buzzword with Angie, implying as it did that she was the one with all the responsibility. She would range from sarcastic ('And there was me thinking we were *partners*') to the outright furious.

'Well, I'm here now. I bet there's a lot of ironing waiting for me,' said Simmy quickly.

'I did it,' said Russell smugly.

'There's not much to do at the moment,' Angie admitted. 'They've all been here a night or two already, so no need for new sheets and towels.' She took her daughter's hand in a startling display of affection. 'It's lovely about you and Christopher. I'm happy for you. I just hope it's not going to be a proper wedding. I can't bear to go through all that again. Every time I try to imagine myself as the bride's mother, I think of Charlotte Rampling in *Melancholia*.'

'That's you, all right,' said Russell, with feeling. Angie had been even more of a curmudgeon than usual at Simmy's wedding to Tony, drinking too much and making critical remarks about the Brown relatives.

She stayed an hour at Beck View, finding a few small tasks such as tidying the downstairs room that was full of games and old saggy furniture and spare clothing, designed for guests to use on days when even the most intrepid would not venture outside. She played with her father's long-suffering Lakeland terrier, taking him into the modest garden and throwing a ball a few times. It was a calming interlude, where emotions were in abeyance and she had nothing urgent to think about. Her mother's grudging words had been taken without umbrage, and her father's good humour and clarity had come as a relief. As far as this little part of the world was concerned, everything seemed quite all right.

# Chapter Seven

Once again in Troutbeck, things felt rather different. She had given Christopher all too little thought throughout the day, and now these thoughts seemed to be banked up, pushing against a flimsy wall that was about to give way. Something very strange had taken place the previous day and he had not given her as much information as he might have. And he had not treated her as his closest and most beloved other. This must be rectified. So she phoned him.

'Hey!' he said, in response. 'I was just going to call you. I had the phone in my hand already.'

She pushed away the tiny voice that asked itself whether this was true. 'How are you? I mean – what's been happening about Jonathan? The suspense is killing me.'

His laugh contained something like disbelief. 'Why should *you* worry about it? You never even met him. Anyway, nothing else has happened about that today. It's been bedlam at work. Nobody's done half what they should have, while I was away. We've got a sale on Saturday, and the catalogue's never going to be ready in time. The press are here as well, getting in the way.'

'Because of the murder?'

'What? No, of course not, you idiot. Because of that stumpwork thing that sold so well last week. I missed the actual sale, if you remember, on account of being at Manchester airport with you. It was all anyone could talk about yesterday morning when I got to work. It went for fourteen thousand quid. Made a big splash. It's been on the news. They're all nagging us to tell them who the vendor was, and how he got hold of the thing. There's been a few rumours, which caught their attention.'

'What *is* stumpwork?'

'Jacobean embroidery, in a kind of 3D effect – usually biblical subject matter. Highly sought-after. This one's been kept wrapped up, so the colours are fabulous.'

'So, who was the vendor?'

'I'm not supposed to say, but it's sure to get out eventually. And then the shit will hit the fan, to coin a phrase.' He paused, while Simmy said nothing. 'The truth is, it was Jonathan. He picked it up for peanuts somewhere – never did tell us where. Must have been some house

71

clearance job, I reckon, or maybe a car boot sale.'

Simmy's heart started thumping. 'My God, Chris! Why didn't you tell me this yesterday? What if Jonathan got it illegally? Don't you have to check for legal ownership before you sell something? Do the police know he was the vendor? Isn't that the obvious reason why he was killed? Somebody wanting the thing back – or—'

'Or what? How does that work? What would be the point?'

Her mind was working fast. 'The money! They'd be after the money.'

'Which he hadn't been paid yet. He would have got it at the end of this week. That had nothing to do with him being killed. There's no way the thing could have made anybody want to kill him. Even if somebody begrudged him the profit, that's not grounds for *killing* him, is it?' He sounded almost frantic in his effort to convince her.

'It might be,' she said hesitantly. 'Look, Chris, Ben's at a loose end now. Bonnie's going to tell him about Jonathan, and he'll be checking it all out online as we speak. He's going to want to ask you all about it. He was already keen to come to one of your auctions and see how it all works behind the scenes. If he thinks there's anything that links the murder to your work, he'll be all over you. I won't be able to stop him.'

'Oh,' said Christopher slowly. 'So why did you tell Bonnie about it, then? They'd never have known there'd even been a murder if you'd kept quiet – would they?' He sounded angry. Cold and hard and angry.

'It never occurred to me not to,' she said frankly.

'I'm not good at keeping secrets. It will have been on the news, anyway, and Ben would spot it right away. What are you so cross about? I thought you'd be glad to let them get involved.'

'How could you think that? Didn't I make it plain last night that I very much dislike being under the scrutiny of the police, for any reason? It's bad for the business and is extremely unpleasant for me personally. Jonathan was never exactly a close mate of mine, to tell you the truth. I don't know why the bloody fool came to me for help in the first place. I was an idiot to listen to him. He must have thought I could sort Nick out for him. Now Nick's going to be gunning for me, because I had to mention his name to the cops.'

Simmy gritted her teeth, trying to ignore the obvious change of emphasis, along with a sense that the story had somehow changed. 'Ben can help with that, if you explain it to him.'

'How? How can he? Tell me that.'

'Stop it,' she said. 'I don't like the way this is going. Two days ago, you asked me to marry you – remember? That presupposes that we're on the same side in everything that matters. It implies things like love and sharing and commitment, and all those big words. It requires us to be in a *relationship* that comes before everything else. For the past five minutes, you haven't sounded as if that means very much to you at all.'

'Okay,' he said, with panic in his voice. 'You're right. I'm sorry. It's the phone – nothing comes across properly. I'm in a flap, to be honest. And you seem so far away,' he finished pathetically. 'I really wish I hadn't missed you last night.'

'That was partly my fault,' she conceded, feeling slightly better. 'And I know the situation isn't ideal. Things are busy for me, as well. There was a flood of orders today, which are going to keep me at it all week. It looks as if we're both fully occupied until Sunday. I was hoping to be at your auction on Saturday, remember? I'm not sure how I'll make it, now.'

'Right,' he said. 'But we can't go on like this, can we? If we lived together in Grasmere or somewhere, we'd come together every evening. See each other every morning. There'd be all the time we need to talk and share and all that stuff.'

'I know. We should do it now. Quick as we can. If you want to.'

'I want to – but it could take six months for you to sell that house. You might lose on it, only being there a few years. You realise I'm practically a pauper, don't you? Nothing to sell. No savings. A battered old Volvo is all I've got to my name.'

'And absolutely brilliant prospects,' she reminded him. 'Just a few more old embroideries going for fourteen thousand, and you'll be rolling in money.' She had a thought. 'My mother read about it in the paper. She says your commission must have been substantial.'

He groaned. 'Which takes me right back to where we began. What do you think the police are going to make of that little detail, then?'

She caught up in a couple of seconds. 'They can't think it

74

was a motive for killing Jonathan, can they? What happens to the money, now he's dead?'

'I don't know – but it sure as hell doesn't stay in my bank account, whether he's alive *or* dead.'

The conversation ended with some rather forced endearments on both sides. Christopher didn't do romance, as Simmy had already understood. In that respect, if no other, he resembled Angie. The theory beloved by couple counsellors recurred to her: everybody married their mother. She had first heard it ten or fifteen years ago and insisted vigorously that it did not apply to her and Tony. She had never found one trait in him that was like Angie. But Christopher was different from Tony, and therefore perhaps closer to her mother than she quite liked.

Another realisation was gradually dawning, which caused her some distress: Christopher did not really like or understand Ben. The sharp remarks about him had increased over the months, so that Simmy had unconsciously reduced her references to him when talking to Chris. This instinctive avoidance of discomfort could not go on. She valued Ben enormously, even taking a tiny sliver of credit for the way he was turning out. She had watched him mature from a clever but unfocused seventeen-year-old to a brilliant and driven school-leaver. He knew what he wanted; he knew his own strengths. He had found Bonnie through Simmy and formed a bond that appeared to everyone as wholly positive. The unlikely pair filled each other's gaps and protected each other's vulnerabilities almost magically. They provided insights into worlds that would otherwise have been closed to them both. They had tremendous fun together, designing games and projects that absorbed every spare moment.

The fact that Christopher failed to grasp what a glorious triumph this was made Simmy worry about his judgement. He saw Bonnie as a damaged rootless teenager, entertaining, certainly, but in no way of any real significance. And he saw Ben as a geek, blundering through life clutching a smartphone, dreaming of Latin quotes and biochemical analyses. The past adventures, where all three of them had come close to the most painfully real aspects of violent death, were dismissed as examples of mischance that meant little. Even when his own father was at the centre of just such an episode, Christopher had given minimal thought to the individuals who found themselves involved. All he had cared about was taking up with Simmy again and keeping himself clear of police interest.

But Simmy was determined not to judge him and find him wanting. She accepted that her bond with Ben and Bonnie was unusual and difficult to understand. They were seen by some as surrogate children, given that she was easily old enough to be their mother. Others had the impression that Simmy was behaving childishly, joining in games that she should have grown out of. And DI Moxon swung between exasperation, concern and admiration as all four of them groped for the evidence and theories needed to solve the latest murder.

The absence of Moxon from this incident in Grasmere was a source of regret. A new detective would be suspicious and resistant to any interventions from Ben Harkness. So, it seemed, would Christopher. If he had his way, the death of his friend would be ignored as far as possible. And here, Simmy was brought up against a brick wall of incomprehension. How was it possible that Chris seemed so unconcerned to identify and punish the heartless killer? Normal human curiosity should surely overcome all other feelings? Perhaps he was trying to protect *her*, she suddenly realised. He knew how reluctant she had been to be dragged into the two murder investigations that had occurred since he had met her again. In Staveley she had unwittingly walked right into the middle of a particularly unpleasant crime. And when Christopher's own parents had died within weeks of each other, Simmy had again been immersed in the whole business.

There were so many issues swirling round, apparently unconnected. Her visceral desire for a baby, somewhat tempered by the desperation of poor Flo; her parents' increasing need of her help; the constant threat of the shop being either too busy or not busy enough. She felt again the warm weight of baby Lucy on her lap and knew her hormones had been stirred by it. She knew that she wanted Christopher as the father of her longed-for child – but perhaps only because he was willing and available, with nobody else in sight. She feared the complications and commitments that would be inevitable if they did start a baby. That, she admitted to herself, had been the case for a few months already. Instead of focusing on her assumed fertile days, and organising accordingly, she had let their usual weekly routine continue without protest, almost relieved when his visits coincided repeatedly with the wrong moments in her cycle. It was all too frightening, with the hand of fate hanging ominously above her head. If she could just have bundled up little Lucy May and taken her home to be her, Simmy's, baby without further discussion, that would have been ideal. As it was, she was faced with nine months of terror that her body would fail again and stifle another helpless infant before it could see the light of day.

How much easier, then, to be diverted into a puzzle as to who killed a man she'd never known, for reasons that were unlikely to arouse much emotion. Ben and Bonnie would delightedly throw themselves into searching for clues, reasons, timings – as far as the authorities would allow them access to such information. Ben's facility with the Internet meant he would quickly discover a wealth of detail about the dead man's life and work. He would spend a day at the auction rooms, chatting to anyone who seemed interesting.

They were not such terrible problems to have, she reminded herself. She had never expected Christopher to be perfect, after all. And he did seem to be amenable to correction, which was a plus. She was aware that she favoured a certain 'type' of man: somebody light on commitment – especially when it came to work. A man who chafed under authority and liked to take charge of his own life. This was certainly true of Ninian Tripp and Chris, and partially so of Tony. All three were on a spectrum in that regard, with Christopher in the middle. None was given to high drama or heavy drinking. She pulled herself up at that point. Making comparisons felt invidious. Ninian had never been a serious candidate for marriage and family. Tony was firmly in the past. The only one she ought to be thinking about was Christopher Henderson, born on the same day as her, both familiar and unknowable, the love of her life and yet still testing the quality of her trust in him.

There could be no guarantees, of course. It was cowardly to want them. All big decisions had an element of blind faith within them. You stepped into the void, unsure whether your foot would connect with solid ground or send you hurtling into an abyss. Either way, in the long run, both options were better than dithering on the edge, not moving at all.

She woke on Wednesday, feeling slightly Groundhog-Day-ish, as the sun filtered through high cloud and she mentally ran through all the tasks awaiting her at the shop. There was also a sense of limbo, with very little scope for direct action on her own behalf. Other people had to make the next move. Although she *could* go and see Flo again. They had parted on an agreement to meet again, having made one of those connections that women are so prone to. She could even make enquiries about selling her house, as Christopher had urged. There was always something a person could do to make things happen, and Simmy Brown felt a certain obligation to do just that.

The long days lent themselves to action. When the sun stayed in the sky until nine o'clock, there was no excuse for hiding away indoors and procrastinating. Equally, the mornings began so early that by seven you felt half the day was already wasted if you hadn't got up and begun some task or project. You could not convincingly argue shortage of time in June. Perhaps this alone explained her father's increased energy and interest in life. Always one to rise early and immerse himself in activity, the past year or so had seen him alarmingly lethargic. Now, there appeared to be grounds for hoping he might not, after all, have been on a one-way downhill slope to old age and dementia.

So she left home before eight and was in the shop by twenty past. She propped the door open and took half her plants outside to decorate the patch of pavement in front of the shop. Colour and scent radiated across the street, brightening the heart of Windermere considerably. Concentrating on more exotic blooms that very few people could grow for themselves, she hoped to attract a better number of customers than in recent weeks.

Bonnie was also early, standing in admiration of the pavement display before going into the shop. 'Ben's coming at twelve,' she said. 'Hope that'll be okay.'

'There's no way of knowing, is there? We might be knee-deep in orders by then. Even deeper than we are already, I mean.'

'And Corinne says, do you want to go for a drink tomorrow? She wants to ask you about Lanzarote. It's meant to be sunny for the rest of the week, and she says you could sit outside somewhere.'

'Okay,' said Simmy, somewhat lost for words. 'We sat outside in Hawkshead last year – when Ben was . . . you know. I don't think we've had a proper chat since then.'

'That's what she said. I just hope she doesn't want to talk about me.'

'Why would she?'

'Who knows?' the girl shrugged. 'She sometimes thinks she's being a bit slack, parent-wise. She was always forgetting to go to parents' evenings at school and then feeling bad about it. Mind you, she was at the place enough as it was, with me being such a challenge for them.'

'She won't want to talk about you. Is she thinking of going to the Canaries, then?'

'That's what she says. Can't think how she'd afford it. The state's not paying her for me any more, which leaves a big hole. I give her a lot of what I earn here, but it's not nearly as much as it was.'

'Lanzarote isn't cheap,' said Simmy ruefully. 'Last week cost serious money.'

'Tell her that, then,' said Bonnie. 'She'll probably phone you this evening with some ideas of where to go.'

The morning was very much quieter than Tuesday had been. The sun never quite dispersed the cloud, and there was a breeze that must have made sailing on the various lakes quite a temptation. When Ben showed up, he was welcomed as a break from an hour of monotony. Simmy had constructed the funeral tributes and was waiting for the next day to make the displays for the hotel. Timing was everything with flowers, and as delivery was not required before Friday, it was too soon to start arranging them.

'Sorry about the driving test,' said Simmy, knowing

better than to pretend the failure had never happened. 'Better luck next time.'

'It's a lottery,' said the boy with a scowl. 'There's no fairness to it at all.'

'What happened?'

'According to the thick-headed examiner, I didn't slow down sufficiently for a potential hazard ahead. That's the exact wording. In fact, there *was* no hazard. I could see quite clearly that the bloke was indicating to go left, before getting to where I was meant to turn off as well. So, I just carried on in a normal way. Wrong. You're not supposed to believe people when they indicate. Where's the sense in that?'

'Your instructor should have told you that,' said Simmy.

'He did, sort of, but every situation's different, and I used my common sense. Never a good idea these days. And then there was this idiot who stopped to let me out, at a junction. I knew he had the right of way, so I waved him to keep going ahead of me. Wrong again. I ask you – the rules are *perfectly* clear about that. I didn't do anything wrong. It's madness to penalise me for that. I still think that what I did was the safest option.' He growled angrily. 'The whole thing's a lottery,' he said again. 'And a conspiracy to make you fork out twice for the test fee.'

'Never mind,' crooned Bonnie. 'We can forget about it for a bit. What about this thing in Grasmere? We haven't found anything online about it,' she told Simmy. 'Are you sure it really happened?'

'I've only got Chris's word for it,' laughed Simmy, before

the startling thought hit her that perhaps it *had* all been a mistake somehow. 'But I don't think he'd invent something like that. He saw the body for himself. He *found* it.'

'In Grasmere, right?' Ben said.

'Yes. I'm not entirely clear about the whole story, but he was in an empty house, and Chris went to find him there. I mean, it's not actually *empty* but nobody lives in it. An old lady died, leaving it full of her possessions. Jonathan – that's the man who was killed – was going to clear it when the legal people said he could. At least – I think that's right. But there's something about her not wanting him to do it because he did something to upset her dog. But he knew where to find a key to the house, and went there for a look round, with Chris roped in as some sort of independent witness, to verify that he wasn't stealing anything. The old lady was called Kathleen,' she added, proud of herself for recalling that detail.

Ben took a deep breath. 'Can we go back to the beginning? This happened on Monday, did it? What time?'

'I don't know. Chris didn't call me until five in the afternoon, but a lot had happened by then. I guess it must have been in the middle of the day sometime.'

'Shouldn't he have been at work?'

'I got the impression this *was* work. The stuff from the house was meant to be going to the Keswick auction. Anyway, there's a suspect called Nick, who had a grudge against Jonathan, because he thought he'd reported him to the tax people. But Chris says it wouldn't have been him who did it. But he did give his name to the police. They took him all the way to Penrith for questioning.'

'Christopher gave this man's name to the police?' Ben was incredulous. 'Why? Does he hate him?'

'I don't think so.' She bit back Christopher's remark about feeling he could have been in Mexico, where she supposed the police were fairly brutal and out of control. Instead she said, 'He was probably just being helpful. I imagine plenty of other people know about Nick as well.'

'But he can't be sure any of them would have dropped the poor bloke in it. Isn't he scared that Nick's going to kill him now, as well?'

'As well as what?' Bonnie interrupted. 'Simmy just said Nick didn't do the murder.'

'Have you met any of these people?' Ben asked.

'No. Except there was an old man who Chris knows in Grasmere. We went to see him a little while ago. I think he was friendly with Kathleen who died, and Chris put Jonathan onto him when the house had to be cleared. Kathleen left a sort of unofficial will saying this old chap – he's called Philip – should handle that side of things. But it's not a proper will, so everything had to be frozen until some sort of important official solicitor did the probate and all that.' She went over this garbled statement in her head. 'Sorry that's so vague.'

Ben was rapidly thumbing his ever-present smartphone. 'Treasury solicitor,' he announced within seconds. 'It's all here. If she died intestate, there'll be strenuous efforts to find her next of kin. There's always somebody, of course. A fifth cousin in Tasmania, or a great-nephew in Kathmandu. The possibilities are endless.'

'Are you reading that or making it up?' asked Bonnie, trying to look over his arm at the device.

'I'm embellishing,' he said airily. 'The law says there have to be genuine efforts made to trace relatives. When did she die?' he asked Simmy.

'I don't know exactly. About a year ago, I think. I get the impression there was a bit of bother early on, with Jonathan falling out with Kathleen, but still really wanting to do the clearance.' She frowned. 'I might have got that wrong, but it does fit with everything Chris told me.'

'So now they've had the go-ahead to clear the house, have they? And that's why the dead man was there on Monday, and Christopher was meeting him?' He gave Simmy a careful look. 'So the cops might be thinking your boyfriend has some explaining to do. Did he tell you how the deed was done? What was the murder weapon?'

'Throttled with a belt,' said Simmy faintly.

'Hm.'

Bonnie giggled. 'This is where you should take a long draw on your pipe,' she said. 'The Sherlock Holmes act doesn't work without it.'

Ben ignored her. 'Sounds as if it must have been a man who did it,' he judged. 'But can't assume that. We need to go to Grasmere,' he announced decisively, and even more Sherlock-Holmes-ily.

'Why? How? They won't let you anywhere near the house. You can't go asking questions of people in the street. You haven't got a car.' Simmy reeled off objections in a panic. 'And Chris's annoyed that I told you about it in the first place,' she finished lamely.

'Christopher's going to have to get used to me, if he's sticking around.'

Simmy took a deep breath. 'He's sticking around all right. We're getting married – probably sometime this autumn.'

# Chapter Eight

The stunned silence lasted three seconds at most. 'Married? Why? Are you pregnant?' Bonnie blurted.

Simmy did not smile. 'Don't you start,' she said. 'My father asked the same thing.'

'Sorry. But . . . I didn't think . . . You never said . . .'

'Stop digging, Bon,' her boyfriend advised. 'She's old enough to know what she's doing.'

'This is not at all the reaction I was hoping for,' sighed Simmy. 'So far, nobody's shown much enthusiasm. Although my mother did her best, I have to admit.'

Bonnie pouted. 'Who else knows?'

'Only my parents. Don't worry – you're next on the list. Even though you don't deserve it.'

'So – where will you live? Will you close down the shop? Are you selling the Troutbeck house?' Ben's mind was visibly sifting implications. 'You're *not* pregnant, I take it?'

'Mind your own business. Besides, we're not talking about me. You were saying you wanted to go to Grasmere. If you behave yourselves, I suppose I could take you this evening. As you'll have worked out by now, it's the most obvious place for me and Chris to live – halfway between here and Keswick. I want to have a look at the houses. I've only been there a couple of times.'

'Will Christopher be there this evening as well?' asked Bonnie.

'We haven't made any plans, but he knows you'll be wanting to talk to him. I tried to warn him last night, in fact.'

'Good – so phone now and tell him you want to meet up with him. Suggest a drink or meal or something. We need *loads* more information about this Nick person, and the man he might have killed.'

Simmy quailed at the prospect of the two youngsters bombarding Christopher with questions, theories, outrageous notions. For all his extensive travelling and multitude of offbeat jobs, she was beginning to wonder just how much he'd learnt about people. As the eldest of a family of five, he might be expected to be reasonably wise when it came to understanding human behaviour – but there had been little evidence of that so far in their adult relationship.

'He won't mind, will he?' asked Bonnie innocently.

'He might find it a bit . . . full on,' said Simmy. 'He won't be offended or anything. He's quite easy-going about most things. But he might take it the wrong way.'

'You mean he won't get why it's any of our business,' supplied Ben. 'Which is very reasonable, because it's not, if you look at it in one way. But doesn't he realise by now that I've got very good *professional* reasons to get involved? I need to learn everything I can about how police investigations work, as near to first-hand as possible. You must have told him that, surely?'

'I've tried. He knows you're starting the degree course in forensics this year, and he thinks it's very impressive. But it's not so easy to explain why you want to interfere in real crimes, here in your home town.'

'Interfere?' Ben was outraged. 'I've *helped*. So has Bonnie.'

'I know. But you've also been in real danger. And most of the time, you were working from your room, making flowcharts and spreadsheets and all that theoretical stuff.'

'*Right!*' the boy almost shouted. 'So what's his problem, if I want to gather some notes about this thing in Grasmere? It's no skin off his nose.'

'As they say,' put in Bonnie with a laugh.

'I didn't say there was a problem,' defended Simmy. 'I'll phone him now and see if he can be there this evening. Satisfied?'

A well-timed customer saved her from further need to justify her man to these bright-eyed amateur detectives. She disliked having to speak for Chris, unsure as to what he would actually think or say.

Ben and Bonnie squashed themselves into the small room at the back and ate sandwiches while Simmy sold tulips to a woman who appeared regularly, full of whimsical ideas for centrepieces for the dinner parties she apparently gave every couple of weeks. This time, she was envisaging a flamboyant exhibition of tulips in every possible colour. 'I can absolutely *see* it,' she raved. 'Yellow, orange, blue, purple, red, pink, white, black – what else? Have you got them in all those colours?'

'Well, no,' Simmy confessed. 'Tulips have finished for this year, so they'll nearly all be imported. Let's have a look.' Together they scanned the buckets of cut flowers arranged around the shop. 'No purple or black,' she noted. 'But there's enough for a really nice show, all the same.'

The woman sighed and took whatever was available. 'Maybe I'll try and get some more somewhere else,' she muttered darkly.

'And good luck to her,' said Bonnie, half a minute later, having heard everything from the back room. 'Stupid woman.'

'I rather like her,' said Simmy. 'She's got a wonderful imagination.'

'You like everybody,' said Bonnie, not for the first time.

'I like most people,' Simmy corrected. 'And there's nothing wrong with that.'

'I should go,' said Ben, wistfully. 'Are we definite for Grasmere, then? I can be back here at five and we can go then.'

'I don't know,' Simmy said. 'There won't be any point if Chris can't make it.' She thought of the time she'd spent with Flo and her baby only a mile from Grasmere and regretted that she wouldn't have a chance to visit her again, with Ben and Bonnie alongside. If she and Chris were soon to live there, she could go and see the mother and child regularly. It suddenly seemed the most appealing prospect she could imagine. She would have a local friend – which she did not in Troutbeck.

'Yes, there will. You can have a look round for houses for sale, and we can get some idea of what exactly happened on Monday. There'll be police tape, or even an incident room. There's no substitute for being on the spot,' said Ben sententiously.

'All right, then,' said Simmy, remembering how she felt about summer evenings and the obligation to make proper use of them.

'Great! You're a star, Sim – you know that?' It was Bonnie enthusing so loudly. Ben made sounds of agreement, smiling broadly.

'It's really nice up there,' Simmy shrugged. 'I'm happy to get to know it better. Now let's get on with some work.'

Ben was on the doorstep several minutes before five o'clock. Simmy would not be rushed, despite his efforts to hurry her by bringing in the outside plants. Bonnie closed down the computer and locked the door leading to the small yard at the back. Simmy ushered them outside and pulled the shop door shut behind them. 'The car's up Broad Street today,' she said. Every morning she had to seek out a parking space in one of the streets on the eastern side of town, and every afternoon she had to try to remember exactly where she'd left it.

They found it without difficulty and followed a number of other rush-hour drivers northwards. Ambleside was slow, with the added traffic caused by summer visitors, but the road through Rydal and on towards Grasmere was smooth and trouble-free. They were soon looping through the woods of Banerigg, where Simmy had been only two days earlier. 'Isn't it lovely!' sighed Bonnie. She was in the back of the car, looking all round at the views. 'This is where you brought those flowers, isn't it? On Monday?'

'Just up there,' Simmy confirmed, ducking her head at a small side lane. 'Pity there isn't a cottage for sale here.'

'How do you know there isn't?' said Ben.

'The place is so tiny – there are almost no houses here. It would be too good to be true. Chris quite likes the little stone cottages a bit further along here, but I think they're too close to Dove Cottage.'

'Where are we meeting him?' Ben asked.

'In the car park at the top of the town. By a big white hotel.'

'Top of the town,' Ben repeated thoughtfully. 'Does a town have a top?'

'Shut up. I know how to find it, which is the main thing.' And she did, with no difficulty. Ben and Bonnie looked around, pausing to laugh at a sign warning motorists that their satnavs could not be trusted past that point.

'No way is this the top,' said Ben. 'I'd call it the *middle*.'

Simmy and Bonnie both ignored him, and he went on, 'I can just imagine all those huge lorries getting wedged between stone walls. I presume that road just curves around the other side of the lake, without really leading anywhere.' He squinted into the sun. 'We're east of the lake,' he asserted. 'And if I remember rightly, there's another car park north of here, which could make a better claim to be at the top.'

'Stop it,' Bonnie ordered. 'You're just showing off.'

Ben's knowledge of the Lake District was at least as extensive as Russell Straw's. His parents had taken the family to virtually every town and village in Cumbria and beyond, including camping trips and weekend outings. Helen Harkness had instigated lengthy walks on the fells, until prevented from further treks by painful arthritis that struck her at far too early an age. 'Too much sitting at the drawing board,' she explained. Simmy had a lot of respect for Helen Harkness.

Christopher was ten minutes late, and when he finally arrived he looked drawn and ten years older. Ben gave a low whistle, and muttered to Simmy, 'What have you done to him?'

The streets of the small town were generously filled with evening walkers, at least half of them with dogs. Most of the shops were still open, and people were sitting in the open air outside cafes and on low stone walls that bordered a small park. 'It's very like Hawkshead,' Simmy remarked.

'It's not at all like Hawkshead,' Ben argued. 'Bigger, for a start, and much more open.' He pointed to the park. 'You don't get grass in Hawkshead, either.'

They arranged themselves around a small table belonging to a cafe attached to The Inn at Grasmere, which was a substantial building occupying a prime position. The cafe was in a conservatory, with some tables outside. They settled at one of these, noting that the diners on either side of them each had a dog lying at their feet. Christopher smiled at the sight of them, and said, 'Just like France. Or Argentina. There are dogs everywhere in Argentina.' Nobody took him up on this, and they ordered a variety of meals, having agreed that Ben and Bonnie were paying for their own food. 'You know – there's only one proper pub in the whole town,' said Ben. 'So that's different from Hawkshead as well.'

'I don't believe you,' argued Christopher. 'There are at least two on the main road, for a start.'

'I meant *in* the town . . . village . . . whatever they call themselves. And you could argue that all the hotels have bars, which operate more or less the same as pubs – but even so, it's not what some people expect. Now take Patterdale, for example—'

'Why have we come here?' Christopher cut across this prattling. 'I mean to this precise eating place?'

'Because we've never been here before and we like to try new places,' said Ben.

Simmy laughed nervously, aware of an increasingly scratchy atmosphere. 'Sorry, Chris. You'll have to get used to these two, I'm afraid. They mean well. Ben's at a loose end now his exams have finished. He doesn't have to go to school much, apparently, even though it's another month until the end of term for the rest of the school. There's a Leaver's Ball next week, and I think that's about it. Awful, really, the way it all just fizzles out. But Ben always finds something to do.'

'He's going down to the Cotswolds at the beginning of August,' said Bonnie, with a mournful look. 'Some old uncle or third cousin. I can't remember what. But he's always had a soft spot for Ben and wants him to go and visit.'

'Meanwhile Ben's here, with time on his hands,' said Simmy. She faced Christopher directly. 'And he *is* very good at solving murders, you know.'

'You make it sound like a game,' said Christopher stiffly.

'People say that,' Bonnie nodded. 'But we never forget how terrible it is – honestly. Killing another person is the worst thing you can do. We absolutely do know that. You look as if it's been a pretty bad few days, actually.'

'I *found* him. Hardly any distance from where we're sitting now.' Chris rubbed his forehead. 'I keep seeing his face.'

'Post-traumatic stress,' said Ben. 'Flashbacks. Probably perfectly healthy – your brain's working to assimilate what happened. It shouldn't last long, with any luck.' He paused, clearly aware of being on thin ice. 'Did you touch him? Was he still warm? I'm sorry if that's making you feel worse, but it would be really helpful to know.'

'Yes, and yes,' said Christopher. 'Now I really don't want to talk any more about it. I only came because I wanted to see Simmy. We're meant to be looking at houses, aren't we?' He gave her a pleading look.

'Very much so,' she assured him. 'But now Ben and Bonnie are here, won't you at least give them a bit to go on? I've tried to explain who Jonathan is, and Philip and Kathleen something. But I think I might have some of it wrong.'

At that, the food arrived. 'Two omelettes, one cheese, one ham; one Caesar salad and a sausage egg and chips,' rattled off the waitress. 'Any sauces with that?' They all shook their heads and waited for her to go.

Christopher spoke first. 'What's Philip got to do with anything? Why bring him into it?'

'There you are, you see – I am getting it all wrong. Just because Philip lives in Grasmere I've got him involved.' She frowned. 'But he knew Kathleen, and it was in her house that you found Jonathan. So I guess he must have *something* to do with it. Didn't you give him Jonathan's name when he wanted somebody to clear the house?'

Christopher sighed. 'You sound just like the police. Names, reasons, dates. Who was where when, and what did they know? It went on for *hours*.'

'It *takes* hours to get the hang of a story, when you start from nothing,' said Ben. 'You generally have to go quite far into the past to get any sort of handle on it. This lady – Kathleen – for example. I mean, it sounds to me as if it really did start with her, and the stuff she had in her house. And it also sounds as if poor old Jonathan was just a shade too quick to start rummaging around with a view to clearing it. He probably made a few lists of what was worth something, and where he might get the best price for it. Then he'd wait for the all-clear from the treasury solicitor and whisk it all away in a flash. Right?'

'Treasury solicitor?' echoed Christopher.

'Right. That's the person who deals with estates when there's no will. Surely you knew that?'

'I know now. Not normally my area of expertise. I just sell the stuff.'

'Philip,' prompted Bonnie.

'Philip has nothing to do with it,' Christopher repeated. 'He's ninety-one and in a home. It must be twenty years ago or more that Kathleen asked him to be a sort of executor, but they never put it in a proper will. He could easily have washed his hands of the whole thing when she died, but he thought he had a duty to do what he could. It's only a few months ago he asked me to have a look at his own possessions, before he went into the home.'

Ben held up a finger. 'But Kathleen must have already been dead by then. This treasury solicitor business can take a year before they let you have the stuff.'

Christopher blinked and shook his head. 'She must have been, I suppose. We didn't mention her then, as far as I can remember. At least . . . I think I'd just forgotten all about her at that point. I can't remember exactly when she died. Too much has happened in the meantime.' He gave Simmy another look of appeal.

'Hasn't it just,' she replied, in full co-operation.

'It's easily answered,' said Ben blithely, eyes on his clever phone. 'Except, I can't find it.' He sat back and concentrated on the little screen. 'Let me think. There's a place where they usually advertise for long-lost relatives . . . Yes! The *London Gazette*. Here it is. Deceased estates. Hey! This is great! It's all here. Mrs Kathleen Leeson. Born 1926. It's got her address and the details for the solicitor who's taken it all on. They call it an administrator – look. She worked as a midwife. Did you know that? Date of death is 26th June last year.' His excitement at the speed and ease of his discovery affected them all.

'That's amazing,' said Christopher, admiringly. 'I wonder whether anybody ever replied.'

'You'll get to hear if they do,' said Bonnie. 'Assuming they want to sell the house contents at your auction.'

'Big assumption.' He grimaced. 'I'll be tainted now by being involved in the murder.'

'I went with you to look at Philip's things,' said Simmy,

after a short silence. 'Remember? He did seem very frail. He never mentioned being in charge of clearing a friend's house. And surely he would have, because that was what we were talking about. What was to happen to his things, I mean. That seems a bit strange.'

Christopher's face cleared. 'I've got it now. It *was* last summer that Kathleen died. Both my parents were still alive. Philip's actually some distant cousin by marriage, and my mother asked me to help him with Kathleen's possessions. But I never actually went to the house. I don't remember what stopped me.' He looked remorseful.

'He can't have been too upset with you, if he got back to you about his own things,' Simmy reassured him.

'When was that?' asked Ben.

'In the spring sometime. Simmy and I went for a look. But he didn't have anything worth more than a few quid, so I wasn't much use to him.'

'But did he already know Jonathan, from last year?' Bonnie asked. 'Didn't the police want to know about all this?'

'I didn't say anything to them about Philip. Why would I?'

'He's part of the story,' said Bonnie severely.

Ben had produced a medium-sized hard-backed notebook from the rucksack he always carried. It had been his schoolbag throughout his time in the sixth form and was now almost part of his body. Simmy could think of only a handful of occasions when she'd seen him without it. 'Good thinking,' he applauded his girlfriend.

'He's not, though,' insisted Christopher. 'I've no idea when he first met Jon. All I did was make one phone call last summer, when I think I gave Philip Jon's name and number as a better person to help him than I could be. That's why I can barely remember it. It didn't come to anything, anyway, because of the lack of a will. For the Lord's sake, this is going in circles, the same as it did in Penrith. For all I know Jon wasn't even killed here. Whoever did it might have just dumped him in the house after he was dead.'

'What difference would that make?' Ben demanded. 'It still makes the house and its contents part of the picture. Had he started clearing it, do you know? Did he bring a van? And why was it *you* who found him?'

Christopher again appealed silently to Simmy for rescue. She grimaced sympathetically, and said, 'You'd better answer him, if you want this to stop. How were your sausages?' However traumatised he might be, Christopher had polished off his food at high speed.

'My omelette wasn't bad,' said Bonnie.

'My salad was nothing special, but I wouldn't complain about it,' agreed Simmy.

'I didn't even notice,' admitted Christopher. 'But I'm no gourmet.'

Ben was writing in his notebook, waiting for the food talk to stop. 'Well?' he prompted the older man.

'I really have no idea what he was doing. His van was parked in the cul-de-sac – that doesn't mean he meant to collect anything. It was his only means of transport. Jon phoned me on Monday morning and said would I come and meet him at the house, because it couldn't be much longer before the all-clear, and he wanted to be ahead of any competition. He was never one to hang about.'

Ben wrote busily. 'How did he get in?'

'He knew where there was still a spare key.'

Ben raised his eyebrows. 'So that proves he was known to Mrs Leeson last year. Why are you trying to make us think otherwise?'

Christopher sat back, glaring at the boy. 'I'm not doing any such thing All I'm trying to do is stick to the facts, without making wild guesses.'

'Jonathan called you on Sunday,' Simmy said suddenly. 'In a state about something. The business with Nick – right?'

Ben winced at this hijacking of his interrogation but made no attempt to interrupt. He merely waved his pencil in reluctant encouragement.

Christopher, however, seemed glad of her question. 'Nick was miles away, all day Monday. No way could it have been him.'

'But you gave his name to the police, didn't you?' said Bonnie. 'Because he had some grudge against Jonathan.'

'Yes, I did. But since then I've heard that Nick was way over in Leeds, all day Monday. He's in the clear.'

'Oh.' Ben made a note. 'His alibi will have been checked by now, then.'

Christopher addressed Simmy. 'Jon was worried about Nick being pissed off with him. That was mostly what he called about on Sunday. When the cops asked me straight out whether I knew of any trouble, I didn't see any option but to tell them. Somebody else would have, if I hadn't. It wasn't exactly a secret. And now it doesn't matter, anyway. It's got nothing to do with Jon being killed.'

Nobody seemed sure where to go after that. A silence

fell. 'Have we finished?' Ben asked, indicating the empty plates. 'Or does anybody want pudding?'

'What about the tapestry thing?' Simmy said, having taken on Ben's role as prompter. She was the link between Chris and the other two, or perhaps a conduit. She had passed on what she could remember of the events of Sunday and Monday, risking her fiancé's wrath at her disclosures.

Christopher sighed again. 'Stumpwork,' he corrected. 'It's nothing like a tapestry. Or needlepoint, come to that – which is the correct term for what people call tapestries these days. I could explain, but it's really not relevant.'

Ben waved his pencil again.

'It sold for umpteen thousand pounds, while we were away,' Simmy elaborated. 'Chris's auction house sold it for Jonathan. My mum saw it in the paper and asked me about it.'

'Aha!' said Ben. 'Now we're getting somewhere. What happens to the money, now Jonathan's dead?'

'He's got a wife,' said Christopher, to everyone's surprise. 'She's called Valerie and lives in Carlisle. He left her about five years ago, but I don't think there was ever a divorce. I met her a while ago, actually. They're fairly amicable – just can't live together. I think there's a new boyfriend moved in. Jon wasn't too happy about that.'

'Men!' tutted Bonnie. 'They always want to have their cake and eat it.'

'Sounds like a quote from Corinne,' smiled Ben. 'In this case, I'd say it's more a matter of dog in the manger. There's no logic to it, but it's very common.'

'So, Valerie gets the money,' Simmy said. 'Does that make her a suspect? Is she big and strong?'

'She is, quite. But there's no way she'd kill him.' Christopher was emphatic.

'Oh!' Simmy's sudden cry made everyone jump. 'There's Flo,' she went on, before getting up from her seat. 'Hey – hello again!'

A woman pushing a baby buggy was passing the open area where the four were sitting, keeping well to the side of the street, which had no pavement. She paused, hearing her name, then smiled. 'Oh, hello,' she said.

Within seconds Simmy was bending over the buggy, where the baby was slumped, fast asleep. 'How's she been?'

'She's fine while we're in motion. I've walked all the way from home. We're going to see Daddy – beard him in his den, sort of thing.' Anxiety crossed the woman's face. 'But I'm not sure he'll be very pleased. He might not want to be distracted if he's in the middle of something.'

# Chapter Nine

'Why? Where is he?' Simmy asked.

'He's got an office in an old converted chapel, just around the corner from here. He said he'd be working late again. Quite honestly, I've got rather sick of it. I blame you, really. You made me see how spineless I've been since Lucy May was born. She's his child too – he needs to spend more time with her and take on some of the hassle.'

'Quite right,' said Simmy supportively. At the same time, she found herself all too well aware of the stereotype, in which the wife walks in on a steamy session involving the husband and his secretary. 'What does he do, anyway?'

'He's area manager for CaniCare. You know – the charity that rescues dogs and gets vet care for them and finds new homes. It's a big outfit now. They've got shops all over the north-west.'

'Is there one in Grasmere?'

'No.' Flo looked around herself, with an expression that said, *When have you ever seen charity shops in Grasmere?* 'But there's one in Ambleside, and another in Keswick. It's only been in existence for two years, and it's already huge. Everybody loves dogs, you see.'

'But you haven't got one?'

The woman laughed. 'No. I'm not that crazy about them, personally. If they're big they scare me, and if they're little they annoy me.'

'I'm a bit the same,' said Simmy. 'Oh, sorry – these are my friends. Ben and Bonnie – and Chris. He's my fiancé. This is Flo – and Lucy May,' she told the others. Christopher had turned away, apparently examining his left thumbnail with great interest. He gave Flo a quick glance and a nod, saying nothing. She said a general 'Hello' to the three of them, and then Simmy started talking again.

'We're thinking of moving up here, actually. You don't know any houses for sale, do you? Or rent, I suppose.'

'There's one or two, I think. I haven't been taking much notice lately. It'd be nice to have you living close by,' she added simply.

Christopher had got to his feet and now approached, holding out his hand for a formal shake. 'Pleased to meet you,' he said. 'How old's the little one?'

Flo gave him a thoughtful look before answering,

'Three and a half weeks. We've got to go to a check-up on Friday. I'm dreading it. They're sure to say she's not gaining enough weight.'

'Screw 'em,' he said blithely. 'What do they know? She looks fine to me.'

*And what do* you *know?* Simmy wondered silently.

Flo laughed. 'I'm so glad I bumped into you. I couldn't bear to waste another evening just sitting about worrying and trying to keep the little beast quiet. I'll have to keep moving, though, or she'll start off again. I never expected to become such a *slave*,' she wailed, in mock distress. 'You never think it'll happen to you, when people tell all those melodramatic stories about new babies.'

Christopher met Simmy's eye with a grimace. 'There must be compensations,' he said.

'Not many, so far. But I guess it has to get better. Once she starts talking, I'm sure I'll find her delightful.'

Ben and Bonnie were still at the table. 'We haven't paid,' Ben called now, waving a slip of paper that was presumably the bill.

'Oops,' said Christopher, and went back to the youngsters.

'Bye, then,' said Flo.

'Phone me,' said Simmy urgently, walking along with her. 'The shop's in Windermere. Persimmon Petals. There was a card with the flowers. That's got my mobile number on it as well. I'd love to keep in touch.'

'Me too. I can introduce you to a couple of women here, if this is where you're going to live. And you should meet Scott. He knows practically everybody in town. He grew up here, you see, and spent most of his life here as well.'

A thought struck Simmy. 'He didn't live in that same house, did he? With his previous wife?'

Flo cast her eyes upwards in a mixture of self-disparagement and resignation. 'How did you guess? Classic, isn't it? I redecorated it, and bought new carpets and things, but somehow it still isn't really mine. It was all very logical, and it's a lovely house, but . . .'

'Simmy!' Christopher was calling her, and she realised she'd walked a hundred yards or so as she talked to Flo.

'Better go,' she said. 'Good luck with Scott.'

'Thanks. I might need it.'

Ben was talking earnestly to Christopher when Simmy rejoined them. 'This needlework thing – what was it exactly? Where did Jonathan get it from? It sounds like something a person might kill for.' He seemed very young to Simmy, manifesting his more insensitive geeky side, just when she most wanted him not to. Chris was clearly not inclined to answer the questions being thrown at him.

'Leave him alone,' said Simmy. 'I'm sorry I ever mentioned the thing now.'

'Lucky you did,' said Ben. 'It's bound to be relevant.'

'It's not,' said Chris.

'Did the police ask you about it? Did they know it was Jonathan's? It was your auction house that sold it, after all.'

'He brought it in months ago, wanting us to value it. I had no idea, so passed him on to Oliver. He got very excited and said it could fetch five grand on a good day. It was entered for the sale the weekend before last, when Simmy and I were away. I forgot all about it until Monday, when Oliver caught me, and said it'd gone for fourteen thousand. He was feeling a bit silly for undervaluing it – but happy about the commission, of course. And the publicity didn't hurt.'

'Didn't Jonathan say where he got it from?'

'He hinted that it was a car boot sale. Picked it up for almost nothing. But he wouldn't say exactly.'

'I don't blame him,' said Bonnie. 'People are going to be cross with him.'

Christopher shook his head. 'It's fair game. Happens all the time. I know a man who finds something worth hundreds just about every week, amongst jumbles of junk on some old lady's stall. Vinaigrettes are the thing, just now. Nobody knew what they were, and they let them go for peanuts. Except, as of a month or so ago, they've become popular. There was one on the TV and now everybody recognises them.'

'I don't know what they are,' said Simmy. 'But fourteen thousand is a bit different from hundreds. Didn't Jonathan have a moral obligation to try to share it with the poor person who innocently sold it to him?'

'Not at all.' Chris was vehement. 'I told you – it's all part of the game. There wouldn't be any dealers if they weren't allowed to hope for a big profit once in a while. They have to make a living. He deserved the cash for having recognised the thing for what it was. That's how it all *works*.' He was speaking loudly, attracting attention from people in the street.

Simmy was still not sure she agreed. She was put in mind of her mother's abhorrence of agents of any sort. Dealers seemed to fall into the same category. 'It sounds dodgy to me,' she said boldly. 'Dealers are just parasitic middle men, as my mother would say.'

'Vinaigrettes are tiny little objects containing a sponge soaked in vinegar,' said Ben, informatively. 'They were used in the eighteenth and early nineteenth centuries to ameliorate the worst of the smells out in the streets. Made of silver, and sometimes gold. They come in lots of different shapes – animals, boxes, all sorts. People collect them.'

'They sound lovely,' said Simmy, in wonder, thoroughly distracted.

'They are,' agreed Chris.

Ben was fingering his phone and showed Simmy the results. The eBay website displayed a long page of the very things described. It was a revelation. 'Wow!' she gasped. 'I want to collect them.'

'Too late,' her fiancé advised her. 'You need to be onto the next thing. Something you can buy for a quid and keep safe until the world wakes up and wants them. The trick is to stay a couple of steps ahead.'

'You're right. It's a game,' said Simmy, thinking again that there was something unsavoury tucked beneath the excitement and competition surrounding the business. 'Makes you wonder whether people value the things for their own sakes.'

Chris looked at her as if she'd directly criticised him. His grey eyes seemed to shrink into his head, and lines appeared at the sides of his mouth. 'Don't say that.'

'Sorry. I don't know anything about it, really.'

He changed the subject. 'How are those two getting home?'

'I'll have to take them.' She bit back the *obviously*. In fact, the buses ran frequently enough to be a viable alternative, but she had no intention of abandoning her charges. 'But we can have an hour or so exploring the town, if you like. They can amuse themselves well enough.'

Ben heard her and flapped a hand in careless complicity. It was approaching seven-thirty, the sky still as light as midday. 'We'll stroll along to the lake and talk everything through,' he said. 'It doesn't feel as if we've got anything like the full picture yet. We can go up that lane past the car park. See you at the car at half past eight, okay?'

'Be careful,' said Simmy, in spite of herself. Ben had found himself in jeopardy on the banks of another lake, less than a year before. Even though he seemed so much older now, there were still moments of vulnerability.

'Simmy!' Bonnie protested with a squeal.

'Sorry,' said Simmy again, thinking she must be getting more like her mother than she ever expected to, if people were so affected by things she said.

The couples separated, one pair heading north and the other south. 'We could go as far as the cemetery,' Christopher suggested. 'There are one or two nice houses along the way. We can imagine how it would be to live here.'

'Lovely,' she gushed. 'It does have a nice atmosphere, doesn't it. My father says Walter Scott was very fond of it.'

'Touristy, though. They get coachloads of Chinese, apparently.'

'Really?'

'They go to Dove Cottage and come into town for cream teas. Poor old Jon hated them. Going back to what you said before, he was a dealer who really did appreciate the things for themselves, you know. He would finger them, and bone on about the workmanship, and quality of the materials. He couldn't stand modern plastic junk. It hurt him the way young people show no respect for good old things. He worried that half of it would just get thrown out over the next fifty years or so. I guess you could say he's well out of it, as far as that goes.'

'No, you can't say that. How old was he?'

'Late fifties, I s'pose. Looked more. He'd had a hard life. Never held down a proper job. Lived on his wits. A bit of a type, you could say. The saleroom's full of them.'

'You liked him,' she realised.

'I couldn't help liking him, most of the time. But I still wish he'd called someone else, instead of me.'

'You sounded quite critical of him on Sunday,' she remarked.

'I don't think I did,' he said irritably.

'What's this street called?' She looked round for a sign. Yet again she was retreating from sensitive territory, to avoid wounding Christopher's feelings. She had to stop doing it, she told herself.

'Broadgate. It goes up to the main road. There aren't many likely properties this side of the road, though. We'd be extremely lucky to find one for sale. I had a quick google today and found one at half a million quid and a couple of tiny flats. It's better the other side – they're building some new ones as well, I notice.'

'What about renting?' The prospect of selling her Troutbeck house was weighing heavily. Perhaps she could

110

let it out and use the money to fund somewhere in Grasmere. Would that sound silly if she voiced it?

'Or we could rent,' he agreed easily. 'That'd be quicker to organise. I doubt there's anything available, though.'

'It's lovely here, isn't it?' She stood still, gazing all round herself. The landscape was different from that of Troutbeck, the fells more craggy, with more level ground between them. They had passed a small field with a large house on the far side of it, and a steeply rising fell behind it. The church stood at the southern side of the settlement, with large hotels providing the major landmarks. The main business was near the church, with touristy shops and the ubiquitous tea rooms on both sides of the street. They had walked northwards from there, along a fairly wide street with shops along one side and no sign of any ordinary residential houses. Nor could she see any Chinese tourists. All gone back to a big hotel for the night, she assumed. Grasmere had very little by way of night life, as far as she could see. The restaurants she'd paused to inspect all closed at nine o'clock.

'Bonnie was quiet,' said Christopher suddenly. 'Doesn't she like me?'

Simmy smiled. 'It's not that. She's always ill at ease where food's concerned. Eating with other people is a strain for her. She had very bad anorexia only a few years ago, and I doubt if she'll ever be altogether normal about it. Ben's been fantastically good for her. He's so gentle and understanding. It makes you want to cry, sometimes.'

'Good Lord – I had no idea. Does *everybody* have some terrible dark experience in their past? You with your baby, my dad with his . . . well, you know.'

'But not you, right?'

He grimaced. 'I expect I could come up with a few nasty moments if I tried. I haven't told you everything about my travelling years. There was this Mayan bloke, in Guatemala. Face like a block of wood. He took a dislike to me and followed me around for a day or two. I got totally paranoid about it, ending up gibbering in a forest.'

'Mayan? Didn't they die out centuries ago?'

'If they did, he must have been a ghost. That's quite likely, actually. Although Guatemala has more than its share of hard men. They're like golems, or robots. Think nothing of killing you – and each other. Remember never to ride on the buses in Guatemala City, okay?'

'You'll have to remind me.'

They had walked past a playground, and into a street called Swan Lane. Ahead she could see the traffic passing on the main road, with houses beyond. 'Okay,' she said. 'I've got my bearings now. But I'm not sure I really would like to live here full time, you know. There's something so terribly self-conscious about it. Worse than Ambleside, even.'

'Well, maybe we'll have to think about Keswick, then. That's got heaps of properties for sale, and it's a lot more user-friendly, with supermarkets and all the other services. Doctors, schools, trains . . .'

'Too far from Windermere,' she objected. 'I'd have to drive fifty miles every day.'

'More like forty-five,' he corrected her. 'But I admit it wouldn't be much fun.'

The hour passed quickly, with less than effective attention shown to the impossibly scanty supply of housing in Grasmere. It seemed enough that they had restored an emotional equilibrium between them, bringing themselves back to the easy intimacy they'd enjoyed during their holiday. Nagging at the back of Simmy's mind was the knowledge that Ben would expect her to extract further details regarding the murder from Chris, but she ignored it. Chris clearly didn't want to talk about it, and she understood that he had only agreed to meet the young pair because she'd asked him to, and they came as a package. If he wanted to see Simmy, he had to take them as well, at least on this particular evening.

But suddenly he took her by surprise by saying, 'There really aren't any obvious suspects, apart from Nick. And even he wasn't angry enough to kill anybody. Lots of people found Jon annoying, but that's a million miles from murder. As I understand it, this sort of killing implies that the person thought he had something to gain. That doesn't work with any of the things I know about Jon. Even with the money from the stumpwork he didn't have much. And he hadn't *got* that money yet.'

'There are other motives. Revenge, for one. And jealousy. Did he have a girlfriend? Has he been carrying on with somebody's wife?'

'Not to my knowledge. He was rather scruffy. I'm not sure women found him very appealing.'

'Can we see the house? Could you bear it?'

'We can't go in.' Christopher looked scandalised. 'Why do you want to go there?'

'I don't know. Curiosity, I suppose.'

'Well, all right. It's back down in the centre of town. A

113

minute or two from where we left the car. Funny Ben didn't want to have a look as well.'

'Oh, he did. He'll have known where it was before we got here.'

Chris led her back the way they'd come, past the car park, and took her to within twenty yards of a modest stone house down a small road opposite the school. Blue police tape still barred entry through the front gate. 'Bit surplus to requirements, don't you think?' he said.

'Does it bother you, being here again so soon?'

'A bit. Mainly, I can hardly believe it really happened. It seems like a ghastly dream. I've already forgotten the details, like you do with a dream. I still can't make any proper sense of it. I've run through it a hundred times, trying to think who could have done it, and why. Anybody would, I suppose. It's not just your friend Ben.'

'The police were lucky to get your statement so quickly, while it was still vivid in your mind. It *was* you who called them, wasn't it?'

'More or less. I came dashing out of the house and bumped into a man just about here. I took him back in with me, and he made the call. He stayed with me till the cops came, but when we explained that it was only me who'd found Jon, and he had nothing to do with it, they pretty much lost interest in him.'

'Who was he? Did you get his name?'

Christopher shrugged irritably. 'I think he knew who I was – lots of people do, of course. He gave his details to the cops.'

Simmy absorbed this scanty information with some

114

unease. Wasn't this man a potential suspect, hovering nearby to see who found the body of the man he'd killed? But would he then let himself be drawn into the aftermath to find himself questioned by the police? Highly unlikely, she decided. 'What was he doing, exactly? When you came rushing out of the house?' She looked round. 'He can't have been a passer-by, can he? This is a cul-de-sac. It doesn't go anywhere.'

Christopher showed no sign of being caught out. He rubbed his cheek and said, 'I don't know. He seemed to be just walking along. I grabbed him. I wasn't at all together, like I always thought I'd be if something like this happened. I was a real mess. He gave me a few funny looks, I can tell you.'

'Did he think you'd killed Jonathan? It must have seemed very odd to him. Was he scared? How old was he?'

Still, Christopher seemed patient and unworried by her questions. 'I don't think he was scared. He'd be about middle fifties, maybe. And I think he believed what I told him. I was a *mess*,' he said again.

Simmy was fairly sure that somebody who'd just committed murder *would* be in an emotional mess. She looked at her future husband and then put a hand on his arm. 'Is that why you left it so long before calling me? Because you were a mess?' It still rankled, she noted, the way he'd failed to keep her informed. 'Because you had to convince everybody that it wasn't you who killed him?'

'What? No – well, maybe. There was never the right moment. The whole afternoon just vanished in a horrible swirling nightmare. They obviously thought I must have done it. They took my fingerprints and DNA.' He shuddered. 'I felt like a criminal. But they'll have my car on camera somewhere, showing I could only have been in Grasmere for a few minutes. I'm hoping they can work out that Jon had been dead for at least an hour before I got there.'

'They won't be able to, Chris. It's a myth about pinpointing the time of death. Especially as they won't have got a police doctor to him for quite a while after you found him. Did you touch him?'

He nodded wearily. 'Of course I did. I tried to loosen the belt. I think I slapped his face. Stupid things like that.'

'Oh dear.' She risked a further step in her questioning, prompted by a nagging sense that he was withholding something. 'I've forgotten why you agreed to come here in the first place. That is, I presume you probably wanted to have a look at the house contents as soon as you could, just as Jonathan did. But it does seem very quick – there was no suggestion of meeting Jonathan here when you spoke to him on Sunday, was there?'

He looked directly at her and reached for her hand. 'We were all waiting for the call from that treasury person, if Ben's right that that's who handles it. Me, Philip, Jonathan – all of us. It was especially unfinished business for poor old Philip. But it's complicated for him in that home, even though he's got his own phone. In the old days, they'd have sent a letter, but now it's all emails and phone calls. So, we gave them my details, so I could deal with it for him. I was going to go and see him as soon as we knew anything, and before that I wanted to catch Jonathan and make sure we were all up to speed. I was planning to go and have a chat with Philip anyway, after seeing Jon.'

Yet again, Simmy took a little time to process all this. One detail had snagged her attention. 'Surely they *do* still send letters? Doesn't there have to be a piece of paper to show all the authorities here?' She had another thought. 'And didn't you say Jon wanted you as some sort of protection?'

'He was a bit jumpy when he phoned, yes.'

'So *when* did he call you?'

'Come on, Sim. Trust me, okay? It's exactly as I've told you. There's no mystery to it. And I've been through it so many times already.' She became freshly aware of how ravaged he looked. But she still couldn't entirely abandon her need to understand what had happened.

'It sounds awfully like a mad dash for the poor old lady's possessions. Like a swarm of locusts. There must have been some sort of fight over who got first dibs and Jonathan came out worst.'

Now Christopher openly groaned. 'Absolutely not like that in any way. For a start, there had to be authorisation from whoever they'd found to inherit the proceeds. That hadn't happened, as far as I know. If there is anybody, that is. I still have no idea about that.'

'And I still don't really get why you and Jonathan both showed up here on Monday? There's got to be something you're not telling me.'

'Please, *please* stop,' he begged. 'I've told you everything. There's no reason to think Jon was doing anything underhand. He'd used the key when he shouldn't, that's all. He didn't have any proper right to go into the house, but in practice nobody's going to care. There is nobody, anyway, who'd have been around to stop him. Just faceless bureaucracy. Jon knew the ropes; he'd seen the same sort of thing before.'

'And who kept Philip up to speed, if you never got there on Monday?'

Christopher heaved a sigh. 'Nobody. I phoned the home yesterday and they said he's got a virus, and they're trying to keep him quietly in bed for a few days. He's woozy, apparently, and they don't think he should have visitors. Certainly not if they're bringing bad news.'

'But how could anybody have known Jonathan would be at the house? Whoever killed him obviously knew he was there.'

'Good question.'

The remark came not from Christopher, but Ben Harkness, who had come up behind them without being seen. 'Nice little house, isn't it?' he went on. 'Just the thing for you two to live in.'

# *Chapter Ten*

All four looked from face to face as the idea elicited different reactions. Christopher flushed, once the implications sank in, and said, 'What the hell are you suggesting?'

Simmy gave the house a closer scrutiny, seeing for the first time the fine quality of the stonework and the generous size of the windows. There was a garden at the front and shady trees. She allowed herself to wonder what it might be like as a home. 'Come on, Chris. You can't pretend it's a new idea. You mentioned it yourself only yesterday.'

'Things are different now,' said Christopher tightly.

Bonnie laughed, and said, 'Trust you,' to her boyfriend.

'Nobody wants to live in a house where there's been a murder, do they? That means it'll go cheap when they sell it.'

'Precisely,' said Ben smugly. Then he turned to Christopher. 'What's wrong with the idea, anyway?'

'The timing's not great, for one thing. And it sounds bad, don't you think? As if I might have had my eye on the place for a while.'

'But it is rather nice, I must admit,' said Simmy wistfully.

Ben chewed his upper lip for a few moments. 'No, but that wouldn't matter. It's not Jonathan's house, is it? Do we know whether they ever did find a distant relative who gets it?'

Christopher took a long breath. 'I have absolutely no idea. I'm just an auctioneer, remember. People bring me things to sell, and I sell them. That's it.'

Ben squared his shoulders. 'Well, I think it's highly likely that a person will be identified with a claim to the estate. The said person will be expected to authorise removal of contents of the house, on condition an exact inventory is made independently, and any item valued at over one hundred pounds or thereabouts should be set aside. Given that proviso, it would normally be assumed that the clearance would be paid for by sale of the contents in whatever way the person doing the clearing chose.'

In spite of himself, Christopher seemed impressed. 'Is that a direct quote?'

Simmy was trying to suppress a thread of resentment at Ben's easy access to arcane facts, when she had got so little out of Christopher.

Ben smiled apologetically. 'Not entirely. I lost the last bit. It just means nobody pays anybody anything, but Jon had to declare anything he thought likely to fetch a decent figure. A hundred is a fair cut-off.'

'But who was going to do the independent valuation?' asked Bonnie.

'Me,' said Christopher, reluctantly. 'Most likely. Eventually.'

Another silence ensued, while this was digested. Simmy took a step or two away from the intense questioning and looked again at the house. There was surely a third cousin, or distant in-law, who would probably put it on the market. The shadowy figure of Kathleen Leeson floated before her mind's eye. An old woman with nobody she loved enough to name in a properly made will to inherit her house and the things inside it. Or had she simply been too lazy or ignorant or deluded to write down what she wanted to happen? What had the old lady really been like? Had everybody shunned her because of a nasty personality? Had she been mentally unbalanced?

It struck Simmy that this was another unpleasant consequence of childlessness. If you had even one child, that made such matters so much more simple. It seemed that such an oversight put you into a category that society had difficulty in dealing with. It was against nature; against good sense. Everybody should have a child. Or failing that, a very special and beloved niece or nephew. Or a ward, or adoptee, or protégé. A person from a younger generation whose interests you chose to encourage in some way. *Like me with Bonnie*, she

121

thought, ignoring the fact that Bonnie already had a foster mother who treasured her.

'What would the old woman have wanted?' she said aloud.

'She didn't want to have to think about it,' Chris answered swiftly. 'She didn't see it as her problem.'

'She was right,' said Ben. 'Irresponsible and lazy, but right. Although she must have known poor old Philip wouldn't be up to it, either.'

'Probably just a bit doolally,' said Bonnie.

'There's *loads* to think about, anyway,' said Ben with satisfaction. 'Oh – and where's the incident room? Didn't they say there was one set up in town somewhere?'

'It'll be in the village hall,' said Christopher. 'It's further along Broadgate from where we just walked. Tucked away on the right. I forgot all about it.'

'Why didn't they interview you there on Monday, then, instead of trogging all the way to Penrith?' asked Ben.

'Because they didn't set it up until yesterday.'

'How do you know?' asked Bonnie, trying not to sound confrontational.

The reply was short and sharp. 'Because I've made it my business to know.'

'It's weird that it's not Moxon,' said Simmy, finding herself hankering for the familiar detective.

'They might ship him in, if they need help,' said Ben. 'From what I've heard this evening, there aren't many viable suspects. They'll be going door-to-door looking for witnesses to unusual activity in the house. As well as exhaustive forensics at the scene,' he finished with

122

satisfaction. 'In there – that's where the main clues are going to be.' He jittered on the spot. 'Wish I could be in there with them.'

'They're not there now,' said Bonnie.

Again, they all gazed at the house, from the opposite side of the little street. The people of Grasmere evidently saw no reason to visit the scene of their local crime, leaving the street almost deserted. 'It's nearly nine o'clock,' Simmy announced. 'We should go. Thanks, Chris, for coming to meet us. Are you going to be all right?'

He put his arms round her. 'Of course I am. I should be flattered that you're giving me so much attention – all of you. It's annoying at times, but I do feel . . . sort of *coddled*, in a daft way.'

'Like an egg?' said Ben. 'Coddled eggs were a favourite with the Victorians.'

'Shut up, Ben,' said Simmy and Bonnie in unison.

The list of suspects still felt thin and short. In the car home Simmy had filled the youngsters in on the apparently innocent bystander who had called the police on Monday. 'It can't have been him, can it?' she said.

'Seems unlikely,' Ben agreed. 'But the police will be keeping an eye on him. Some killers like to play that sort of game – they think they're far too clever to be caught, so they take risks. The thing they don't realise is that the police actually aren't half as stupid as most people think.'

'No,' said Simmy, doubtfully. 'Although they are sometimes.'

'Anyway,' Ben went on briskly. 'What's with this old bloke in the home? What's his name again?'

'Philip. What about him?'

'He seems to be in the middle of things. You've met him, haven't you?'

'Back in March, yes. Chris and I went to his house and looked at his Airfix models. He wanted Chris to value them, and some other bits. He was going into the home in a week or two, and his house had to be sold.'

'No family?'

'Presumably not. Same as poor old Kathleen.'

'And were they valuable? His things, I mean.'

'Sadly no, according to Chris. He was pretty disappointed.'

'He's got another lady friend,' said Bonnie unexpectedly. 'Corinne knows her.'

'This is a bit sudden,' said Ben. 'When did you remember that? Does Corinne know about Philip and his friendship with the Leeson lady as well?'

'It just came to me. We were talking about the murder last night. Corinne knows everybody, even in Grasmere. That is – she knows how they connect. She's never met Philip, but the girlfriend's a man-mad loud-mouth, to quote Corinne.'

'What's her name?' asked Simmy.

'Daphne. She lives at Rydal. She was after Philip for years when his wife died. She's quite a bit younger than him. He would never agree to live with her, but they're quite pally. There was some sort of incident between her and Kathleen a while ago now. Fighting over Philip, Corinne says.'

'Wow!' Ben's excitement was palpable. 'There's scope for a good grudge there, then. Though we'd have to work out where Jonathan fitted in.'

Bonnie's face went blank, and she shrugged. 'No idea about that.'

'Something to do with Kathleen's things going off to auction,' said Ben. 'Must be. And that drags Christopher into it.' He was quiet for a moment, before saying, 'You know, Christopher really didn't want to tell us much, did he? There must be more connections than he told us about.'

Simmy felt stirrings of an excitement to match Ben's, combined with defensiveness on Christopher's behalf. 'That stumpwork thing! What if somebody thought they ought to have had it, for some reason? That's the linking element, surely? Jonathan getting all the money for something that should never have been his. And we still don't know where he got it.'

'Hang on.' Ben raised a hand. 'What does that have to do with Philip or Kathleen?'

'Um . . . nothing, I suppose. It just jumped into my mind when you said something about connections. Won't the police think it's relevant, once they find out it was Jonathan who sold it?'

'It adds a nice extra layer for investigation,' said Ben happily. 'And well done, Bonnie, for remembering about the Daphne person.'

Bonnie smiled modestly. 'And Simmy can get the whole story out of Corinne tomorrow evening, can't she? They're going off for a girlie natter somewhere.'

Simmy had forgotten about her date with Bonnie's foster mother. 'So I am,' she said. 'But I still don't know where.' They were almost in Windermere. 'Where do you want me to drop you?' she asked Bonnie. 'Yours or Ben's?'

'Ben's,' said Bonnie. 'Listen – Corinne's going to text you. I think she's got somewhere in Ambleside in mind for your meet.'

Thursday was still not as sunny as it might have been. The middle of June, with the farmers striving to gather in their hay, ought always to be bright and warm. Flaming June, as Russell Straw observed every year, was almost certainly an example of good British irony. June almost never flamed. It drizzled and floundered in varying degrees of cloud.

Simmy got to the shop in a wary mood. The four-way conversations of the previous evening had raised far more questions than they resolved. The murder of Jonathan felt much more of a threat to her own personal hopes and dreams than she had initially imagined. Ben and Bonnie would require her to remain centrally involved, as they examined every detail they could ascertain from Christopher and the Internet. Not that she was anywhere near as reluctant to participate as she had been on earlier occasions. This time, she felt needed. Christopher was made uneasy, even frightened, by many of the implications. His nature was that of a maverick, where rules went ignored if they didn't suit him – not too unlike his own description of Jonathan, she realised. Christopher disliked the police with the same instinctive response as Angie Straw's. He regarded them as bad news, to be avoided as much as possible. Simmy understood that his afternoon in Penrith, being interviewed as a potential suspect in a murder, must have been deeply unpleasant. So much so, that he still hadn't told her anything about it. Ben's comment on the dearth of real information from Christopher recurred to her, with fresh impact. Was there something he was deliberately concealing, or did he just hate talking about it?

Her wariness, she realised, was more on behalf of Chris than for herself. Her role was to protect and console him as far as she could. There was a sense that he might be in danger; that he might know the person who had killed his friend, and who just might have reason to kill Chris as well. This thought had come to her during the night, loud and clear, but also illogical. Whatever the motive for the murder, she could see no credible way that it could extend to her fiancé. And yet . . . there were so many aspects to the story that she didn't understand. Even the relationship between the auctioneer and the house clearer was obscure. It could not be very long-standing, since Chris had only lived in the area for three years. Jonathan had a wife, albeit estranged. He spent much of his time in a big blue van, crossing the country in search of valuables. There had to be a dozen auctioneers he dealt with regularly, who probably regarded themselves as his friends, just as Christopher had. He must know scores of people. And any one of them could have wanted him dead for their own impenetrable reasons.

Such musings quickly ran into trouble, though. The house in Grasmere was too obviously part of the reason for the killing. It was a local matter, and that meant Christopher would know the people concerned. They would know him and have theories about his role in the whole business.

'You don't look very happy,' Bonnie observed, half an hour after the shop opened. 'I thought we made brilliant progress last night. Christopher didn't seem to mind all the questions – did he?'

'As far as I know he was okay with it.'

'We thought he might never want to go to Grasmere again, after Monday. It takes some people that way, you know. I mean – finding a dead body like that. The trauma stays with them for years. But he seems pretty well balanced. Ben was impressed.'

'He wants us to live in Grasmere. There's not really anywhere else that would work, so if we're both to carry on with what we're doing now, it's more or less got to be there.'

Bonnie nodded. 'It's a nice place, except for all the tourists.'

'We've got tourists here in Windermere.'

Bonnie gave her a look. 'Hardly. Not compared to all that Wordsworth stuff. It never stops. Great coachloads of them. And not one capable of quoting a single line of his poetry. Ludicrous, when you think about it.'

'Must be the same in Stratford. They all go there but haven't any idea about Shakespeare.'

'Corinne went to London last month – did I say? She walked across Westminster Bridge, to get to Waterloo Station, and said it was absolutely *thick* with people taking photos of Big Ben. Hundreds of them, all going home with the same picture. Makes you wonder what they think they're doing.'

'Talking of Corinne, she still hasn't said what's happening this evening. Are we supposed to be having a meal, as well as a drink?'

'Not sure. I'd guess just a drink and a packet of crisps.'

'If she hasn't texted or phoned by lunchtime, I'll call her.'

Bonnie seemed uneasy at being a go-between, which Simmy found irritating, since the initial message had come from her. 'What's the matter?' she asked.

'I haven't seen Corinne since yesterday morning, so I don't know what she's thinking, okay? You should call her. That's the best idea.'

'I will,' said Simmy, before three customers all came in together and the phone rang. New orders appeared on the computer, and Simmy realised she had to devote a considerable amount of time to making funeral tributes for the following day. The morning passed in a blur. 'Should I order extra flowers for Saturday?' she wondered aloud.

'Oh!' Bonnie clapped a hand over her mouth. 'I forgot. Ben wants to go to the auction in Keswick. He was hoping you could take him.'

'What – all day?'

'If possible. We thought Tanya and I could probably manage the shop. The thing is, he thinks he needs to see how it all works if he's to get any proper understanding of the people involved in the murder. He wants to watch it all in action.'

Tanya was Ben's younger sister, only fourteen, but impressively capable. She had helped out during the Mother's Day rush, making a great difference to the workload. She'd come in again during the May half-term. 'Well . . .' said Simmy.

'She'd love to do it. And it would be a nice break for you.'

'I've just *had* a break. I was in the Canary Islands for a week, remember.'

'Well, we're happy to hold the fort on Saturdays, every now and then. Tanya's good company and she can cope with most of the work.'

'It's tempting,' said Simmy, with a rush of good cheer at the prospect of regular free Saturdays, if the two girls really could manage. 'I'd love to spend all day at the auction.'

'Do it, then. What time does it start?'

'Ten. But we need to look at all the things for sale, for at least an hour beforehand. We ought to leave here soon after eight, if we can manage it.'

'No problem,' said Bonnie, fishing out her phone to inform her boyfriend of his good luck.

'I've just remembered something,' said Simmy, with a shock. 'Talking about the auction – I'm supposed to be going to some little village hall sale with Chris this evening. In Kirkby Lonsdale. I think he must have forgotten as well. We were going to have to leave here soon after three. You would have had to close up for me.'

'I still can. But what about Corinne? You need to find out what Chris is doing,' Bonnie advised.

'Yes.' Simmy reached for her phone. 'What else have I forgotten? Another thing to do with auctions. There's too much going on,' she wailed. 'My poor head can't keep up.'

'You should write it all down,' said the girl complacently. 'Keep a little notebook.'

'You mean one of those gadgets that tells you where you're meant to be? Isn't that an app?'

'No, I mean a real notebook. Ben's works really well.'

'I'd only lose it or forget to look at it.' She slapped her head. 'I *know* there's something.'

'Take it a step at a time. Is it some reason why you can't go on Saturday?'

'It might be . . . my parents often want me there on Saturday afternoons . . . got it! I told my dad I'd take him to Keswick again sometime soon. I might even have said it would be this weekend. I'm sure my mother said he was expecting to go on Saturday. But he could well have forgotten. He could come with me and Ben, couldn't he? I'd better phone and ask him.'

'Phone Christopher first about this evening.'

'Yes, Mum.'

It turned out that Christopher had indeed forgotten about Kirkby Lonsdale, and no longer wanted to go. Russell Straw had made a rare commitment to a friend to go for a walk from Staveley to Kentmere, expected to take much of Saturday. He too had forgotten his conversation about the auction.

'So that's all right,' sighed Simmy, wondering why she didn't feel more offended at the way people never seemed to want to go anywhere with her.

# Chapter Eleven

In the event, the arrangement with Corinne was very simply made. They were to go to Ambleside in separate cars and meet at the top of the town (unlike Grasmere, Ambleside really did have a 'top'), where cafes were available in abundance. While Bowness might have been just as convenient, there was a calmer atmosphere in Ambleside. People would be returning from ambitious fell-top walks, tired and hungry. There were dogs slumped under the outdoor tables and small children struggling to stay awake. While it was still term time, nobody between the ages of five and sixteen would be on holiday, which in itself created a relative tranquillity.

Corinne had purple hair and often wore clothes to match. When Simmy thought of her, it was in those shades. Even her skin seemed rather reddish at times. She had brown eyes and wide hips. Over twenty years she had fostered dozens of children, but now in her early fifties she wanted to spread her wings and do something different. Only Bonnie and a younger boy remained, and the boy had a grandmother who was preparing to take him on full-time.

Simmy quickly spotted her, standing in the middle of the paved area by the postbox, as designated. Across the road was the Ambleside Salutation, which Simmy and her father found irresistibly appealing, despite never having been inside, or availed themselves of the spa it provided. The two women kissed briefly, and then stood back awkwardly. 'We could get pizza at Zeffirellis,' Corinne suggested. 'And eat them in the park.'

'Okay.' Simmy had no wish to argue, despite rating pizza a long way down her list of favourites. 'What about drink, though?'

'Sorted.' Corinne showed her the contents of an old-fashioned shopping bag woven from straw. Several cans of fizzy drinks, lager and cider were visible. 'I went to Tesco just now.'

It was unorthodox and almost uncivilised compared to the meal of the previous evening, but Simmy was no snob. She enjoyed the other woman's lack of convention, at least in small doses. 'Brilliant,' she said.

Twenty minutes later they were on a park bench with the makeshift meal laid out between them. A mild breeze was blowing up from the lake, the sky still hazy as it had been all day. 'They say it'll rain tomorrow,' said Simmy, channelling her weather-obsessed father. 'Bonnie says you want to pick my brains about Lanzarote.'

'Not so much. That's just what I told her. Really, it's her I want to talk about – I couldn't tell her that, though, could I?' She paused, then took a swig of the canned lager. 'With Ben going off to Newcastle in a few months, she's going to be wanting to go with him, don't you think?'

'Has she said so?'

'Not exactly. She'd have to find a job and somewhere to live. He'll have a place in a hall or whatever they call it, for the first year. His mother's insisting on that. But if Bonnie *doesn't* go, he'll be coming back here every weekend, and Helen won't want that, either.'

'No.' Simmy had been thinking along similar lines for most of the year. 'I don't want to lose her from the shop, obviously. But I can see it's not a long-term prospect for her.'

'No. Well, she seems to think your life's going to change soon as well. I need to check it out with you – if I persuade her to stay here, she'll want to hang onto the job with you. Everything depends on that.'

'Does it? Why? She could get something else easily enough.'

'No!' The word emerged with some force. 'That's just it. What else could she do? She's got no exams worth a shit. She's not the most reliable kid in the world, either. There'd be nothing but stacking supermarket shelves or telesales. Believe me – I've been there. And she's worth more than that.'

'Of course she is. So, you're asking me to guarantee her a job for – how long? Three years, until Ben graduates?'

Corinne laughed. 'That would be pushing it. Just till Christmas would be a good start.'

Simmy began to understand why Bonnie had been embarrassed about this meeting. She must have suspected that she was going to be the main topic of conversation. 'Well, if it helps, I've got no intention of changing anything to do with the shop. I might be moving house soon, but that won't affect my work. Chris Henderson and I are engaged, actually.'

Corinne nodded. 'I know. Though I don't see a ring.'

'We'll get one soon. It's all been a bit chaotic. There was this murder in Grasmere—'

'I know all about that,' Corinne interrupted. 'There's a funny old girl called Daphne Schofield, who I see now and then. She called me on Tuesday about it. And, of course, Ben and Bonnie had to get nosing around, didn't they? Like always.'

'It's been horrible for Chris.'

'He found the body, right? And he knows Philip, who's mates with Daphne. Or was. Sounds to me as if he's not got much longer. She was well out of that, if you ask me. Though she might have ended up with his house, I s'pose. And she'd have loved to give Kathleen Leeson a smack in the eye by stealing her boyfriend.'

Simmy was becoming aware of a kind of dance in which attractive old houses were increasingly falling empty as their aged inhabitants died off. The question of who inherited them and their contents was not always straightforward.

135

Sometimes, scandalously, they stood empty for months or years on end while matters of inheritance were sorted out.

'Sounds like a real cat fight.'

Corinne shrugged. 'No, not really. All very ladylike and civilised. And Daphne isn't one to hold a grudge. She's just lonely, basically. Can't face life without a man. She doesn't care about houses, to be fair. She knows what a burden a big house can be. The thing is, these old people live so long that their children are often over seventy, and don't want the bother of clearing out decades of stuff before they can sell them. You'd think the old parents would have the sense to just pass everything down to the next generation, wouldn't you? The grandchildren, I mean. They'd have more use for it. But it never seems to happen like that.' She sighed. 'So, when are you getting married, then?'

'No date yet. We'll probably rent a house or flat together in Grasmere, to start with.'

'And keep your Troutbeck place?'

'Rent it out, maybe. Or try to sell it in the autumn. He hasn't got anything to sell, luckily.'

Corinne cocked her head. 'So, you've got more behind you than he has. What's he been doing all this time?'

'Travelling, mainly. Living hand to mouth. But he's settled down now. Seems to be loving the job with the auction house. He got promoted a few months ago – it could all work out really well. He might end up owning the whole business eventually.'

'Nice. Everybody loves an auction. And you'll be wanting a baby or two,' she added without changing gear.

Simmy swallowed back the automatic evasive reply. It

was intrusive, impertinent, insensitive – but kindly meant. There was no doubt that Bonnie gossiped about her, passing on bits of news, reporting conversations, speculations. 'That would be nice,' she said faintly.

'And he seems a decent bloke. Good parent and all that, from what I hear. Never seen him myself. Been married before, has he?'

'We both have. But he's never had kids. I think he'd be good with them. He's got nieces and nephews.'

'Time running out,' Corinne observed. 'I know how that goes. Bonnie won't have told you I had a wobble, six or seven years ago – big crisis at the time.'

'Oh?'

'Yeah.' Simmy had a sense that Corinne would have liked to light a cigarette at this point. Her fingers twitched, and she gave herself a little shake. Then she consoled herself with a large bite of pizza. 'Had a chap who said he was desperate for a kid, and how about it. You know – after all this fostering, you'd think I'd have had enough. But I never did have any of my own. Daft, really. So there I was, forty-three and suddenly going all out to get a baby. When it didn't work, he dumped me.'

'Bonnie never said anything about that.'

'She didn't know the details. He never moved in – the social workers wouldn't have liked that. The thing is, it taught me a lot.' She gave Simmy a searching look. 'You'd have to be sure you weren't marrying him just to get a kid or two.'

Simmy could feel herself flushing. 'You mean, because I might have left it too late?'

'More or less, yes. You can't take anything for granted.'

'I know. Are you saying I might go off Chris if we end up without any children?'

'No, no. But it can happen. You should be careful.' The older woman munched thoughtfully and finished her lager. 'Listen to me! What am I saying? Must be getting old. You go for it, love. There're never any guarantees in life, after all. The whole thing's one bloody great risk.'

Simmy laughed. 'That's true. Well, I said yes when he proposed, so I guess I'm committed. Poor old Chris – the killing of his friend has knocked everything else out of his head anyway. I hope they find who did it soon.'

'So do I. Bonnie's there in Helm Road every waking moment until they work it out.' She flinched at her own words. 'They always make it feel like a game – they forget some poor person's *dead*.'

'I know it seems like that. But really, they *do* care about people's feelings. And this time, they've only got a little bit of the picture. There's no way they can understand what really happened. Although that might change on Saturday.'

'What happens then?'

'I'm taking Ben to Keswick for the auction. Bonnie and Tanya are minding the shop. It'll be good practice – or something. Melanie did it for weeks when I was out of action last year, and she wasn't much older than Bonnie at the time.'

'Should be okay for a morning,' said Corinne dubiously. 'Do you want me to drop in and see they're managing okay?'

'That would be great, if you've got time. I'll make sure I get as much done tomorrow as I can, so it probably won't be busy. Bonnie can make up sprays and birthday flowers – the sort of thing people want on the spot. I can't think of much that can go wrong – but that could just be lack of imagination on my part.'

'Tanya's sensible, as far as I can see. I've only met her once, though.'

'She is. The other sisters say she's turning into Ben. She joined in with his spreadsheets and whatnot when there was that business in Staveley a few months ago.'

The pizza was all gone, and the sun was lost behind a grey cloud. The breeze was turning chilly. 'So, you wanted to ask me if I could guarantee work for Bonnie, after Ben goes? Is that right?'

'Pretty much. And I thought a catch-up would be good.' Corinne gave Simmy an affectionate look that was almost maternal. 'I thought you might want to dump a few things on me, as well. Your dad not being himself these days, and the new boyfriend, and people getting themselves murdered. It feels as if it's one thing after another, and you never get a chance to work through it all. Now there's this Grasmere thing, before you've properly got back from holiday.'

'That's very sweet of you, but I don't think you need worry. I mean – I seem to be bearing up quite nicely. The only thing . . . well, the *biggest* thing is the baby issue. I met this woman on Monday with a baby. Then we saw her again last night. She lives outside Grasmere. I stayed ages with the baby on my lap. It was lovely.' She sighed.

'There's nothing like it,' Corinne agreed. 'That warm solid little body. Plays havoc with a person's hormones.'

'You can say that again. Everything *tingled* with it.'

'You should have shouted for your Christopher there and then. You'd have started your own baby that night, if you had.'

Simmy laughed, half-appalled, half-relieved. 'The trouble is, he was answering police questions in Penrith at the time. I don't think he'd have been up for it.'

'Well, get cracking, that's my advice. Don't wait for the ring or the licence. First things first.'

'I know,' said Simmy.

They wandered back to where they'd met, because Corinne had parked on a small patch beside a pub, where it said 'No Parking'.

'It's okay – they know me,' she said heedlessly.

'Oh!' Simmy's eye had been caught by a shop sign. 'That must be the charity shop Flo was talking about.' The sign announced 'CaniCare – your local charity for dogs'.

'Always scope for more doggy charity,' said Corinne, who had been a keen dog breeder in her time. 'This one's everybody's favourite round here. They've got a rescue place up near Cockermouth.'

'Her husband works for them,' Simmy went on. She pressed her face to the window of the closed shop. 'Looks as if they've got lots of nice stuff. The place is packed. Bric-a-brac mostly. Hardly any books, that I can see.'

'They get all kinds of donations from old ladies, apparently. I heard of one in Coniston who left everything she possessed to them when she died.'

'Gosh! Imagine liking dogs as much as that.'

140

Corinne waggled her head, to indicate a level of disagreement that she was too polite to express.

'Well, better go.' Simmy's own car was legally parked in the big car park round the bend towards the main road out of town. 'Thanks for the chat. It was lovely to catch up.'

Back in Troutbeck, she phoned Christopher. 'Had a good day?' she asked him.

'Not particularly. How about you?'

'Fine, thanks. I've just had pizza and lager with Corinne. You know, Bonnie's foster mother.'

'Oh yeah? What did she want?'

'Nothing, really. Just a chat. She made me think, actually. About a lot of things.'

'That sounds ominous.'

'It shouldn't.' Something snagged at her; a sense that there was a faint hint of insult in his response. 'Can't I think without you getting worried?'

'Depends, I suppose.'

'Well, there's nothing to bother you. Have the police been back again today? What's happening with the investigation?'

'No idea. All I know is that Valerie dropped in this afternoon, wondering if he'd left any of his stuff with us. She's determined to trace every single thing that belonged to him. Heartless cow she is. Made me wish he'd left a will in favour of some girlfriend somewhere.'

'Or a dogs' home,' said Simmy lightly.

'No chance of that. Jon hated dogs. Must have been bitten as a kid or something. He'd cross the road to avoid them.'

'That wouldn't go down too well in Grasmere. The place seems to expect everyone to love dogs.'

'Right. Philip had one, until last year. So did his friend Kathleen. I think that's how they met in the first place, come to think of it.'

'Do you know a woman called Daphne? Apparently, she's another of Philip's lady friends. He seems to have been quite popular. But Corinne says he's really poorly now. She thinks he might not last much longer.'

'Oh God! I'll have to go and see the poor old boy, then. And no – never heard of a Daphne. Let's hope *she* hasn't got a house that'll need clearing as well.'

'Why? Doesn't your business depend on it?'

'Up to a point. But I don't need any more trouble in that direction for a while.'

His mood was not helping the conversation to flow. She had a long list of things she wanted to talk about with him: houses, rings, sweet nothings – and murder. But he seemed intent on closing down every avenue she tried.

'Oh! I nearly forgot to tell you,' she said suddenly. 'Ben and I are coming to your sale on Saturday. All day. Bonnie and Tanya are running the shop for me. Corinne thinks they'll be fine. Ben wants to see how it all works. You might have to show him round at the end and answer some questions.'

There was a silence for a long five seconds. 'What time will you get here?'

'Before nine, I hope. We want to have a good look at all the lots first. It's my dad's birthday soon. I could buy him something.'

'If I have to show your friend around, it'd best be then, then. Early on, I mean. I'll be knackered when it finishes – and hungry – and you might be fed up with it all by the afternoon.'

'Whatever's best for you. You don't sound too keen on the idea. Is there something I'm not getting?'

'That boy. I've said it before – he gets on my nerves. Thinks he's so clever, God's gift to the forces of law and order, when it's got nothing whatsoever to do with him. Can't he just leave it?'

'He *is* clever, Chris. And he's not getting in anyone's way. The Penrith police won't even know he's interested – unless he comes up with something they've missed.'

'How will he know what they've missed?'

'Good question.' She tried to laugh. 'I can see how he might be irritating, but I thought after last night you'd got a better idea of what he's like. Everybody loves him when they get to know him. When we thought we'd lost him, last year . . . it was so *awful*. Just thinking about the world without him was heart-wrenching.'

'Okay. I've got the message. It probably sounds as if I'm jealous of a kid half my age. He just gets my back up somehow.'

'That's a shame, because I don't think you can get out of talking to him on Saturday. Not unless you can find somebody else to show him round.'

'I might just do that. Josephine could maybe do it. She always likes to show off the computer stuff.'

Simmy had barely heard of Josephine before. 'Is she new?'

'What? No, no. She was here from the start – years

before me. She designed the whole system. You must know who she is.'

'Yes,' said Simmy vaguely. Had he deliberately failed to mention the woman up to now? Was there some reason why, if so? 'I look forward to meeting her,' she added.

'Good. I'll speak to you tomorrow, then.' He sounded weary and distracted. Simmy did her best not to take it personally. Chris had a lot to contend with, she repeated to herself. But actually – how was that an excuse? What stopped him from pouring it all out to her, his future wife? Why was he so hung up on Ben, who meant nothing but good? Didn't everybody want the same thing?

'That'll be nice,' she said. 'And Chris – I love you, you know. I'm here for you. Everything's going to be all right.'

'And I love you,' he said. 'That's not in question.' And he rang off before she could ask him just what *was* in question, then.

'Tanya's coming in after school,' said Bonnie next morning. 'You can go over everything for tomorrow. She's excited about it.'

'Should I have checked first with Helen?' Simmy suddenly worried. 'I should, shouldn't I?'

'She's fine with it. But maybe a quick call would be an idea.'

'Right. What's Ben doing today?'

Bonnie grimaced. 'He's really into it now. Searching the Internet and finding a whole lot of fascinating stuff that I don't think is at all relevant. He's been making one of his spreadsheets as well. The weird thing is, we've never met *anyone* connected with the case. Not even the SIO. They're all just names. That's never happened before. I mean – last time, we were right in the middle of everything. We went to their *houses*. You as well as me and Ben.'

'And the time before that you found the body,' said Simmy with a pang. These two young people had experienced far more than they should have done. Death, danger, horror, betrayal. And yet they remained so bright-eyed and sunny-tempered.

'Yeah,' said Bonnie.

'I don't imagine any of the characters involved will be in Keswick tomorrow, either.'

'Oh yes they will. At least, the Nick person probably will be. He's got to carry on as usual, hasn't he – even if he's the killer.'

'He's not, though. Chris says he can prove he was somewhere else, miles away.'

'Whatever. Ben still wants to have a look at him. Besides, practically everybody there will have known Jonathan. They'll have ideas and bits of the story. They're bound to be talking about it. I wish I was going to be there,' she concluded regretfully.

'You're being very noble,' Simmy told her. 'But there's no way we can both go.'

The frustrations of youth were all too obvious. Transport was an abiding difficulty, as well as finances and adult expectations. The long summer months loomed ahead, promising a mixture of gloriously free time and severe constraints as to what was feasible in the way of activities.

145

'It's not that, is it?' said Bonnie. 'It's us not being able to drive. If Corinne wasn't being such a pain about it, I could learn in her car. But she won't let me. And we can't afford proper lessons.'

The idea of delicate little Bonnie at the wheel of a car sent shivers through Simmy. And yet she was almost eighteen – quite old enough for a licence. 'It'll happen eventually,' she said. 'And don't forget the bikes.'

'That's what Tanya said. "Why don't you both cycle to Keswick?"' She mimicked an exaggerated little-girl voice. 'Has she any idea how long that would take, and how exhausting it would be?'

'People do it, though. They do much greater distances than that, in fact. Has Tanya got a bike as well? Wouldn't she want to go with you if you did that?' Suddenly the constraints appeared to be lifting. Why hadn't she thought of the bicycles before? As well as that, there were plenty of buses crossing the region several times a day.

'We're not doing it. The roads are full of tourists. Those coaches are lethal. We'd be crushed against a stone wall somewhere. And you can't take any *stuff* on a bike.'

Simmy gave up, more than half-glad that the idea had been vetoed. The image of two broken young bodies under the wheels of a large bus full of foreign tourists was too vivid for comfort. She could even see the excited sightseers taking their everlasting pictures of the gory scene. 'You could be right,' she said. 'But you'll get to hear all about the auction. And there's always another time.'

Before the girl could reply, the shop door pinged, and they both turned to greet the expected customer with welcoming smiles.

'Oh! It's you,' said Simmy, her smile growing even broader. 'What a surprise.'

# Chapter Twelve

DI Nolan Moxon returned the smile. 'A welcome one, I hope,' he said.

'I suppose that depends on what you've come to say. But it has been a while, hasn't it.'

'Three months,' he nodded. 'And here we are again.'

'Are we? I mean – is this about the thing in Grasmere? I didn't think you were part of the investigation. Isn't it the Penrith people this time?'

'They've asked us for assistance. It's a big job. And there's no hard and fast boundaries when something like this happens.'

'Oh.' She thought of Christopher and his resistance to the police. Then she thought of Ben and his latest spreadsheet. And she realised that Moxon would have instantly linked all the different individuals together and drawn an obvious deduction. 'I should have known.'

'You should. Your boyfriend found the body, for a start. And I've just learnt that young Mr Harkness is planning to spend all day tomorrow at Mr Henderson's auction rooms. With a certain Mrs Brown. Just like old times,' he finished, with a sigh.

'You've spoken to Ben?'

'Fifteen minutes ago. Following a hunch, you might say.'

'A pretty obvious one,' put in Bonnie, who had pressed close to the two adults, shamelessly assuming their conversation included her.

'All right, young lady. No need for that.' He gave her a fatherly look, aiming for stern authority, but his affection for her made it difficult. 'It's a strange business. The poor man was killed very violently, and yet nobody can find any reason for such an act. In broad daylight, too, as far as they can tell.'

'Everybody knew him, according to Chris,' said Simmy. 'He must have done something to upset someone. Something awful, I mean.'

'Indeed,' said Moxon, as if this was obvious. Which it was, Simmy realised.

'Ben's working on it,' said Bonnie with pride.

'So I understand. Impressive, as always.' He addressed Simmy, their eyes meeting over Bonnie's head. 'You'll be sorry it was your boyfriend who found him,' he said carefully. 'Must seem like a jinx.'

She took a small breath. 'Well, oddly enough, it doesn't. I mean – I am sorry it was Chris, of course. He's seriously upset about it. But for myself, I don't feel nearly as resistant as I have before. It helps not to know any of the people. Never even met Jonathan. The only person I know in Grasmere is a woman called Flo, with a baby. And I only met her this week.'

'When you say "any of the people", who do you mean, exactly?'

She laughed. 'Good question. Bonnie was just saying the same thing. There really *aren't* any people, are there? No suspects. No witnesses. At least, as far as we know, of course.'

'There's Mr Henderson,' said Moxon, with extreme caution.

'What do you mean?'

'You'll have thought about it for yourself by now. From what he said to the Penrith people, he arranged to meet Mr Woolley in that house. He knew he would be there. Then another man called the police to report a death. A man who knew who Christopher Henderson was, having been to his salerooms. That meant there was no sense in Mr Henderson trying to leave the scene before the police arrived, even if he really wanted to. You can see how that might look.'

'Woolley? Is that his surname? Did I know that?' Her brain had gone into paralysis at these ghastly insinuations, leaving her nothing sensible to say.

'Simmy,' Bonnie reproached her. 'You've got to focus. What DI Moxon says is obvious, really. Ben and I were just saying last night. It could look quite bad for your

Christopher. That'll be why they kept him so long in Penrith on Monday.'

'But they let him go. They obviously don't think he did anything.'

'They know where to find him, though. They'll have told him not to go anywhere outside the area.'

Simmy eyed Moxon anxiously. 'Is that what you came here to tell me?'

'Partly. Look – I'm on your side, as far as I can be. I credit you with more sense than to take up with a murderer. You know enough by now to understand that the police have to follow the evidence, especially in the first days of an investigation. And up to now, there's not a lot of it around. Fingerprints in the house, bits of other stuff for forensics to play with, issues about money and a few dodgy deals. There's the wife, and the man who'd been making threats.'

'Nick,' nodded Simmy. 'He's got an alibi.'

'Right. D'you know him?'

She shook her head. 'But Jonathan was worried about Nick on Sunday. He phoned Chris about it.'

'Worried how?'

'Scared for his own safety, apparently. Chris will have told the Penrith people all about that. You just said it yourself – Nick was making threats.'

'Do you know what they were about?'

'I gather Jonathan reported Nick to the Inland Revenue. Or somebody did, and Nick assumed it was Jonathan. He makes a lot of money from his dealing, according to Chris.'

Moxon wriggled his shoulders uncomfortably. 'Not as

much as Mr Woolley did. He's had one or two very nice sales lately.'

'The stumpwork,' Simmy said. 'I know all about that.'

'Oh, do you? That's more than we do, then. Tell me – where did he get it in the first place?'

She gave an embarrassed laugh. 'Sorry. No idea. He wouldn't tell anyone.'

'Must have been stolen,' said Bonnie, wide-eyed. 'So, when it got in the news, the rightful owner tracked him down and killed him.'

Moxon gave her another of his fatherly looks. 'Hardly,' he said.

'Oh? Why not?'

'I can think of at least five reasons. First, the auction house wouldn't agree to sell it if there was any suggestion that it was stolen. Secondly, no halfway-sensible thief would sell it so publicly. Thirdly, the rightful owner would surely devote his efforts to getting it back, not killing the person who robbed him—'

'All right,' the girl interrupted him. 'I get the point.'

'Maybe he was brutal to somebody's dog,' Simmy suggested, more in an effort to calm the scratchy atmosphere than to offer any real contribution. 'I gather he didn't like them.'

It worked. The others both stared at her in bemusement. 'How do you know that?' asked Moxon.

'Chris told me last night. I can't remember how it came up. The woman with the baby, perhaps. Her husband works for a dog charity. I saw one of their shops in Ambleside yesterday.' She was prattling, still quivering from the impossible idea that the police suspected Christopher of murder. If she could sow suggestions that would lead attention elsewhere, that felt at least slightly positive. 'It's not entirely stupid, is it – to think somebody held a grudge against him because he did something awful to their pet?'

'Nobody's said a word to that effect,' said Moxon. 'Not as far as I know, anyway. I haven't seen the whole file, I must admit.'

'I'll need to tell Ben about the dog thing,' said Bonnie, importantly. 'It's new information.'

'The thing is,' said the detective heavily, 'the Penrith people have a strong impression that Mr Henderson is concealing something. They're very experienced interviewers up there, and their main man swears there's some big factor he's keeping to himself. I came here to ask you to try to persuade him to pass on to us the whole story. It's in his own interest, even if it involves dropping himself in a bit of trouble in the process. No trouble's as serious as murder, after all.'

Simmy swallowed hard. 'You're saying that as things stand, he's looking like a suspect, because he's keeping something back? If he is, it'll be to protect somebody else, not himself.'

'Very possibly. I leave that with you. Lots of people hold things back from the police, of course. But when it's a murder investigation, we can't let it go. You'll understand that. But he apparently doesn't.'

'All right,' said Simmy faintly.

Moxon looked at his watch and adopted a less serious

expression. 'You're quiet for a Friday,' he observed, glancing round the shop.

Simmy made a matching effort to regain her composure. 'It's only eleven o'clock. It'll get busier any minute now. I've got quite a lot to do, actually. I was away all last week, and I still have a few jobs to catch up with on the computer. Plus, there's a funeral this afternoon. I've got less than an hour to get the flowers for that delivered.' She glanced at the laptop. 'And I think I said I'd go to one of the hotels on the Ambleside road to talk about flowers. I'm getting terribly forgetful. Bonnie says I ought to keep a notebook.'

'For work, or life in general?'

'Both, I suppose.'

'Did you say you'd been away? Where did you go? I thought you'd got a bit of a tan.' He was looking at her bare forearms, which were a shade or two browner than usual.

'Lanzarote. It's got the perfect climate, all year round. Although Chris says Tangier is even more perfect. I'm not sure I'd agree with him. The food doesn't sound my sort of thing, for a start.'

The detective shook his head. 'Never been to either, so I can't comment.'

'Customer,' said Bonnie perkily, just before the doorbell pinged. 'Mrs Hyacinth,' she added in a whisper.

Simmy rolled her eyes warningly and turned to greet their regular Friday purchaser of scented flowers for the weekend. It had been a while since she actually bought hyacinths, but the name had stuck.

'Better go, then,' said Moxon. 'Nice to see you again.'

Simmy forced a smile that was the palest shadow of the one she'd given him when he first arrived. He made a rueful grimace, clearly quite aware of the change he'd brought about with his words.

The shop phone rang while Simmy was serving the customer and Bonnie took the call. 'Newby Bridge?' she said. 'No problem. Any particular time?' She jotted details on a pad. Half-watching her, Simmy hoped the scribble would be legible. For somebody with a flair for design and presentation, the girl's writing was dreadful.

Moxon's departure was discreet and rapid. It was twenty minutes before Simmy and her assistant had a chance to talk about his visit. 'It was nice to see him,' said Simmy. 'At first, anyway. I didn't like being told they think Chris killed that man.'

'He didn't say that exactly. He wants you to get Chris to come clean about whatever he's keeping back. I don't think you need worry that it's any worse than that. Remember how scared Ben and I were last year, because it was us who found the body. They never really thought we'd done it, but they've got to follow the evidence, like Moxo just said.'

'But they knew you. They don't know Chris. And when you hear about his life and what's he's done, it probably doesn't inspire a lot of confidence.'

'Don't worry,' Bonnie insisted. 'He's pretty respectable, really.'

Simmy wanted to believe her. She assured herself she was being silly. But disobedient thoughts kept popping up to disturb her. Chris's manner all week had been disconcerting. Of course he hadn't killed his friend, but it was increasingly clear that he had been deeply affected by the death. That wasn't surprising. It was a trauma, a great shock, and he would take time to recover from it. His new role as Simmy's fiancé came second to the horror of finding a strangled man. But there was more than that. Chris was scared. Perhaps also guilty and angry. There were perhaps implications for his business, cans of worms that the police were sure to open. Already there was the accusation of tax dodging. And a hint that the auctioneer might have sold an item whose provenance was suspicious. She could easily envisage the intent questioning and observation that Ben Harkness would indulge in the following day at the auction. Nothing would escape him. And she, Simmy, would be cast as his sidekick. Instead of the sweetly subtle tricks that Bonnie was so good at, there would be tall, awkward Simmy Brown, blundering into conversations and accidentally bidding for priceless Chinese vases.

The day became busy as predicted, with three new deliveries to make, a trip down to Newby Bridge with the order taken by Bonnie, and a lengthy phone call from a guesthouse close to her parents' B&B wanting a lavish floral display for a special group due to arrive shortly from Singapore. Quite why this required such excessive preparations never became clear, but Simmy had more sense than to argue.

Bonnie had accessed the online auction catalogue, and repeatedly read out descriptions of some of the lots, as well as calling Simmy to look at the photographs of them. 'Such lovely things!' the girl marvelled. 'Hundreds of lovely things. But who's going to buy a "large collection of shells from the South Pacific"? Guide price thirty to fifty quid. I mean – I can understand someone wanting to collect the things for themselves, but who wants someone else's collection? Where's the fun in that?'

'My guess would be somebody like the woman from the guesthouse I've just been talking to. She'd arrange them in the bathroom, for decoration. But think of the *dust*,' Simmy sighed. 'What a lot of work people give themselves.'

'Mm. And how about this? "Carving in ivory of a tiger attacking a buffalo. Chinese. Possibly eighteenth century." Are they allowed to sell ivory? Isn't that just making it more desirable? All those poor elephants.'

Simmy had only a moderate concern for elephants, and the picture of the carving looked quite appealing. 'It's okay if it's antique, I think.'

'So, people make fake antiques out of newly chopped-off tusks. Obviously. They'll do anything for money. This one's worth five hundred pounds!'

'People can be very nasty,' Simmy sighed in resigned agreement. The truth of this assertion had made itself more and more apparent since she had become a florist, discovering in the process that flowers could be used maliciously, and almost nobody could be trusted.

'So – I forgot to ask – how did it go with Corinne last night? Did you talk about me?' Despite the bouncy tone, there was a wary look in the girl's eyes.

'A bit. She wanted to know how secure your job is here.'

'What? Why? You're not going to fire me, are you?'

Simmy laughed. 'I wasn't planning to, no. Actually, we

got onto me and Chris almost from the start. She's quite wise, isn't she?'

'Is she? I wouldn't take too much notice of her advice where men are concerned. She's made nearly as much of a mess in that department as my mother has.'

'I don't believe that.'

'You should. The difference is, that Corinne always kept her men right away from the kids. We never saw them. She put us first every time.' She looked out of the window, her eyes unfocused. 'She must have given up quite a lot for us, when you think about it.'

'I don't think she regrets it. She's proud of all her foster kids.'

'Not all – but we weren't a bad bunch, on the whole. It never occurred to us that she could have had her own children. Most foster parents have some of their own, after all.'

'Does she ever talk about that?'

'Not to me. I suppose it might be that she knew from quite young that there was some reason she'd never manage a baby of her own, and that's why she went in for fostering. If I ever thought about it, I more or less assumed that had to be the explanation.'

Simmy said nothing, anxious not to disclose any confidences. Yet again, she was saved by a customer. When that was dealt with, it was almost four o'clock and the working day was winding down.

'Doing anything this evening?' Bonnie asked idly.

'Nope. When do I ever do anything in the evenings? Although I have been out twice this week. That's almost a record.'

'Shame to waste the nice weather.'

158

'I know. Although it's not that nice, really. Not compared to the Canaries, anyway.'

'At least it's light.'

Simmy was reminded of Melanie Todd, her previous assistant, who had tirelessly urged her to socialise. Mel seemed to be physically hurt by the thought of someone spending night after night alone in Troutbeck. When Simmy embarked on a lukewarm relationship with a potter called Ninian, Melanie was disproportionately delighted. But now Simmy had a real live fiancé, and nobody need worry about her any more.

'Well, I'll be out all day tomorrow, won't I? And Chris'll come over on Sunday and we'll go somewhere.'

'You should buy an engagement ring,' Bonnie said solemnly. 'Unless there's a family heirloom somewhere?'

This was a new thought. 'Not that I know of,' she said absently. 'And if there was, I suppose his first wife would have got it. Or one of his brothers' wives.'

'Do they have jewellery at the auction?'

'I think so. But there wouldn't be anything I liked, or that would fit me.' The idea of a second-hand ring of unknown origins repelled her slightly. 'And he's probably not allowed to keep anything back for himself.'

'They do it all the time,' said Bonnie with impressive confidence.

'How do you know that?'

'Ben and I have been watching that old series, *Lovejoy* on Netflix. We saw three episodes last night. They're really good, in a funny way. If you can believe the stories, practically all the things sold at auctions are fakes.'

'I don't suppose that's very true to life, is it?'

'That's what Ben's hoping to find out tomorrow.'

Simmy inwardly quailed on behalf of Christopher, bombarded with questions about murky background deals and auctioneers creaming off the best things for themselves. Then she remembered that the mysterious Josephine was more likely to bear the brunt of it. She could explain her role to Ben during the drive to Keswick next morning. 'I'm not at all sure I'm doing the right thing,' she said. 'It sounds as if Ben's going to make a real nuisance of himself.'

'Don't worry about it,' breezed Bonnie. 'Just let him get on with it.'

# Chapter Thirteen

Friday evening turned out to be considerably more eventful than Simmy had anticipated. Staying half an hour late in the shop, trying to prepare for all eventualities next day, she found herself running through the hazy details of the Grasmere murder yet again. Moxon's unexpected involvement made a significant difference, she discovered – although not altogether in a good way. He had come to tell her that her fiancé was a 'person of interest' in the investigation, having guessed that she would not have fully grasped this unsavoury fact. He had meant it kindly, and she would rather hear news like that from him than anybody else, but it was still unpleasant.

She was also forced to confront the realisation that the antique business was fertile soil for crime. Fraud, tax evasion, theft – and even murder, it seemed – were all part of the picture. This concerned her, particularly after discovering that floristry was also not immune to malice and deception. Was there any sort of business that only saw the lighter, kinder side of human nature? Gardening, surely – despite the storylines in the television series *Rosemary and Thyme*. Midwifery came to mind. Pain, fear and occasional tragedy were part of it, but never any deliberate aggression or malevolence, that she could imagine. Even her ex-husband's aberrant behaviour towards one of their midwives was not actually malicious.

But, she insisted to herself, there was no harm in Christopher. He was a good person, quick to make friends, slow to anger. He was as far from a cold-hearted killer as it was possible to be. Moxon's words had firmed up Simmy's determination to ensure that justice prevailed, and the real murderer was caught. And for that, Ben Harkness was likely to come in very useful.

The phone interrupted her thoughts. It was close to six o'clock, which was an odd time for someone to call the shop. 'Hello?' she said, expecting some sort of recording or call centre asking to speak to the manager.

'Oh, hello. You're still there. I didn't realise it was so late until just now.'

'Flo? Are you all right?'

'More or less. No worse than usual. It's the low point of the day, like when you were here on Monday. I found a forum where everybody said babies are their most horrible at six o'clock. Just when their fathers come home and want everything to be peaches and cream. That's why I was walking the streets on Wednesday. But I've turned my ankle this afternoon, stupidly, and can't walk very far. Just one darn thing after another, as they say.'

'Poor you. When does Scott get home?'

'Your guess is as good as mine. He wasn't thrilled when we showed up on Wednesday and told me not to do it again.' Her voice dropped, and Simmy detected something alarming in the tone.

'That's not fair,' she said indignantly. 'Leaving you on your own so much.'

'I think I prefer that to having him around, actually. He's all dark looks and long sighs when he is here. There's something wrong at work, I think. But he won't talk about it. Just says it's not me and I'm doing a great job with the baby.'

'That's something, I suppose.'

'Not nearly enough. He's changed precisely three nappies since she was born and taken her out to the lake once. That amounts to roughly one per cent of the work, by my calculations.'

'Oh dear,' said Simmy feebly.

'Gosh, I'm sorry to go on like this. You hardly know me, and here I am moaning about my life. Ignore me. I actually called to see if you'd like to come over sometime, and we can do something together? But you probably work full-time in your shop, don't you?'

Simmy's natural goodwill towards all and sundry was

finding itself sorely tested. The twisted ankle meant the woman needed a chauffeur, presumably. Did 'do something' mean being driven out to some Lakeland beauty spot, or a local pub – or what? How would the baby be factored into such an excursion? 'Well, yes, I do. Five and a half days a week, in fact. And I mostly spend the other day and a half with my fiancé. That only leaves evenings, doesn't it?'

'You could come here one evening, then. How are you fixed next week?'

'I can't say for sure. It's all a bit difficult at the moment. I have to help my parents—'

'It's the same with everybody,' Flo spat, suddenly angry. 'Nobody's got a minute to spare in their insanely busy lives. Not even my husband, father of this wretched child. It's absolute madness.'

'I *would* like to see you,' said Simmy, in all sincerity. 'I think your baby's lovely. But I daren't promise a specific evening without talking to one or two people first. I can call you on Monday and fix something.'

'All right, then.' The tone was grudging. 'I'm sorry to be so needy. I'm not usually like this, you know.'

'That's okay. You're having a hard time, there all on your own. Anybody would feel the same. It must be boring much of the time.'

'Right. The funny thing is – the baby's bored, as well. She perks right up when we see other people or go somewhere new. We're driving each other crazy.'

'It won't last for ever,' said Simmy, sounding hopelessly clichéd in her own ears.

* * *

She drove home, trying to clear her head of every thought but the central issue of the following day. No sooner was she inside her house and boiling the kettle than the phone jingled again. 'Hey, it's me,' said Ben. 'I've been trying to get you. First it was engaged and then it went to voicemail.'

'Sorry, it was that woman with the baby in Grasmere. What do you want? You're not cancelling tomorrow, are you?'

'Course not. Have you got your laptop there?'

'Not the main one. I had to leave it at the shop for Bonnie tomorrow. I've got my old one, though. It still works, but it hasn't got the shop stuff on it.'

'Good. Get onto the Internet, then, and have a look at the sale catalogue for tomorrow. They've got seven hundred and fifty lots. All those things! It'll be amazing. We've got to buy something, you know. And there won't be time for a proper look round, before they get started. There's pictures and guide prices, so you could pick out anything you fancy.'

'I'm not sure I want to, Ben. Bonnie showed me some of it already. I'd much rather see the actual objects. Why do we have to buy anything, anyway? There's no rule that says we have to, is there?'

'No. Obviously not. But we'll want to have something to show for the day, won't we? You *should* look at the catalogue,' he urged. 'There's such a huge range. Statues, stamps, old tablecloths, oriental carvings, pictures, china, toys, medals . . . I'm just flipping down the pages and those are what jump out. There's *loads* of things.'

'I know. I have been before, remember. I've seen what it's like.'

'Oh.'

She felt bad for deflating his excitement, but his efforts to force her to share it were irritating. Coming on the heels of Flo's disappointment, it made Simmy feel conscience-stricken at being so uncooperative. 'Yes, well, as I say, there'll be time enough tomorrow.'

'All right, then. Bonnie tells me you saw Moxo this afternoon,' he went on. 'Must be taking the thing seriously, if they're drafting in people from outside their patch.'

'It's not very *far* outside. They must work together all the time.' She hoped to deflect him from enquiring too deeply into the detective's reason for calling on her – despite knowing that Bonnie would already have explained. She recalled how Ben himself had felt that Christopher was not disclosing the whole truth.

It seemed that her strategy had worked. 'Mm,' said Ben, 'perhaps you're right.' The details of how various police forces operated were unclear to Simmy, and evidently to Ben as well. The only consistent person they'd had dealings with was DI Moxon, throughout all their adventures. Most likely, he was the only one with any patience for the annoying amateur sleuths, however helpful they might occasionally prove to be.

'Well, I'll see you tomorrow. I'm going now.' She was hungry, as well as irritable. If she didn't hurry, Christopher would make his nightly call, and she'd be wishing she could eat and talk at the same time.

As it was, the phone gave her no more than time to put

the kettle on and cut a slice of bread. It was seven-fifteen – early for Chris. 'Hello?' she said.

'Oh . . . hello. Is that the lady from the flower shop? Persimmon Petals? The phone message gave this number for out-of-hours calls.'

'That's right.' Bonnie had persuaded her that she should make herself available at all times, for urgent flower matters. Now she decided that it had been a bad idea.

'I *am* sorry to trouble you.' The voice was a quavering old lady's, and Simmy steeled herself to be patient. 'But I thought perhaps you could help me. I sent flowers to my granddaughter in Grasmere earlier this week. It seems I should have used a florist closer to hand, but I liked the sound of your name. Persimmon Petals. It has a nice ring.'

'Great-Granny Sarah,' said Simmy. 'I remember.'

'Oh, that's good. Florence phoned me to say thank you, the next day, and told me how friendly you were, and how she is left on her own a lot by that fool of a husband. Well, I shouldn't say that. Most people think Florence is the foolish one for marrying him. But she did sound in a bad way. The baby cries a lot and the district nurse doesn't sound to be up to the job. I've spent three days worrying about it and wishing I could be with her. But with my hips . . . and I'm due to have a cataract removed next week, and really it just isn't possible.'

'I'm sure she doesn't expect—'

'I'd be more trouble than I'm worth,' the old lady interrupted. 'I know that. So – this is going to sound so dreadfully impertinent – I was hoping you might have a few hours free to drop in and chat with her. I don't know why it is, but the women she thought were her friends in the area don't seem to be available when she needs them.'

'The thing is, Flo phoned me herself a little while ago, asking me the same thing. And I hate to say it, but I'm another of those busy women. I bumped into her and the baby in Grasmere on Wednesday evening and we exchanged phone numbers. And I think the baby's adorable. I will do my best to go and see them – but my free time really is very limited. Plus, of course, it's likely to be at the times when her husband's at home. Sundays and evenings.'

'Don't be too sure of that. Florence tells me he's just decided to keep the shop in Ambleside open right through the weekend, to catch the summer visitors. That means extra work, and you can't always rely on the volunteers – some of them are almost as old as me!' She chuckled. 'He seems to be intent on staying away from home as much as he can. Makes me furious.'

'I saw the shop yesterday evening. CaniCare – that's right, isn't it?'

'Did you go in?'

'No, it was closed for the day. It looked as if it had some interesting things, though.'

'I gather it's a favourite with rich old women. They get all kinds of wonders dumped on them. Scott's even persuaded *me* to let them have a lot of my things when the time comes. It does seem like a good cause and he's absolutely passionate about it.'

Simmy eyed her slice of bread and felt her stomach churn in anticipation. 'I'm afraid I'll have to go now,' she said, feeling mean. 'I was just about to have my supper.'

'Oh, I'm sorry. Of course. I'll let you go. I hope you're not offended by my calling you?'

'Of course not. It's very sweet of you to be so concerned. And I will try and get to Grasmere one evening next week, if I can. I haven't got very many friends myself, to be honest. I'd be glad to see more of Flo. It's just . . .'

'Yes, I know, dear. Everybody's always so busy. It's the way of the world these days.'

Simmy laughed and finished the call.

The final call was, as expected, from Christopher. *And I love you* had been his closing words, twenty-four hours earlier. She had had a great many conversations in the course of that time, but his words had remained warm and comforting at the back of her mind. Whatever happened, they would face the troubles of the world together. Hearing his voice now, she felt strong and purposeful in her new identity as half of a couple.

'Had a good day?' she asked as a matter of routine.

'Not too bad, I guess. The main event was Nick showing up to the viewing. That was a surprise. He says he's not going to let officialdom stop him, and if he's had up for tax dodging, then so should a hundred other people be. He's really fired up about it.'

'Did he know about Jonathan?'

'Obviously he did. The cops had him in for questioning, same as me. Lucky for him, he could prove he was up north Sunday and Monday.'

'But he doesn't know it was you who gave them his name?'

169

'Hey! Come on! What's that supposed to mean? It was hardly a secret, after all.'

'What wasn't? That Jonathan reported him to the taxman? Or that you suggested he had a motive for murder? I'm starting to feel sorry for the poor chap. Everybody seems to be dropping him in it, one way or another.'

'You don't understand.' His voice had changed from cheerful to defeated in seconds, and Simmy blamed herself. 'Nick doesn't hold grudges. He's like a stereotypical Irishman, except he's originally Welsh, I think. Nothing bothers him for long. Yes, he flares up quite a lot, but it all dies down again in a few days. Anyway, you can see for yourself, if you're still going to be here tomorrow. I'll introduce you.'

She chose to take this at face value, and then tried to raise his spirits with a change of subject. 'Thanks. I'll look forward to that. So – are you coming here on Sunday, as usual? Any ideas about what we should do? What about tomorrow evening, if I'm in Keswick all day, anyway?'

'Actually . . . don't take this the wrong way, but I am going to have to cry off, at least for Sunday morning. I've got a stack of valuations to catch up on, for a start. Things that can't wait another day. And I had a call from Valerie Woolley, Jon's wife. She wants me to talk her through exactly what happened when I found him on Monday. That's not going to be a barrel of laughs, is it? I don't know what she thinks she has to gain from it, but I imagine I'm in for a grilling rather like the one I got from your friend Ben.'

'She's probably imagining all kinds of ghastly things and hopes the reality will be less awful. It usually is, don't you think?'

'I don't know. I think I'm rather deficient where imagination is concerned. When my dad died, I didn't have the slightest wish to hear the details.'

'Oh, well. When are you seeing her, then? Sometime on Sunday?'

'She's coming to Keswick at eleven. She probably thinks I'll take her out to lunch, but I won't if I can help it. Why the hell should I, when all's said and done? She's not even his wife in any real sense. She's lucky if she gets whatever he's left.'

'She will, though, won't she? There isn't anybody else, is there?'

'Not that I know of. Well, she can darn well pay for the funeral out of whatever she inherits. And she can make all the arrangements.'

It occurred to Simmy with a pang that if her ex-husband died suddenly, she might want to know how it happened, even if it was years since she last saw him. But she would definitely leave it up to his siblings to take charge of the funeral; she was unlikely to even want to attend.

'What if I came up there and we all had lunch together?' It was an impulsive and irrational idea, which she instantly regretted.

'You don't want to come all this way twice, do you? Or do you mean you could stay over on Saturday night?'

'That would be lovely – but I'll have to take Ben home after the auction. Unless we can find him a bus.'

'Or a ride. I can think of a few people who might well

171

be going that way. Pack a toothbrush, just in case. The way things are going, you never know where you're going to be from one day to the next.'

He did want to see her, then. Only when that became clear did she realise she'd been doubting him. He had shifted from the relaxed attentive lover he'd been on holiday to a short-tempered and impatient stranger. Except that the earlier version still popped up at regular intervals, to provide reassurance that it was other matters causing his changed manner. Which was not at all surprising, she kept reminding herself. She was probably not her usual self, either. Where were the comforting words, the willingness to listen that she ought to be offering? Instead, she foisted Ben and Bonnie on to the wretched man, and asked far too many questions.

'That would be great,' she enthused. 'Let's hope we can make it work.'

'I think we can dump Valerie Woolley before it gets to lunchtime. I don't owe her a thing.'

*You do, though*, Simmy thought. He had been there at the scene of Jonathan's death. However accidental his presence might have been, that conferred on him a degree of responsibility. He had a unique knowledge that he had a duty to share with anyone who'd cared for the dead man. Not only that, but he was central to the investigations conducted by the police. 'Poor woman,' she said. 'You'll have to go gently with her.'

'You wouldn't say that if you'd heard her today. It sounded to me as if she thinks I was the one who killed him.'

Simmy made a sound to indicate scornful disbelief

and moved on to the usual end-of-call formula. The see-you-tomorrow and have-a-good-night, and the final declarations of love. Somehow, she ended up feeling rather less contented than she had the night before.

# Chapter Fourteen

Saturday was warmer than previous days, but the sky still fell short of a clear summer blue. There was high cloud yet again, but the early morning was just as insistently inviting as the late evening had been. It felt wasteful and ungrateful to remain inside when the outdoor world was so bathed in light. The prospect of spending the whole day in an auction room increased the sense of having got something wrong. She left the house soon after seven and reached Bowness in record time. Even so, Ben was at the door before she was out of the car. They greeted each other brightly. 'Nice day,' said Simmy. 'Seems a shame to spend it indoors.'

But Ben was of a wholly different opinion. The notion of seizing every balmy day was quite alien to him. At his age, there were thousands of such days still to come, so what was the point of regretting just one? 'It might mean there are fewer people there today, though,' he acknowledged. 'They'll be wanting to do outdoorsy things, the same as you.'

Simmy accepted the implication that she was essentially just one of the crowd, with no natural tendencies to swim against the tide. 'Oh, well,' she sighed. 'We'll be there nice and early at this rate. They open at eight. We might be the first in.'

'Great! That gives us time to have a really good look at all the lots.' He had printed out the catalogue he'd found on the auction house's website and made meaningful jottings in the margins. 'I might try and get a present for Bonnie's birthday. I was going to order something online, but this'd be much more interesting.'

'Good idea. You'll get a buyer's number, then?'

'Right.'

She glanced over at him and saw a faint frown of confusion on his face. 'You know what that means, don't you? I thought you'd been watching it all on telly.'

'I know the theory. But they might want proof of identity, and a credit card. I should have brought some cash.'

'I can't believe you didn't think all this through already.'

'I've been busy,' he replied shortly.

'Well, you can use my card and pay me back,' she said easily. 'And listen – I'm hoping to stay in Keswick overnight, so if we can find you a lift home, that would be good. Chris thinks there's sure to be people driving back down this way after the sale.'

'What? You'd consign me to the care of a total stranger, would you?' The sarcasm could not entirely conceal the flicker of alarm in his voice. 'What about the bus?'

'You're welcome to get a bus if you want to, but it'll take ages. A car would be much quicker. If we can't find anybody with a car, I'll take you. Don't panic.' She wanted to add – *You're eighteen, not thirteen. Why are you being such a baby?* But she remembered what had happened to him the previous year and realised she was being the insensitive one, and Ben wasn't behaving unreasonably.

'Okay. There's a lot to do before then, anyway. My head's bursting with it all. And it's odd without Bonnie.' He sighed. 'I hope Tanya behaves herself. She can be a bit of a ditz sometimes.'

'She was really good last time. All they have to do is sell flowers,' Simmy said optimistically.

'Yeah. And answer the phone, stay patient with total idiots, not get the names of the flowers confused and write everything down. Oh – and let's hope there isn't an armed robbery while they're in charge.'

'Shut up. You're just trying to get me worried.'

'Sorry. Anyway, if I have to get the bus I will. It's my own fault for failing the driving test. Serves me right for thinking I knew better than the examiner. Well – I *did* know better, but I should have just pretended. Story of my life.'

'Chris phoned last night and said that Nick man's going to be there today. The one they all think must have had a grudge against Jonathan. But now Chris says he's really a decent chap and wouldn't stay cross for long. It'll be interesting to see what he's like.'

'That's good. Who else, I wonder? I mean – how many other possible killers are going to show up? There's a good chance some will, given that the murder has to have something to do with the antique business. Or house clearances, at least. Did I tell you my dad says he'd have loved to do that for a living, instead of teaching? He's a secret collector, you know, but my mum won't let him accumulate much clutter. He's got a whole drawer full of tiepins and another one with cufflinks. We've no idea where he gets them from.'

As far as Simmy had been able to discover, David Harkness was a shadowy figure in the family home. She had never spoken to him, although he had been in the living room once when she visited, his legs up on a pouffe and football on the television. In his late fifties, he was increasingly exhausted by the demands of his job at the local comprehensive, according to Bonnie. She had hinted that she thought he might also be depressed. Her fondness for him was tinged with diffidence; there had never been a father figure in her own life, and she was unsure how best to approach him.

They were through Ambleside and heading towards Rydal. The sun was already high in the sky, and the gardens they passed were riotous with colour. Simmy made a vague sound in response to Ben's disclosures about his father, but no more than that.

'Okay,' Ben went on. 'So, what's the plan exactly?'

'Don't ask me. I'm just the driver. This is your project, not mine.'

'It's not a *project*. It's an investigation. But you've been before. You know your way around already. It's all going to be new to me.'

'There's a woman called Josephine who does all the computer stuff. Chris thinks you should talk to her mostly.'

'That's because he thinks I'm going to be there to find out how the system works for buying and selling. Doesn't he?'

'I don't know what he thinks. He probably assumes you're hoping to get some ideas about the murder. He's not daft, you know.'

'I never said he was. And I *do* want to understand the whole process because it's likely to be relevant. Didn't we say all this already?'

'You asked me what the plan was.'

'Okay. I meant, where are we going to sit? Are we both going to bid for things? Is Chris going to have any time off to talk to us, or does he just keep on going all day? Is he the only auctioneer? Do you know any of the regular bidders by name? Who's friends with who? All that sort of thing.'

Simmy felt weak. She had given very little thought to the precise details of the day. 'I've been twice,' she said. 'The first time was with my father, just after the Bowness murder. And I went up again after work one Saturday and just sat at the back, watching Chris in action. I have no idea who any of the people are, except for Hannah. She's Chris's sister, and goes quite a lot, I think. I have got one answer for you, though – he does keep going all day. It's about seven hours without a break.'

'Impressive. And frustrating. No chance of talking to him.'
'We told you that.'

They arrived just before eight. Being so early added considerably to the sense of adventure for both of them. A woman was pulling open the big gate to let cars through. Simmy and Ben were third in the queue. A big notice on the gatepost said, SALE TODAY 10 A.M. VIEWING FROM 8 A.M.

'Nice to be prompt,' said Ben, which Simmy took as a patronising piece of praise for her timekeeping and speedy driving.

They queued again at the reception desk, where two women were greeting people as they arrived. Doors were opening and closing on all sides as people went in and out of mysterious smaller rooms. 'One of those is Chris's office,' whispered Simmy. There was no sign of the man himself. Ben was given a form to complete before being allocated a bidder's number. Simmy gave her name and was told she was already in the system, but would be given a new number, since it was over a month since she last put in a bid. 'Makes sense,' said Ben. 'Otherwise they'd get into five figures in no time.'

Simmy was still trying to work out that piece of mathematical logic when they went through into the saleroom.

Everything was as before in the overall layout, but the nature of the objects for sale had changed dramatically. There was a huge sofa at the front, and two smaller ones in the middle of the room. Arranged all around them were chairs of every kind. Deep sagging armchairs, mahogany dining chairs, cane-seated bedroom chairs and a very worm-eaten ornately carved thing that was more like a throne than a chair. It had a worn leather seat. 'Once used by Anne Boleyn, I should think,' said Ben. For a moment, Simmy believed him.

On three sides there were shelves and tables stacked with objects large and small, as well as more hanging on the walls. Clocks, old books, suitcases, records, statuettes, stuffed animals in glass cases, pictures, musical instruments, old radios, old sewing machines, bags of embroidered linens, rolled-up rugs and carpets, chess sets – and a whole section of china and porcelain. On the fourth side was the auctioneer's rostrum flanked by two lower tables for computers. 'They have online bidding, don't they?' said Ben.

'I guess so,' said Simmy uncertainly, trying to remember what Chris had told her.

Also, near the fourth wall, in front of the auctioneer and his assistants, stood a row of glass cabinets containing the more valuable or easily damaged items. Jewellery, coins, stamps, tiny oriental carvings, pill boxes, delicate porcelain figures. Ben flipped through his catalogue and found Lot 432. 'Hey, listen to this. "Snake Charmer by Rosenthal, Germany. Guide price £1800 to £2000." It's rather nice, don't you think? I could get that for Bonnie.'

'Did you say two thousand pounds?' Again, for a moment she believed him when he said he might buy it. The piece was indeed compelling. A girl in flimsy garments was bending over, one finger extended, pointing down at a cobra just in front of her. Her other finger was against her lips in a hushing gesture. The elegant suppleness of her body had an erotic charge. Simmy gazed at it longingly.

'It's worth it, look. It's fantastic. You couldn't lend me a couple of grand, could you?'

'In your dreams.' But how great would it be to own the thing. Already she was glimpsing the intense appeal of the whole auction experience. The urgent desire for such a lovely object as this, the fierce contest against other bidders, the temptation to buy it at any cost – and the associated wheeling and dealing that must surely accompany such irresistible drives. 'Let's see if we can find Chris,' she said. 'Remember what we came for.'

They selected two upright chairs with padded seats and reserved them by putting their number cards on the seats, as they saw others had done. There were eight or ten potential bidders sitting with their catalogues, intently studying the contents. Conversation was muted; it was a large space with a high ceiling, so little could be overheard. 'I wonder if Nick's here yet,' muttered Simmy.

Ben was paying no attention to her, eagerly scanning his catalogue. 'Who?' he said, belatedly aware that she had spoken.

She reminded him as they went back to the reception desk, which had an office behind it, both sides of the window now full of people. Potential buyers were arriving in large numbers, thronging the waiting area. All the seats in the office were occupied by busy staff members. Outside, the car park appeared to be full.

'There he is,' Ben said, tapping Simmy on the back. 'Look.'

She turned and met Christopher's eyes, over the shoulder

of one of the reception women. He waved and smiled, and she felt warmed by the welcome. He disappeared for a moment, and then a door opened and two seconds later he was giving her a hug. 'You got here, then,' he said, with a little laugh. 'Hello, Ben. How's it going?'

'Fine. This is all very interesting.' He turned in a half-circle, looking all round at the people, the posters and the busy office. 'This is typical, is it?'

Christopher made a rueful face. 'Good question. Actually, this is a lot busier than usual. We're not sure why.'

'Notoriety? They've heard about the Grasmere murder, and made the connection with the auction. Do you think?'

A man close by gave Ben a look. 'Murder?' he said, with a frown. 'Did somebody get murdered?'

'Don't worry about it,' said Ben. He ducked his head in self-reproach. 'Sorry,' he muttered to Christopher, who was looking decidedly displeased.

'Probably not that,' said Simmy. 'Maybe it's because you were in the paper about that stumpwork. It makes you seem glamorous.'

'I've got no objection to that,' Christopher conceded. 'But look – we can't stand here. We'd better go into my office. I've got an hour and a half before it all kicks off. I don't usually get here until after nine.' He was working his way through the crowd towards the door he'd come in through. 'It's just along here.'

'You came early specially for us,' said Ben, trotting along behind the others. 'That's nice.'

Christopher shrugged and gave Simmy a smile. They had arrived at another door, which opened into a small room with a computer and telephone. Nobody sat down. 'Have you had a look in the saleroom?' Christopher asked.

Simmy nodded. 'We both want that snake charmer.'

'The Rosenthal? Gorgeous, isn't it. I could live with it myself.'

'You're not allowed to buy it, are you?' Ben asked. 'Isn't that forbidden?'

'Why would it be? My money's as good as anyone's.'

'Yes, but – how would that work? You can't bid while you're doing the auctioneer thing, can you?'

'It varies. I can make it look as if it's an online bid or get someone else to bid for me. It's all quite kosher.'

Ben looked unconvinced. 'It's not exactly upfront, though, is it?'

Christopher sighed and shook his head. 'Nothing's exactly upfront in this business. People don't want it known what they're buying or selling. Mostly it's just a game, like it's always been. Sometimes they're embarrassed if they've paid too little – or too much.'

Ben waggled his head in ambivalent judgement on this uncertain morality. 'Well, that's not the main business in hand, is it?' he said, squaring his shoulders. 'We want to try and spot anything that could explain why a man got murdered.'

Simmy had a thought. 'Will the police be here, doing the same thing?' she wondered.

Christopher went pale. 'Nobody's said anything to me.'

'They wouldn't, would they?' said Ben. 'They'd send a plain clothes sergeant to watch the goings-on.'

'I wish you hadn't said that. Now I'm going to be searching the bidders for an undercover cop. It'll distract

183

me. You have no idea of the level of concentration it takes to do a good job.'

'I look forward to finding out,' said Ben, with a formal little nod. 'Simmy tells me you're remarkably good at it.'

'He works the room,' said Simmy proudly. 'I never knew what that meant before. It's a pleasure to watch him.'

'I should go,' said Christopher suddenly. 'Josephine's going to want me. There's always something at the last minute.'

'Show us which one she is,' said Simmy. 'Ben's going to want to talk to her, if he gets a chance.'

They all trooped back to the reception area, which was less busy than before. Christopher pointed out a woman sitting at a computer at the back of the open office behind the reception windows. She was around fifty, with a careless haircut and shapeless figure. 'She's our guiding angel,' said Christopher, quite loudly. 'We'd be lost without her. Hey, Jo! I'm talking about you.' He leant over the counter in her direction.

The woman turned, met his eyes and smiled adoringly. *Uh-oh*, thought Simmy.

'This is Simmy. You've heard me mention her. And Ben. He's here on a sort of research project. He's off to university in the autumn, doing forensic something-or-other.'

Josephine shook her head slightly, as if trying to connect antiques to forensics, and failing. 'Hello,' she said. She gave Simmy a long look that was very far from friendly. The reason for it was painfully obvious, and quite disconcerting, even if it was an almost comical cliché. The frumpy middle-aged employee nursing a passion for her charismatic boss. There must be a

184

thousand instances of it in Cumbria alone. But, like the powerful emotions of teenaged girls, it was not safe to ignore the yearnings of older women. Trouble of many sorts could arise from it, in both cases.

'Pleased to meet you,' Simmy told the woman, with the most pleasant smile she could muster.

'Go and find somewhere to sit,' Christopher advised them. 'I know we don't start for another hour, nearly, but the seats fill up quickly. You can watch everything better if you sit near the back. That way, it's more obvious who's bidding.'

'We've already bagged places,' said Ben. 'We want to try and spot Nick – the man who Jonathan reported to the tax people.'

Christopher rolled his eyes and glanced around for anyone overhearing them. 'You mean, the man with the solid alibi?'

'Right,' Ben nodded. 'But it might not be conclusive. Maybe he has a son or brother or wife who was angry on his behalf.'

'Stop it,' Simmy hissed at him. 'Come and sit down and behave yourself.' She grinned disarmingly at her fiancé and pushed the boy ahead of her.

Ben was soon distracted by the appearance of a picture show on a monitor mounted on the wall above the podium. The lots were being shown, one by one, with ten seconds accorded to each. Ben was matching them to the description in his catalogue, with intense interest.

Simmy's gaze was also on the monitor. 'Gosh – that looks nice,' she breathed, as a *cloisonné* vase was shown.

It was red and orange and yellow, big and shiny, with a dragon design. 'Must be Chinese, I suppose.'

'Japanese.' Ben tapped his catalogue. 'Guide price only a hundred quid. Must be more modern than it looks.'

His careless remark about friends or relations of the ill-used Nick had given her pause. Had the police formed the same idea? Could you be so murderously angry on behalf of someone else – whose grievance was scarcely serious enough to justify murder in the first place? Her thoughts returned yet again to the Grasmere house and its significance as the scene of the crime. Along with those thoughts came the inevitable acknowledgement that her Christopher had also gone to that same house, for reasons she still wasn't sure she fully understood. It had to appear suspicious to the police; so much so that it was almost surprising that Chris wasn't in custody or at best out on bail. Instead of being so delicate and sympathetic on this subject, DI Moxon should surely have been explaining just why there was such a level of doubt as to her fiancé's guilt.

Perhaps it had been the accidental bystander who had persuaded them. The man who called 999, because Christopher had been so shocked as to be incapable of doing it himself. 'I told you, didn't I, about the man in the street?' she asked Ben now.

'Who?'

'Pay attention,' she snapped. 'You're leaving me to do all the work here.'

'Sorry. I'm not really. I'm just trying to get the hang of all this.' He gave an all-embracing gesture to indicate the

186

saleroom. 'You never know what's relevant. What are you trying to tell me?'

'The man outside the house, when Christopher found Jonathan. He called the police. They'll have interviewed him.'

Ben's attention was finally captured. He turned sideways on his chair to look at her. 'Did he hang around, then, until they showed up?'

'Yes, but they didn't seem very interested in him, according to Chris, when they realised he hadn't seen anything useful.'

'They can't have known that until they'd questioned him properly. And if he was just passing by, he won't have been able to say much to exonerate Chris.'

There had been one row of empty seats behind them when they sat down. Now people were filling them, too. Simmy had been aware of somebody immediately behind her for the past few minutes and had unconsciously been trying to speak more quietly. But Ben had a loud voice, which got louder when he was excited. Before she could say more, a man pushed his head between them. 'That was me,' he said. 'If you're talking about last Monday afternoon in Grasmere.'

They both twisted round to look at him. 'Pardon?' said Simmy.

'The name's Pruitt. I'm the chap who called the police for Mr Henderson. I gather you know quite a lot about what happened.'

Neither Simmy nor Ben could think of anything to say. They looked at each other, then back at the man. *We were too loud*, Simmy reproached herself, trying

187

to remember exactly what they'd said. 'We know Mr Henderson,' she said.

'I haven't seen you here before.'

'You come regularly, do you?' Ben was regaining his composure and clearly thinking fast. 'In that case, Christopher must know *you*. He's sure to recognise all his usual buyers.'

'I've only been a couple of times since he took over. I used to come to every sale when it was Oliver.'

'But you knew who he was, on Monday.'

'I did, yes.'

Ben's eyes were flickering from side to side. Simmy recognised the signs and tried to guess what he was thinking. Something not quite right, something concealed and now needlessly revealed. What did it mean? She looked at the man, the angle between them stiff and awkward. 'Why don't you come and sit here, so we can talk properly?' she said, patting the empty chair beside her. It was small and hard.

'I won't, thank you. I prefer the back row, where I can see everything that's going on. And I'm keeping this seat for someone. She's just gone for some coffee.'

He was a solid man, of middle height and middle age. His grey-black hair was cut short, lying in crinkly ridges flat on his head. He could have been a pub landlord or an AA man, Simmy decided. He had none of the weary disillusion of a teacher, nor the apprehensive manner of a social worker. He seemed to expect people to like him. Had Christopher liked him, she wondered, in those intimate Grasmere moments?

'Did you know Jonathan, then?' Ben asked, with startling directness. 'The man who was killed, that is. The one whose body you saw on Monday.'

Mr Pruitt blinked, but did not flinch. 'I can't say I recognised him. But then, I didn't look very closely. He wasn't a pretty sight. I might have seen him here, but I can't say for sure.'

A woman then put in an appearance, carrying two mugs of coffee. She stared curiously at Simmy and Ben, casting questioning looks at Mr Pruitt. 'Hello, Sal,' he said. 'I've been chatting to a pair of newcomers to the salerooms, wanting to know the drill.'

'It's not complicated,' she remarked. 'You'll pick it up soon enough.'

The woman named Sal was much younger than Mr Pruitt and appeared to be intimately acquainted with him. It seemed to Simmy that he was averse to Sal's being included in any discussion of his involvement with Monday's drama. Something in his face confirmed this. He sat back and avoided Simmy's eyes.

There was still half an hour to go before the auction started. The smell of the coffee appealed to Simmy, and she decided to get some for herself. There was a small shed-like building that served basic snacks, on the far side of the car park. It offered seating for a dozen or so, squashed close together, but they were happy for customers to take their cups and plates into the saleroom, to be returned later. 'I'm going to get a drink,' she told Ben. 'Do you want one?'

'Tea, I suppose,' he said, without enthusiasm. He'd

taken a notebook out of his bag and was making jottings in it. The bag was the one he'd used for school and the sight of it reminded Simmy of how young he still was. Still too young to appreciate coffee, or to fully understand the effect he had on other people. She could feel Mr Pruitt's unsatisfied curiosity as to just who they both were and how they were related. Ben's note-taking must only be increasing his confusion.

Waiting in the short queue, she scanned the people at the few tables, most of them studying their auction catalogues, pen in hand. How seriously did they take the sale? How important was the day for their incomes? Did they depend on buying cheap and selling dear, in the whole uncertain business? Was it sometimes so crucial to their survival that they would resort to crime to get what they needed? On the numerous television programmes featuring antique shops, fairs and auctions, everyone looked relaxed and mildly amateurish, as if it was more of a hobby or a game than a means of earning a living. That was not the impression she gained from the people around her. They were badly dressed, ill-shaven, hollow-eyed, for the most part. Although most were chatting amiably, there was a definite atmosphere of earnestness in the air. None of these people appeared to be here for the fun of it.

'Won't get anything as good as that stumpwork again for a while,' she heard one man say. His neighbour just nodded, with a grimace that seemed to say *And even that was a fluke.*

She took the drinks back to the saleroom, settling down on her 1920s upright chair and wondering whether she could manage to stay there all day without developing backache. 'If we left a bit early, I could drive you home and then come back before Chris has sold everything,' she muttered to Ben.

'How early?'

'Two-thirty? Three? We'll have seen more than enough by then.'

'You don't know that. We might have seen enough by midday. On the other hand, we could stay till five and be none the wiser. We've got no idea.'

'That's true.' So true, in fact, that she realised she didn't really know what, if anything, the boy was hoping to witness during his day at the auction. He had been a lot less proactive than expected so far. She'd assumed he would go round asking questions of the staff and making pages of notes. As it was, he had hardly taken his eyes off his catalogue and the monitor on the wall.

'So many *things*,' he murmured. 'Who on earth buys them all? Where do they go? Where did they come from? There's a story behind every one of them. It's overwhelming.' He shook his head. 'The world must be so full of *stuff*. How many auctions like this happen across the country every week? Fifty? A hundred? All that buying and selling! I feel as if I'm on a different planet.'

'I know. I had the same thoughts when I came here the first time.'

A bell rang, and Christopher appeared from a side door and took his place on the podium. People settled down. Two men in overalls positioned themselves in front of shelves in one corner of the room. Two women sat at

191

computers close to the podium, but on a lower level. Chris had a monitor of his own. 'That'll be for the online bids,' whispered Ben. Simmy noticed that he had sketched the whole set-up in his little book.

'Where's Nick?' she muttered. 'I forgot to ask Chris to point him out.'

'Too late now,' said Ben.

With a brief preamble about commission rates, the necessity of having a buyer's number and a projected finishing time of five o'clock, the whole proceedings got under way. The men in overalls indicated the lot that Christopher announced – lifting it up if it wasn't too big and turning so that everyone could see it. At the same time a photograph of it appeared on the wall-mounted screen, and when the bidding was finished and Christopher's little hammer had tapped the table, the final price was also displayed. The pace was brisk and Simmy could see that it had to be finely balanced. Too fast and potential bidders might still be dithering when the hammer came down. Too slow and the buyers became restless. The opening to each lot caught her interest. Chris would name a figure, which she presumed was at the lower end of the estimated value, and very seldom did anyone take him up on it. He would drop, often considerably, until a bidder almost always materialised, often at a figure of only one or two pounds. Then, almost miraculously it seemed to her, they would be back to a point just above the first figure he had mentioned. Did it always go like that, she wondered, or was it just this saleroom that followed this pattern? There were occasions when the original sum was doubled or more, as well as instances where the lot went for a small fraction of it. But mostly, it turned out to be prophetic. She found herself doubting the truth of the claim that auctions were wildly unpredictable.

In no time at all it was past twelve o'clock and Christopher had sold one hundred and ninety lots. Ben wrote down the final price of each one in his catalogue. He sometimes added brief notes as well. Simmy watched the faces. Once a person had made their opening bid, almost always with a flourish of the catalogue or number card, they went on bidding with subtle nods, winks or flick of a finger. The reason for such discretion escaped her. The auctioneer looked right at them, even saying, 'The bid's with the lady in the second row,' or similar. Everybody knew who the bidder was.

'The Rosenthal won't come up for ages yet,' said Ben. 'Sometime between two and half past is my guess.'

'You're not really thinking of buying it, are you? I wouldn't mind it myself, actually.' She had little idea of how the Harkness family finances worked, but Helen was a successful architect and her husband a senior teacher. It was not impossible that Ben had enough cash at his disposal to buy a valuable piece of porcelain. The notion of young Ben or even Bonnie owing it was oddly painful. *I want it myself*, she thought with surprise. *If anybody's having it, I want it to be me.*

'Only in my dreams,' he admitted. 'I was imagining I could buy it and keep it secret and give it to Bonnie when we get married.'

'Nice idea,' she said lightly. 'But I'm going to want a

sandwich soon. I need to take these cups back and go to the loo, as well.'

'Doesn't Christopher ever need a break? How can he work right through for seven hours?'

'Good question.' She gave her fiancé a long look. He was selling a large painting of a flock of sheep, constantly scanning the room for bidders, reacting quickly when one was located, making everything seem relaxed and easy, and yet wasting not a second. Behind her she sensed a flurry and saw Chris home in on it from his rostrum. Instead of smoothly taking in the new bid, he hesitated. Then he looked harder at the person in question and stammered, 'New bid, eighty-five pounds. Any more? Ninety to anyone?' The words were right, but the delivery was faulty. He seemed to have forgotten what came next. 'Eighty-five pounds,' he said again. 'Bidder at the back of the room.' There was a silence, although Simmy didn't think anyone had noticed anything unusual. 'Sorry, then. That's a no sale. The vendor wants more than that for it.' And he gave a double-tap with his hammer to indicate a failed sale, the bidding too low for the reserve price.

It was the first time the Pruitt man had made a bid. He and Sal had remained quietly still all morning, and Simmy had almost forgotten about them. Their seats were low-slung armchairs, and they must have remained invisible until one of them rose up to make a bid. And Christopher had suddenly recognised the man from the Grasmere street and been thrown into confusion.

'What's the matter with him?' muttered Ben.

'What do you think? Isn't it obvious?' she snapped

back, before lowering her voice. 'He didn't expect to see you-know-who behind us.'

'Took his time to recognise him.'

Simmy didn't grace this with a reply. 'Lunch,' she insisted, after a few moments.

Leaving their bidding numbers and Ben's backpack to save the seats, they went out to the little cafe. They bought sandwiches and drinks, and grabbed the last two places. Ben flipped through his notebook. 'Stumpwork,' he said suddenly. 'I googled it and couldn't find anyone paying more than a couple of thousand for even the oldest pieces. How did Jonathan's fetch so much? Did you say it was *fourteen* thousand?'

'That's what the papers said. It was very special. Something that several collectors all wanted, I suppose.'

'Maybe it had gold doubloons stitched into it.'

She laughed. 'Someone would have noticed, don't you think?'

'Why don't we know where it came from? Where did Jonathan get it? The papers must have asked him that.'

'They didn't, because they didn't know who the vendor was. It was meant to be a secret. Chris only told me on Tuesday.'

'Ah.' Ben became thoughtful. 'So, it was still a secret up to when Jonathan was killed.'

'We've been over this.' She rolled her eyes, trying to convey to him that everything they said was clearly heard by all the other people having their lunch. It seemed unwise to speak so openly about Jonathan Woolley.

But Ben evidently had no such qualms. 'Well, I think there's more story to it. Who bought it?'

'The V&A,' came a voice from the next table. 'It was an online bid. An American museum wanted it as well, but they dropped out. It's a hugely valuable piece of embroidery. Part of a sequence, they think. There are two others that look similar already in London.'

# Chapter Fifteen

Ben and Simmy stared at the woman who was speaking so freely. 'Oh,' said Ben. 'Thanks.'

'My pleasure. Pity Chris Henderson didn't realise its value. Oliver nearly had a heart attack when the bidding kept going up the way it did. He'd valued the thing at five thousand, and he thought that was pushing it.'

'So, Jonathan must have been shocked as well,' said Ben slowly. 'He didn't know he'd got such a valuable thing.'

'Apparently.' The woman shrugged. She had dyed orange hair and looked to be about fifty. Simmy noticed her hands in particular. They were large and expressive, with long fingers and short nails. She seemed happy to share information and went on, 'Some of us guessed Jonathan was the vendor, but when we asked him about it, he wouldn't say where he got it or what he paid for it originally. A couple of hundred, most likely. Could have been even less.'

'Chris is my fiancé,' said Simmy, in a spirit of disclosure. 'He was with me on Lanzarote – that's why he missed the sale.'

'I guessed that's who you were – the way you were looking at him all morning.'

Simmy smiled faintly and blushed. 'He's very good at it, isn't he.'

'Not bad. I'm Beverley, by the way. I'm a regular here.' Four or five other people had been frankly following the conversation. Now two men made sounds of friendly approval, endorsing the woman's claim to familiarity. 'It's a small world,' she added.

'Are you a dealer – or a collector?' Ben asked her.

'Both, I guess you could say. Just trying to scrape a living, same as these guys.' Her accent was faintly American, or possibly Canadian, Simmy thought. 'I send stuff back to the States, mostly. They're not as bored with china and porcelain as you folks are here. And they've still got space in their homes for some decent furniture.'

'You're American, then?' Ben's questions were generally very direct.

'Originally, yeah. I've been here for twenty-five years now, married to a Brit, but I go back so much it keeps the accent alive.'

'So you must have been miffed when the stumpwork went to a British buyer.'

Beverley shrugged. 'Couldn't care less. So far out of my league, I just enjoyed the show.'

Simmy took a good long breath. 'Do you know Nick?' she asked.

'Nick? Which one? There's three I can think of.'

'Don't tease the lady, Bev,' said one of the listening men. 'There's only one Nick anybody's interested in.'

'Okay. Nick with the tax issues, right? He's here today. The one who was bidding for that tin trunk – remember? Lot 99. And the set of leather suitcases. He can sell them in London.'

Simmy racked her brains. 'What does he look like?'

'Long hair. Stubble. Tall.'

It rang no bells. 'I don't think I noticed him.'

'I did,' said Ben suddenly. He flipped through his catalogue. 'He paid sixty pounds for the trunk and fifty for the suitcases. I wrote it down.'

'Good prices. He'll double that.'

'And declare the profit to the Inland Revenue?' said Ben cheekily.

'Of course,' said Beverley with a straight face.

'How much trouble is he in with them?' asked Simmy.

'Who knows? Nobody's going to broadcast that sort of thing, are they? He's pretty sick about it, I can tell you that. He didn't do anything that we haven't all done. It was a gutless thing someone did, reporting him like that.'

'Somebody with a grudge against him, then?' said Ben.

Beverley pursed her lips. 'Cuts both ways,' she said

obscurely. 'If you start looking for grudges, they can go back a lot further than you think.'

'A feud!' said Ben, excitedly.

'If you like.'

Simmy was worrying that they were missing too much of the auction. 'We should get back,' she said. 'It's nearly half past twelve.'

'Okay.' He stood up and began to squeeze between people at the other tables. He clutched his notepad to his chest. Simmy threw a friendly smile at the informative woman and followed him back to the saleroom.

To their surprise, nothing was happening when they got back. Christopher's podium was empty and both the computer operatives were also absent. 'What happened?' Simmy asked Mr Pruitt, who was sitting on his own.

'Comfort break. Twenty minutes. They always do it around now. Health and safety rules, presumably.'

Not many of the buyers had left their seats. A few were eating sandwiches, and one couple even had a thermos. A minute or two later, the woman from the cafe came in and sat down next to Mr Pruitt. 'Hello again,' she said.

Simmy and Ben both blinked. This was a different woman to the one who had sat with Mr Pruitt during the morning. He had swapped the youngish Sal for the older Beverley, apparently in an arrangement that suited everybody. 'Sal gone home?' asked Beverley.

He nodded. 'This is my wife,' he told Simmy and Ben.

'We met just now in the cafe,' said Simmy.

'Not bidding for anything?' Mrs Pruitt asked.

'Not yet,' said Simmy.

'They're not too keen on sightseers, you know. Taking up space and not buying anything – a bit out of order, if you ask me.'

Ben opened his mouth to retort, but Simmy caught his eye with a warning look. 'We've still got all afternoon,' she said. 'And there are still a few empty chairs, anyway.' The seats in question were squashed between sofas and not very easy to access. She smiled to remove any hint of defensiveness.

'What's the notebook all about?' asked Mr Pruitt, looking over Ben's shoulder. 'You've been writing in it all morning.'

'Just a little project,' muttered the boy, clapping the book shut. Simmy herself had wondered what he was finding to write down, but she knew better than to try to see. The Pruitts were mutating into less amiable characters. Since Christopher's wobble at the sight of the male half of this couple, she had been asking herself just what had taken place between the two men in Grasmere on Monday.

Christopher was well known across the region, she supposed. His face would be familiar to anybody who'd attended the auction even once. But Grasmere was quite a distance from Keswick, and not everybody went to auctions. Had Mr Pruitt realised instantly who it was who'd found a dead body? From what he said, it seemed probable. Had he known Kathleen Leeson? Or Philip? All of a sudden, he seemed to be a lot more connected to the central questions than had first appeared. And yet – why would he show up here, drawing attention to himself and frightening the auctioneer? Was he trying to threaten

Chris somehow? A host of theories filled her mind, and looking at Ben, she suspected he was having very similar thoughts. Then his mobile summoned him with a text and he hunkered over it for a minute or two. Simmy was too polite to enquire as to the content of the messages, and he said nothing to enlighten her.

Then everything got going again, and they were on Lot Number 260. That was about a third of the total, by the numbers, which suggested that the sale would be over around five, as predicted. Simmy found herself calculating times and logistics, and whether she could sustain an entire afternoon in the saleroom. Then her mobile began to jingle in her bag. Nervously, she looked round. Chris was taking bids, everyone focused on him. But there were also muted conversations going on around the room. Total silence was not demanded. She fished out the phone and answered softly, having seen the caller identified as Bonnie Lawson.

'Hello?'

'Simmy! Thank goodness you answered. Listen – can you come back? We've got trouble here.'

'What trouble? It'll take me an hour. It's nearly time to close up, anyway. What's the matter?' Her voice had risen, and people were staring at her disapprovingly. Ben was looking at her in alarm.

'Tanya cut herself. There's blood everywhere. It's clogged up the computer keyboard, so it doesn't work.'

'Good God, Bonnie! Is she all right?'

'We used the first-aid kit. But there was a man here and he called 999, which was pretty stupid. I'd already phoned Helen and she came right away. So, we didn't need an

202

ambulance. Helen's taken her to the new urgent treatment place in Kendal – they can do stitching.'

'How long ago was this?' The dark looks had become impossible to ignore, so she got up and went out to the reception area as she listened to Bonnie's garbled story.

'An hour, I suppose. I don't know exactly. But I can't close the computer down. And it needs mopping – the floor, I mean. And the table.'

'What on earth was she doing?'

'Cutting some ribbon with a knife. It slipped somehow. I didn't see. But it sliced along her wrist, and it *poured* with blood.' The young voice was shaky and getting worse. 'I can't really cope with blood, actually,' she said faintly. 'I had to *force* myself.'

'Well done,' said Simmy with an effort. 'Poor Tanya.'

'She was very brave. The man who called the ambulance was such an idiot, though. He made it all worse, talking about arteries and tourniquets. He came in about two minutes after it happened, while I was phoning Helen, and making Tanya press a clean pad on the place. That's what you have to do, you know.'

'Yes,' said Simmy, who had been on a one-day first-aid course herself. The kit in the shop contained two big sterile pads for the very purpose. 'That's right.' She remembered, belatedly, how Bonnie had difficulty with anything that could be described as dirty. Blood came under that heading. It all went back to damaging childhood experiences that had made the girl's early teens severely dysfunctional. 'Don't worry, love. Just lock the shop and I'll see to everything. You've been a hero, by the sound of it.'

Ben had followed her out and was flapping and hopping in front of her, trying to get included in the conversation. 'Ben's here,' said Simmy. 'I think he wants to talk to you.'

'In a minute. Are you saying I can go home and just leave everything? I'm not sure I should.' She moaned. 'It's such an awful mess.'

'Yes. It's fine. It's my fault for leaving you. Here – talk to Ben before he explodes.'

The boy snatched the phone, bending over it as if protecting his beloved from further distress. 'Hey, Bon. What happened? . . . Okay. That's okay. I'm not hassling you . . . No, it's fine . . . we'll come back now. Go back to Helm Road, and we'll find you when we get back. Shit, kid – you scared me.' He forced a laugh. 'From what Simmy was saying this end, I couldn't even guess what had happened . . . yes, that's fine. Just . . .' His voice seemed to die away, consumed by emotion. 'Bye, then,' he choked. Then he looked at Simmy. 'She says you'll have to tell me. She doesn't want to say it all again. Did something happen to Tanya?'

'She cut herself. Your mother came and took her to be stitched. Bonnie can't face all the blood in the shop. It's all over the computer, apparently.'

Ben pulled a face. 'That won't be easy to fix. The keys'll be all clogged up.'

'I know. I'll have to borrow yours.' She was teasing, knowing he would never let her use his precious Mac. 'I won't know who's ordered flowers otherwise.'

'Hasn't your mother got one you can use? Or Christopher?'

Christopher! There he was, still ploughing through three or four hundred lots of antiques, with no idea of what was going on. So near and yet so far. She thought quickly. 'I'll leave him a message with Josephine,' she said. Then she took a deep breath. 'Actually, there's not such a great hurry, is there? Nobody needs me right away. I can clean the shop tomorrow. It's probably nothing like as bad as Bonnie thinks. I don't know why she was so anxious for me to go back, really.'

Ben gave her an impatient look. 'She wants *me*,' he said. 'And you're my only way of getting there quickly.'

'That's not what she said. She never mentioned you.' The idea of her role being nothing more than a chauffeur was annoying.

'Well I want to be there, and she knows that. Same difference.'

'Are you two all right?' came a voice from behind the reception counter. They turned to see the stout woman identified as Josephine leaning towards them. There was nobody waiting for attention – the whole area was deserted.

'Oh! Yes, thanks. That is, we've got to leave early. I can't interrupt Christopher, obviously, so perhaps you could tell him there's a bit of a crisis in Windermere, so I've gone to see to it. I'll phone him at five, okay?'

'He might not be finished by five.'

'Well, in that case he won't answer his phone, will he?' It was all starting to feel like too much. Guilt at leaving two young girls in charge of the shop; irritation with Ben who saw her simply as his driver; a sense of having wasted the morning in something that had actually been slightly tedious; uncertainty as to when she would have a chance to get Christopher to herself; it all made for jangled nerves.

'Pity we never saw Nick. I forgot about him. We didn't try to spot him from that woman's description.'

'We got the important stuff, though,' Ben said, sounding pleased. 'About the tax, and all that.'

'Did we?' She tried to remember exactly what they'd been told.

'I'm getting a few theories,' he said. 'Plenty to work with. Once I run it all past Bonnie, it'll be even clearer in my mind.'

'Bully for you,' muttered Simmy, getting into the car.

# *Chapter Sixteen*

As she'd suspected, the bloodstains in the shop were much less gruesome than Bonnie had implied. Even the computer was only moderately spattered. The letters in the middle of the keyboard were somewhat gluey – from F to K were the worst affected. Experimenting with a piece of wire, Simmy found she could get most of it out. When it was dryer, it would flake off fairly easily, she hoped. The floor was similarly splashed, with a larger pool beside the computer table. Why had the wretched girl been cutting ribbon there anyway? And why not with scissors?

The next task was to phone Helen Harkness and ask

after Tanya. It was now almost half past two, and there was every reason to assume the patient was back at home, nicely bandaged and mollified. She tried to think which knife the girl must have been using and remembered with a jolt that there had been a Stanley knife in a drawer below the computer. Its blade was razor sharp and pointed. Would she be in trouble for leaving something so dangerous where a girl so young could find it? And how deep was the cut in her arm? Were any vital nerves affected? The surge of worry came all the more powerfully for having been suppressed for the past hour. Tanya was a nice girl, bright and cheerful. She had a twin sister who had embraced teenage culture and social media with all the usual enthusiasm. But Tanya had seen a different way, inspired by her brother Ben. Encouraged by the history teacher at school, and with Bonnie's unconventional example, she was increasingly ambitious. 'Law,' said Bonnie. 'She wants to do law.'

She made the phone call, using Helen's mobile number. The woman was cool and calm, but not exactly friendly. 'She lost a lot of blood. Bonnie's very upset about it.'

Bonnie! Simmy understood that she was expected to be every bit as worried about the older girl as she was about Tanya. 'Yes,' she said. 'It must have been awful for both of them.'

'I had to drop everything and rush her to that new place in Kendal. Lucky I knew about it.'

'Yes,' said Simmy again. 'But she's all right now, is she?'

'There'll be a scar. She just missed an artery. It's really not nearly as bad as we first thought, but poor Bonnie had a right old meltdown. It made it all seem more of a drama than it need have been.'

'Oh God. I'm so sorry, Helen.'

'Well, it couldn't have been predicted, I suppose. She was trying to be helpful, making up a bouquet for a customer.'

'Not the man who called the ambulance?'

'No – I don't think so. Didn't he show up a few minutes later? Bonnie really took against him.'

'So I gathered. Do we know who he is?'

'Bonnie probably does. He must have given his name when he made the call.'

Simmy looked round the shop and saw a half-finished bunch of flowers on the floor, under the table, splashed with dark-red blood. Roses, lilies, white daisies – where was the customer who had been trying to buy them, she wondered. Had he or she left the order, saying they'd be back when the bouquet was complete? That would be the usual practice. 'Well, I'm terribly sorry. I'll have to give her her pay sometime.' *I hope it won't put her off coming again*, she thought. Clearly, it was too soon to say anything of that sort. Helen was very likely to veto such a suggestion, the way she was feeling.

'I expect he'll be in touch, then,' said Simmy. 'I've got to go now.'

She gathered up the laptop, checked that everything was turned off, the doors locked, the plants provided with water and then left the shop. She'd parked her car in the main street, trusting it would escape the attentions of officials for the ten minutes she intended to leave it. The only orthodox spaces were too far away, in small streets on the outskirts of the town. She got in and then she just sat there, unsure of what to do next. Christopher would still be juggling bids, and she'd had enough of watching him do that. She wondered whether he had noticed her and Ben talking to the Pruitts, and if so, whether it bothered him.

The prospect of another hour's drive along the busy winding road on a Saturday afternoon made her feel weary. She reviewed her options and discovered that every one of them involved doing something for someone else. She could visit her parents and help with ironing or bedmaking. She could visit Tanya and see the damage for herself or call Bonnie and offer reassurance and congratulation on a crisis well handled. She could even drop in on Flo and her baby, on the reasonable chance that they had once more been abandoned by the neglectful Scott. All quite easy and more or less pleasant activities – but none of them what she, Simmy Brown, actually wanted to do.

So, what *did* she want? Something lazy and relaxed, she decided. Something with no agendas or motives that had anything to do with murder enquiries. She had little enough time off from the shop, and what she did have should be spent in peaceful self-indulgence.

But she didn't want to go home, either. That would make too much of a statement. Hiding, escaping, sulking – various negative interpretations of that sort might well be drawn. She could almost hear Bonnie saying *But why did you do that? Shutting yourself away when there's so much going on.*

210

That was the trouble, of course. There was simply too much going on. There had been all week, and it made her breathless. She was going to get married, move house, try for a baby – all thrilling and positive. So why did she feel besieged by other people's expectations? Even Christopher didn't seem to understand the upheaval involved. He was taking it all much too lightly. And yet, she didn't want to bring him down or make everything seem difficult. He wasn't in his usual frame of mind, after the traumatic events of Monday. He hated being the object of police interest. He had to concentrate fiercely to do a good job as an auctioneer, with only a brief break in a seven-hour day. He had glanced at her now and then, but only as a potential bidder. Would he have worried at her sudden departure with Ben? Or did he quickly forget all about it? Had the whole exercise of going to Keswick been foolish, with disastrous consequences for Tanya and Helen being annoyed with her?

She suddenly knew what she wanted to do. It was a summer weekend, the sunshine filtering pleasantly through the high cloud. Her favourite town at times like this was Ambleside. Calmer than Bowness, but more colourful and interesting than Windermere, it offered a good variety of attractions. The evening she'd spent there with Corinne had only enhanced its appeal. It was on the way to Keswick, after all. She could spend an hour strolling around with an ice cream, and then head off northwards to meet her fiancé and tell him what a brilliant auctioneer he was.

\* \* \*

It worked out much as planned. Meandering along the busy streets, she found somewhere to buy an ice cream not far from the statue where she'd met Corinne and leant against a stone wall to eat it, thinking about nothing. People smiled vaguely in her direction, and two separate dogs approached for a brief salutation, dragging their uncomplaining owners after them. Nobody seemed to be in a rush; the holiday mood dominated everything. When the last tip of the cone was finished, she looked around and noticed the CaniCare charity shop a little way down the street. A woman was coming out with a bulky carrier bag, so it was evidently open. Simmy drifted down for a look.

The shop was much more densely stocked than any she'd seen before. It reminded her irresistibly of Christopher's auction room. There were shelves on two sides, rows of clothes on hangers on a third, and the window itself was full of knick-knacks. Down the middle was a table holding boxes and trays of further small items. Plates, old postcards, numerous china ornaments, toys and a lot more that could only be termed 'miscellanea'. The atmosphere was of an Aladdin's cave, heightened by a faint smell of joss sticks and lower-than-usual lighting. Music was playing. Somebody here had a powerful imagination; Bonnie would approve heartily.

Simmy fingered the contents of the first tray she came to. Costume jewellery, silk scarves and ties, old watches and lengths of ribbon were all jumbled together, as if just tipped out of the drawer of an old lady's dressing table. Which it probably had been, she supposed. People donated their deceased relative's house contents to charity, almost as often as they paid someone to clear it all away. They'd pick through it for the best things, and then turn their back on the rest. If a shop like this was willing to take it, then good luck to them.

A man was standing behind the small counter, watching her and another woman who was scanning the shelves of books. Simmy met his eye. He was of middle height and middle age, with a bald patch surrounded by mid-brown hair. He wore spectacles with thin metal frames. 'Wow!' she said. 'What a lot of stuff!'

'Pile it high, sell it cheap,' he said, without a smile. 'That's the motto here.'

'I'm sure it works very well.' She held up a brightly coloured scarf with a Tiffany design. 'This is top quality – and you only want two pounds for it.' That was another quirk she'd already noticed: the prices were all in round figures. Most charity shops inexplicably priced almost everything at a figure ending in nine.

'The thrill of the chase,' said the man, still not smiling. 'And the back room's full – literally full – of a great deal more. It comes in faster than we can process it, and the boss insists we never refuse a donation.'

'You need to hire a hall one day a month and have a big rummage sale,' she suggested.

'Good idea,' said the man with a sigh.

She bought the scarf, and then found a long-sleeved shirt that was exactly what she had been looking for. The total came to five pounds, and she went away very contented.

\* \* \*

It was half past three, and she was forty minutes at most from Keswick. She could easily catch the closing lots of the sale and be there when Christopher stumbled exhaustedly off his podium. They would go to his flat, eat, drink, canoodle . . . a long day would have a perfect ending, with a good helping of luck. It could all go badly wrong, of course, but she clung to her optimistic scenario. They could make the most of the time together, whatever happened, refusing to be victims of circumstance, ignoring other people's troubles at least for a few hours.

The drive was impeded by tourist traffic, especially in the Grasmere area. Walkers and dogs ambled across the road in some places, and cars were parked where they shouldn't be, making it difficult to squeeze past oncoming vehicles. There were also sheep liable to jump out without warning. But none of this bothered Simmy. She enjoyed the sense of having regressed a century or so, where traffic did not dominate every aspect of life and rules were there to be broken. The landscape on both sides of the road was high and rugged – the classic Lakeland scenery that was so beloved by the English. Its very timelessness was the main appeal, so that attempts to erect wind turbines or zipwire rides were rejected almost automatically. There were limits, everyone agreed, and if you didn't preserve at least a few wild areas, what was the point of it all? Or so Simmy's father would argue. Ben would point out that the zipwire, at least, came close to fruition. And quite a few of the lakes that everybody loved were in fact man-made reservoirs, supplying water to big cities further south. Nothing was quite as natural or simple as it seemed.

The car park was barely half-full when she finally arrived at the saleroom. Two men were loading a large pile of objects into a blue van, and another was packing his purchases into a trailer behind his four-wheel drive. If she remembered correctly from her previous day at the sale, the rules permitted buyers to remove their acquisitions from one o'clock onwards. A small team of men and boys located the lots, checked they'd been paid for and assisted with loading them up, even while the auction was still going on. She and Ben had missed that part of the proceedings. Then she noticed, in her wing mirror, a large tin trunk being pushed into the van and realised she was looking at the mysterious Nick at last. He was tall and thin, wearing colourless clothes, sporting a week's worth of stubble and looking exhausted. The man helping him was one of the saleroom staff – a wiry little chap in his sixties who restlessly roamed around looking for people needing assistance, pausing every minute or two to chat to people he clearly regarded as friends.

Simmy was ten yards away, with her back to Nick and his van. Her window was open, and she could hear the grunts and muttered words as the vehicle was forced to accommodate a variety of purchases. The trunk was followed by a hallstand and a rolled-up carpet. Then the men slammed the door shut and stepped back.

'Didn't go as bad as I thought,' said the taller one. 'Wasn't sure how I'd go down, after all that talk.'

'Hmm, hmm,' was all the answer he got, along with a sympathetic shake of the head.

'If you ask me, it's got to be the wife – or something

215

from years back. Or maybe he kicked an old lady's dog once too often and her son saw red.'

The small man chuckled.

'Anyhow, as I told them in there' – he cocked his head towards the saleroom – 'the bit of trouble I had over tax turns out to be a storm in a teacup. Showed them my cash book and so forth, and they've rapped my knuckles and told me to get it right in future. Nothing to raise a sweat over.'

A woman emerged from the reception area, carrying an awkwardly-shaped purchase, and the helpful porter hurried to her aid. Simmy buzzed up her car window and sighed. It was twenty past four and she was thirsty. Perhaps she should first grab a mug of tea in the little cafe before it closed for the day.

'We don't close until everybody's gone,' the woman told her. 'That's nearly six, sometimes.'

Simmy sat with her tea, wondering how Christopher was getting on. She could go and see for herself, but there didn't seem much point. His car was parked in its own special bay, which she could see from where she was sitting. He couldn't go anywhere without her seeing him. But perhaps she ought to text him and tell him where she was.

She got the phone out and turned it on. There were no messages of any significance waiting for her. Her parents might be wondering why they hadn't seen her, but they habitually used the landline phones, either in Troutbeck or at the shop. She began to compose her text to Chris, when there was a jingle to announce a phone call.

It was Christopher. 'Hey – where are you? I've just finished ahead of schedule, and I've found a voicemail from Philip's nursing home. I've got to go to Grasmere right away. Where are you?'

'I'm right outside,' she said, with a little laugh. 'I drove Ben home and then came back up here. What's the matter with Philip?'

'He's dying, and they say he's asking for me.'

# *Chapter Seventeen*

For far too many minutes, Simmy continued to find the situation almost laughably ironic. She knew this was irritating to Christopher, and deeply inappropriate, but it was so wildly unexpected and so ludicrous that she should have to drive straight back to Grasmere yet again, that all she could do was laugh. Chris had come to find her in the cafe, getting himself a much-needed tea and cake, and answering people who came up wanting to talk to him. Finally, she got herself under control.

'Why you?' she asked him. 'What time did they send the message? Why didn't they call the office here and ask them to go and fetch you if it's as urgent as all that.'

He was hoarse and stiff from sitting for so long. He merely shook his head and gulped down the tea. 'Give me a minute,' he croaked. 'I need to go and speak to Josephine.' He was standing beside her little table, dancing from one foot to the other. 'What if he dies before I get there?'

'Why does he want *you*?' she asked again. 'Hasn't he got a lady friend? Is the nursing home right in Grasmere, or somewhere miles up in the fells?'

'I told you – there's hardly anybody else but me who ever visits him. It's only a mile or two out of town.'

'Poor old chap.'

'I hate to keep him waiting. We'll take my car – here's the key. Go and wait in it for me. Are you ready to go in two minutes?'

'I suppose so,' she nodded. 'Can I leave mine here? Will it get locked in or anything?'

'It will, but I've got the key to the gate.' He gave her a look that said *obviously*.

They were on the road just after five, going much too fast for the conditions. 'Watch out for sheep along here,' said Simmy. 'There were some loose when I came up.' Christopher ignored her. They spoke little, despite there being plenty to say. They both needed a spell of quiet, Simmy realised.

The nursing home was two miles outside Grasmere in a converted mansion on a north-facing slope. It was approached by a narrow road bordered by stone walls. 'Should I come in or wait out here for you?' she asked.

'Oh, I don't know. Better come in and see what they say.'

The nursing home still retained its stately home aura, at least in the entrance hall. Carved wooden panelling; hard-wearing marble floor tiles in black, brown and white; a handsome staircase rising in a curve to the upper floors – it all felt very Downton-Abbey-ish. 'Goodness,' said Simmy. 'He must be paying a bit to live here.'

'And the rest,' nodded Christopher. 'Take more than a few Jacobean stumpworks to cover even a year. But he got a good price for his house, and there's some arrangement with the council. They pick up the tab when his own money runs out, apparently.'

Under the influence of Ben Harkness, Simmy found herself imagining council hitmen making sure that day never came.

Chris knew the way to Philip's room and, since there were no staff in evidence, he let Simmy go with him as he headed up the stairs. 'Must be dinner time,' he said. 'They don't like visitors turning up after five.'

They found Philip on the first floor, second room on the left. He was sitting in a big armchair by the window, which was wide open. 'Hey!' said Christopher. 'They said you were on your deathbed.'

'I refuse to lie down and go quietly,' said the old man breathily. 'I dare say I'm good for a few days yet.'

Simmy had no direct experience of the process of dying at the end of a long life. Images from films and books suggested a brief period of deep sleep before the breathing gently stopped. Her father often referred admiringly to one of the Brontë sisters, dying in an upright chair, resisting

220

to the last. Or was that Elizabeth I? In any event, Philip seemed remarkably serene.

'Glad you could get here,' he wheezed. 'And . . .' he looked at Simmy, 'you brought your lady friend.'

'She's my fiancée now. I proposed last weekend.'

'Well done, lad. Take my advice and be sure you have some offspring. It gets very miserable otherwise, I can tell you.'

'We'll do our best,' said Chris, with a rueful glance at Simmy.

'No time to waste,' the old man went on. 'I need to talk about Kathleen's house – that man who was killed there. The dealer.' He ran out of breath, and Simmy felt a flash of panic. It seemed all too likely that he would expire right there before her eyes.

'How did you—?' Chris began to ask, before noticing a local paper on a little table at Philip's elbow. The front page was full of the story of Jonathan's murder. Nobody at the nursing home would think to keep the news away from him. Another paper was visible beneath it, where the story of the valuable stumpwork had been the main excitement. The paper appeared on Thursdays, and Simmy had not seen it yet.

'Did they kill him for that bit of sewing?' Philip said.

'No, no. Why would they?' Christopher leant over him, speaking urgently. 'Jonathan sold it in good faith. We had no idea how much money it would make. That can't have had anything to do with it. It must have been some old grudge.'

'Hmm.' The old man blinked several times, obviously

221

marshalling his thoughts. 'Wasn't it hers, then? She had some good stuff, you know. Showed it to that mate of yours. Seems to me he must have helped himself to it and sold it.'

'No!' Christopher became even more animated. 'It was nothing like that.' He paused, staring at Philip. 'Where did you get the idea that Jon was the vendor, anyway?'

Philip shook his head. 'I don't know for sure. It just seems to fit the facts. I could swear I've seen that piece of handiwork that's in the paper. It's pretty obviously the same one, and he sold it for all that money,' he moaned. 'Kathleen can't have had any idea it was worth anything.'

'Where did *she* get it?' Simmy suddenly asked.

Again, the old man shook his head. 'I've no idea. I only saw it after she was dead. Maybe she got it from her mother. It was in a box with other fancywork.'

Chris put a hand on his friend's arm. 'But why does it worry you so much? Why does it matter now?'

'It's not right. Something's not right.' Philip fought for breath. 'That man being killed in her house. You have to . . . have to . . .'

'Don't worry, old friend. We'll get it all sorted for you. You'll be glad to know that Simmy's got friends who like to play amateur detectives. They're good at it, too. They're doing a lot of investigating to find out who killed poor old Jonathan. We'll be back here in a day or two to explain exactly what happened.'

'Mmm,' sighed the old man, sagging alarmingly in his chair.

'Chris . . .' Simmy said.

'I know. I'll go and get somebody. You stay here.' He

disappeared and Simmy heard him thumping down the stairs. Barely two minutes later he was back with a woman in a green uniform, which made her look like a hospital theatre nurse.

'I didn't know he had visitors,' she said reproachfully.

'We couldn't find anybody,' Christopher said.

'You can't have looked very hard.'

'Never mind that,' Simmy interrupted. 'He's passed out, look.' Privately, she was convinced that Philip had died, and that she and Christopher would probably be blamed for it. She had watched him intently for signs of breathing and had detected no movement while Christopher was fetching help.

'You've exhausted him. He ought to be in bed.' She bent over Philip and laid a finger on his wrist. 'I think he's just fallen asleep. He is very frail, you know. We thought we were going to lose him this morning, but he's hanging on. Did he manage to speak to you?'

'Oh yes. He was very glad to see us.'

'Good. But you should go now. We're not a hospital, you know.'

'What does that mean?'

'It means we don't do much more than basic medical care. But Philip's made a firm request not to be moved unless absolutely necessary. Until very recently, we'd have automatically had him taken to A&E, but we've had a change of policy, not before time.' Her face darkened. 'There have been some very sad consequences over the past few years.'

'Yes, but why does that mean we have to leave?'

'Oh, I see. Well – you're not family, are you? We do sometimes let close relatives stay overnight, but it's not the usual practice. There wouldn't be anywhere to sleep.'

'We're not proposing to stay overnight,' said Simmy. 'Are we?' she checked with Christopher.

He shook his head. 'I guess not. But I hate to just leave him. We never said . . . I mean . . . will he . . . ?'

'You might not see him again,' said the woman frankly. 'Sorry, but that's the reality.'

'All right. Yes. I get it.' He bent over his friend. 'Bye, then, Philip. We'll be going now. You'll be well looked after, I'm sure. Don't worry about anything. It's all going to be set right, I promise you that.' He glanced up at the woman. 'Maybe he can hear me?' he said pleadingly.

'Maybe,' she said. 'He's very relaxed, anyway. Everything's just running down. He's not in any pain, and there's no suggestion that he's scared. He's an example to us all,' she finished fondly.

Simmy was wiping away tears. Christopher put his arm around her shoulders. 'I shouldn't have brought you with me,' he said.

'Yes, you should. I'm glad you did. He's such a nice old chap. I wish I'd got to know him better. I didn't realise . . .'

'How fond I am of him?' He gave a rueful smile. 'Neither did I, till just now. Poor old Philip. Fancy ending your life worrying about a piece of embroidery.'

'That's not what was worrying him. It's the fact of a murder. He wants justice to be done.' She clenched her fists. 'And we've got to see that you keep your promise to him.'

\* \* \*

They were both hungry and unsure as to what to do next. There was a lot to talk about, events moving too fast for proper discussion, which Simmy found frustrating. It was almost frightening, the way every day brought something unexpected that had to be dealt with. The auction had initially seemed a bit dull, compared to the rest of the week – until she thought back and remembered the people in the cafe and the Pruitts in the row behind her and Ben. She hadn't even had a chance to ask him what all those notes were about. Christopher didn't know about Tanya's accident, and Ben didn't know about Philip's revelation. A rerun of their Wednesday evening get-together seemed urgently called-for. She knew she was forgetting something crucial. Did it have to do with Bonnie, she asked herself. Had the girl expected a visit, to check on her welfare after the traumatic exposure to blood?

'Mustn't forget Valerie Woolley tomorrow,' said Christopher, whose thoughts must have been running along similar lines. 'Eleven o'clock. Bloody nuisance.'

'Did she know Philip?'

'What? No, I shouldn't think so. Why would she?'

'I don't know. It's a small world up here. How long had she and Jonathan been separated?'

'Ages. Five years at least. They lived in Keswick, and then she walked out and found a place in Carlisle. I think he kept hoping they could get back together eventually.'

'Maybe they would have done, the way she's so concerned to know what happened to him?'

'She's not a monster. Wouldn't anybody with normal feelings be the same? It doesn't mean she wishes they'd stayed together.'

'I don't know,' said Simmy, wondering again how she'd react if Tony had been murdered, down in Worcestershire. 'What would you do if Sophie was killed?'

'Good question. I shouldn't think anyone would even tell me. We've been divorced for ten years now. Last I heard she was married with three kids.'

'So, what do we do now?' she asked. 'All I really want is to slump in front of the telly with some takeaway. Shocking, I know. You must be just as knackered as me. More, if anything.'

'I'll be okay after a drink and some food.'

'I keep thinking about this time last week. The benefit seems to have worn off much too quickly.'

'It all went wrong on Monday. Nothing's been simple or straightforward since then.' He sighed. 'Even the sale of the stumpwork would have had ramifications, without the Jonathan business.'

'It's all Jonathan business, though – isn't it? It all links up, with him in the middle. Ben's probably got a flowchart that shows exactly that. Or it will when I tell him what Philip just said.'

'Flowchart?'

'That's right. Sometimes he calls it an algorithm. Poor old Moxon has to pretend to understand what he's talking about.'

'I still don't get why a detective inspector should take a schoolboy so seriously. Doesn't he get stick from his superiors about it?'

'Sometimes, I suppose. But Ben's much more help than hindrance – mostly. It wasn't so good when he got into trouble in Hawkshead. We're all still shaking from that. It's made Helen a lot more jittery about Ben's interest in crime.'

They were in Christopher's car, but not going anywhere. 'So why did you dash off halfway through the sale?' he asked her. 'I looked up and you'd gone. Left that man from Grasmere staring right at me, without you to hide behind.'

'Pruitt. He's called Pruitt. Odd chap.'

'It threw me when I recognised him.'

'Yes, I noticed. Anyway. I got a call from Bonnie saying Tanya had cut herself and I should come back and clean up the blood. I didn't really need to rush off like that. It turned out that Bonnie wanted Ben to comfort her, and I had to drive him. She's got a thing about blood and felt all wobbly.'

'Tanya is Ben's sister, right? Is she okay?'

Simmy had to remind herself that Christopher lived an hour away from Windermere and all the people there who formed her own social circle. He couldn't be expected to keep track of them all. In fact, she ought to be pleasantly surprised that he knew how Tanya fitted into the picture. Instead, she felt lonely and slightly scared at the prospect of setting up home with Chris, in the process losing some of the closeness she enjoyed with the others. And yet, it was all going to change anyway when Ben went off to university. 'Right,' she nodded. 'She's fourteen. One of twins. She's a really nice girl – clever, like Ben.'

'Was there much blood?'

'Not really. The laptop keyboard got some of it.'

'Yuck! I'm not great with blood, either, you know.'

'I can probably pick it out when it's dry enough. Funny –

I don't mind it at all. I've never been squeamish about that sort of thing.'

'So, is Tanya okay?' he asked again.

'I think so. It was quite a deep cut, though. She found a Stanley knife and was using it to cut ribbon or string or something. The flowers she was tying up were all over the floor of the shop. I wonder whether the customer came back for them and found the shop locked up.' Yet another thing to be sorted out, she realised.

He reached out and turned the key in the ignition. 'We can't just sit here,' he said. 'We can go back to Keswick, get some fish and chips, and call it a day. There's nothing else we can do for anybody until tomorrow. Let's lock the door and turn off the phones and forget them all.'

'That would be wonderful,' she sighed. 'But please don't drive so fast this time.'

# Chapter Eighteen

Saturday evening did not work out quite as planned. When they got back to the saleroom, Christopher found a note in an envelope pinned to the locked gate, with his name on it. It turned out to be from Josephine, his office manager, with a list of things she felt needed his attention. Reproach rose from every line. 'What an old-fashioned way to communicate,' said Simmy. 'Why didn't she text or email or phone?'

'She's a weird person,' he said. 'Still likes to have everything on paper.'

'Have you got to do anything this evening?' She tried to

read the note over his shoulder, but he was holding it away from her. 'What does she say?'

'It's just business stuff. Somebody's saying we got a lot number wrong, and some other person's gone off with the thing they paid for. We'll have to check the cameras to see where it went.'

'Cameras?'

'That's right.' He pointed to three different spots across the parking area. 'We've got twelve of them, all round the place, inside and out. Every move anyone makes is filmed, from the minute we open the gates on a Saturday.'

'Blimey! That's very Big Brotherish.'

'We don't make any secret of it. It works incredibly well at stopping anyone nicking anything.'

'Okay,' she said doubtfully, thinking of her father's likely response to such levels of surveillance. She didn't think he'd been aware of it during their day at the sale a few months earlier.

'And Josephine says there's a strange car still in the yard, and she wonders if it belongs to somebody I know.' He grinned. 'She means yours.'

'Do you think she knows it's mine?'

'She doesn't miss much.'

'And all she has to do is check the cameras and see who drove it in.' She shivered. 'I don't like that.'

'You're living in the past, Sim. We're all caught on camera all the time. It's an inevitable part of living in Britain. I don't even think about it any more. It did come as a shock, though, when I got back from travelling. Now, if you want to drop out of sight, you have to go to Panama or a remote part of Alaska.'

'I don't think there are many cameras in Windermere.'

'More than you think. They're so cheap now that ordinary citizens put them up on their houses.'

'So – can we go, or do you have to do a job for Josephine?'

'We can go. All this can wait.' He folded the note and flipped it over his shoulder onto the back seat. 'Go and get your car. Drive out in front of me, and I'll lock the gate behind us. I'll get us some supper. You go ahead and make yourself at home. You know where the spare key lives.'

Christopher's flat was the upper floor of a substantial 1930s house on the edge of Keswick. Simmy had been there a number of times, but only once spent the night. She found it unsettling, for some reason. Since his parents had died, he had added various pieces of furniture from their Bowness bungalow, so it had a disorganised, cluttered feel. There were very few books and not a single picture on the walls. When she queried this, he shrugged and said, 'How do you choose? Once you start, you end up covering every wall with them.' She hadn't found a credible answer to that.

His bed was even narrower than hers, which made for uncomfortable nights. Remembering that, she inwardly sighed. Why had she agreed to stay over, anyway, she asked herself. Having got in using the key he kept under a stone halfway down the alleyway between his house and the next, she collapsed onto the sofa. It was good that he trusted her to be there alone, she reflected, even as she felt guilty at the thought. What did she think he might have to hide? It all went back to Moxon's revelations, the previous day. Suspicion was in the air, and Christopher had become tainted with it. Ever since he found the body on Monday, he had behaved differently from how she might have expected. She kept telling herself he was sad, shocked, scared, as well as angry. But he had also shown defensiveness, avoidance and even an odd detachment. When he promised Philip he would do his best to find out the truth, she had been surprised. It had clashed with so much of what he had said and done all week. There were odd little pieces of behaviour that she kept trying to reconcile with the man and his story – and failing. There had been something strange between him and Flo Penrose, for example, and just now his reaction to Philip's news about the stumpwork had been curious, with hindsight. Moxon's concern that Christopher was hiding something was feeling more credible all the time. The alarming thought that she had promised to marry a man she barely knew rendered her silent when he came back with their fish supper.

They ate it with relish, even so. Chris had eaten almost nothing all day, so took more than his share of chips at Simmy's invitation. She watched him, comparing the familiar face with the unknowable mind behind it. Nobody really knew anybody, she told herself. All those thousands of thoughts that flashed through every hour of the day couldn't possibly be revealed to another person, however intimate and honest they might both want to be. The accompanying feelings were seldom easy to put into words, and they too flickered by in a chaotic stream. It was all perfectly normal. Ben would say it was the penalty they all paid for their excessively large brains. Where animals would carelessly huddle together for warmth and safety, communicating quite well enough for their needs, human beings had to analyse and argue and anguish about identity and relationships and what was going to happen next.

'You're quiet,' he said, eventually.

'Yes. There's a lot to process.'

'Is there?'

She looked into his eyes, wondering whether he was teasing, or being deliberately stupid as a way of fending her off. 'You know there is. Why – does it bother you?'

'Does what bother me?'

'The fact that I might start talking about murder, or marriage, or houses or work. All the things we do actually *need* to talk about.'

'I thought we'd decided the main points. We'll go and buy an engagement ring next weekend, if you like.'

'Okay. But you're dodging the issue. Issues. You've just made a promise to Philip that you'll do all you can to find who killed Jonathan. I can't escape the impression that there's a lot more you could be telling me – and the police. You do know, don't you, that they get very annoyed with people who withhold information? Even if it incriminates you, you're supposed to tell them everything you know. Otherwise they can have you for obstructing the course of justice or whatever they call it.'

He chewed slowly, watching her face. His eyes revealed

nothing. 'Do you think I've been lying?' he asked.

'That's not what I said. Of course I don't think that. Lying isn't the same as keeping something back. But you know people from all over the area. They know you. You handle their precious things and do that charismatic auctioneer act. You knew that stumpwork came from Kathleen Leeson's house, didn't you?'

'I promise you I didn't. Not for sure, anyway.'

'Okay. But now you've made that promise to Philip, you've got to make more of an effort to help the investigation – don't you think? You should tell the police everything else that might help. Everything you've been holding back.'

'Which is precisely nothing. I said whatever I thought would make Philip feel better. Anyone would have said the same. He's not going to know, is he? I doubt if he'll ever regain consciousness now. He'll die happy. Isn't that what everyone wants?'

'They want to be able to believe people's promises, I should think. And it's daft to say there's nothing you can do. You know all the people who might have killed your friend. You were on the scene moments after it happened. Don't you think you owe it to *yourself* if not Philip to put in a bit of effort to—'

'Help the police with their enquiries?' he interrupted. 'I did some of that, and it was extremely unpleasant, let me tell you. I told them everything I could think of about Jon's work, social life, marriage. None of it seems to have done the blindest bit of good. Now you've gone all sniffy on me, because I told a dying man what he wanted to hear.'

234

She held her ground. Whatever else she might be feeling, she wasn't the least bit scared of him, as she had occasionally been of Tony. But neither was she sorry for what she'd said. 'Well, all right, but I still think you're ducking out of it. When I tell Ben—'

Again, he interrupted her. 'Oh, I wondered when that was going to come. Your precious Ben can put me to shame every time, can't he! You don't seem to understand that he's a boy, and I'm a grown man. I've got responsibilities. He's got all the time he wants to play his clever games. The way I see it, the police are there to solve murders, not me. They're going to be a lot better at it, too. Ben Harkness doesn't know any of the people involved – he never met Jonathan, never knew what he was like. He'll go home and draw diagrams, and invent theories, and if the police listen to him for more than ten seconds, I'll think they're wasting my taxpayer's money. I've had enough of it, Sim. I want you to talk to me about houses and our wedding, and the babies we want to have. Is that so awful? Eh?'

His voice softened, and he pulled her into him, knocking her empty polystyrene fish container onto the floor. 'I never said I would play detective games with you, did I? Are you going to ditch me because of that? You look as if you might.' He turned her face to his and stared at it. 'You're scaring me, to be absolutely honest.'

It was one of the most revealing speeches she'd ever heard him make, and it turned many of her thoughts on their head. Was she just playing childish games with Ben and Bonnie? It had never felt like that. DI Moxon might have moments of exasperation, but he did take the three of them seriously. Then she began to see that this might well be how it looked to an outsider. And Christopher *was* an outsider, having seen very little of Simmy's friends. He had only visited her parents three times since his own mum and dad had died, despite the two families having been very close in the past. Simmy had taken him there for Sunday lunch on these three occasions. The conversation had not touched on murder investigations, mainly because Simmy and her mother had an agreement to keep such matters away from Russell, if possible. He had an inflated sense of danger, verging on paranoia, and rightly or wrongly they did their best to avoid arousing this fear.

'I'm not going to ditch you,' she said calmly. 'We're going to tackle this whole thing like adults. I can see your point and I hope you can see mine. I agree with you that the murder of a man you knew is not the biggest thing in our lives, but it's pretty high on the list. I don't think we can get on with anything else until we've done our best to get it resolved.'

He was still watching her face. 'How?' he said.

'For a start, by telling Ben what Philip said about the stumpwork. It'll make a big difference to his thinking. And I want space to think things through – I've met some people, heard some talk, had a few ideas. I want to share all that with Ben, because he's so good at making connections, and he can check it out on the Internet and find out all sorts of details that could be relevant. It might look like a game to you, but it's more than that. It's what he *does*.'

Christopher sighed. 'You want space,' he repeated. 'Isn't that code for cooling off a relationship? It feels like rejection, like being pushed away. You came to my sale today, and then dashed off when your friend Bonnie called you. To be honest, I was quite surprised when you came back again. You chatted to the Pruitt – is that his name? – man, and never told me what he said. That man can cause a lot of trouble for me, and there's you being all friendly with him. And then I hear you've been asking about Nick, in the tea room. I can't make sense of what you think you're doing.'

'Oh.' She frowned at the floor. 'How can Mr Pruitt cause trouble?'

'He's the only thing between me and being charged with murder. You must see that. All he has to do is adjust his story a bit, and I'm toast.'

'What story? He saw you come out of the house looking distraught and called the police for you. That's quite bad already, looked at in a certain way. How can he make it worse? And why on earth would he want to?'

'I don't trust him. It feels as if he's got some hold over me, because I was so emotional and messed up after I found Jon. Why was he at the auction? The only answer that makes any sense is that he wanted to have another look at me, for some reason.'

Simmy did not at all like the way this was going. 'I really don't understand why you're scared of him. Maybe I'm being thick, but I can't see how he can possibly cause trouble. More than that – I don't see why he should. If you don't know each other, he's got no reason to tell lies about you, has he? And if he changes his story now, it's him that'll look suspicious, not you.'

Christopher scratched his head vigorously. 'I suppose he must have known Jonathan, from seeing him at the auction. But he never said anything about that on Monday. He left the identification business all up to me. I expect I'm being paranoid – but I can't shake the feeling that he's up to something.'

'He says he used to go to the saleroom quite often before you took over as auctioneer.'

'I don't remember him. I didn't recognise him on Monday. Maybe that annoyed him – do you think?'

'What Ben would want to know is – why was he there in the first place? At Mrs Leeson's house. The street is a dead end, and he didn't have a dog with him, did he? That's what's sinister, surely? Unless he lives right there, of course.' That idea was new, and superficially persuasive.

'I don't think he does. He gave his address when he phoned 999. I think he said Easedale Road, which is a few minutes away.'

'Oh well,' said Simmy defeatedly. 'I suppose it'll all become clear eventually.'

'You think? What if they never find the killer? What if I have to spend the rest of my life dealing with people's suspicions that I had something to do with it? It would rule out any hope of living in Grasmere, for a start.'

Something in his voice made her sit up. 'Chris, now you're scaring *me*. What haven't you told me? I can see it on your face – there's a whole lot more to this than you've said. Isn't there?'

'No, not really. I can't get you to understand what it was like on Monday. Let me try and go through it all again. Everything happened so fast, I couldn't keep up. I couldn't work out any of the implications. I didn't know what I should say or do. There was poor old Jon, in the middle of a perfectly normal day, his face all black and ghastly. I just ran. And there was this man, standing there as if he was waiting for me. For a crazy moment, I thought he was my dad, and I was ten years old again. I grabbed him and *cried*. I put my face on his shoulder and shed real tears. He pushed me away, took me behind a wall and made me explain. It must have been ten minutes before we went back into the house. He didn't recognise me at first, but then it dawned on him that I was the auctioneer. Then he called 999. While we were waiting for the police he kept talking, trying to make me explain why I was there and who Jon was, and how we knew each other. He was nearly as bad as the cops in Penrith, but a lot more gentle. And now I don't remember what I said, or what he must have thought – or what he told the police. They soon let him go, anyway.'

'Okay, stop. I need to think.' She put her hands to her temples and closed her eyes. 'It sounds as if he might have been following you, the way you tell it now. As if he might have been looking for Jonathan as well, even. Don't you think?'

He stared at her. 'When I started thinking like that, I thought I was being paranoid.'

'Why did the police let him go so quickly? That's what sounds odd. Surely he would have seemed to them as significant as you? It would look as if you *both* found the body, wouldn't it?'

'We told them how it was.'

'And they obviously believed you. Did the Pruitt man touch Jonathan, as well as you?'

'I don't know. I remember him staying well back, by the door. I think not.'

She exhaled, letting out tension and frustration. She needed Ben. The narrow bed upstairs was not calling to her in any way, and she found herself wondering whether she'd left it too late to make an excuse to slink off home to Troutbeck. Christopher was draining a large glass of wine and eyeing the bottle speculatively. They'd talked for nearly an hour, all of it about murder, with the worrying result that they seemed to like each other slightly less than before. They hadn't harmonised their emotions, filled each other's gaps, consoled each other's ruffled feelings.

'Valerie Woolley tomorrow,' he groaned, after a few minutes of silence. 'She's going to ask me exactly the same tedious questions that you just subjected me to. I'm tempted to be out when she arrives and avoid her completely.'

'You wouldn't do that,' said Simmy, hopefully.

'Only because she'd keep after me until I gave her what she wants. Did you say you wanted to be with me when I talk to her?'

'I think I did – but now I'm not so sure. Actually, Chris, would it be absolutely dreadful of me if I bunked off home now? I'm not in the mood for sex, to put it bluntly, and there isn't really anywhere for me to sleep. It's been a long day for both of us.'

He looked at her in utter confusion. 'What did I say? What have I done?'

'Nothing, you fool. It's no big deal. I just want my own bed. It's going to be a warm night, and we'll never manage to sleep squashed together in yours. Can't we be adult enough to manage times when we don't both want to be together? We probably need to talk it over sometime soon – the ground rules, and what we both think it means to be married.'

'I know what it means to be married,' he said stiffly.

'Not when it's being married to me, you don't. I've had quite a while on my own now and you've had even longer. Neither of us wants to be joined at the hip, surely?'

'Who knows what they want? Haven't we already sorted that? We only know it when we see it.'

'Okay. So tonight, I want to go home. I don't want you to be upset about it. I realise it looks inconsistent of me, to drive back again for the umpteenth time today, but that's how it is.' She got up from the sofa, gathering the chip boxes as she went. 'Lucky I hardly had any wine.'

'Lucky for you that I did, or I'd have come chasing after you.'

'Like Valerie Woolley might do with you?' she shot back. 'I don't think anybody's going to do any chasing when it comes to it. You stay here, have a nice lazy lie-in and be here when she shows up at eleven. Be nice to her, and then call me when she's gone, and we'll decide about the rest of the day. Okay?'

'No, but I've got the message.'

'Don't sulk, pet,' she said, in a deliberate echo of Frances, his mother. 'You're a big boy now.'

\* \* \*

241

She drove away feeling startlingly pleased with herself. This must be what was meant by *assertiveness*, she thought. State your wishes, accept the other person's reaction, remain calm and don't be manipulated into doing what they want instead. It felt like a formula that should work perfectly between adults.

The only question was – how much of an adult was Christopher Henderson?

## Chapter Nineteen

She sent Ben a text at eight-thirty next morning: *I know it's a bit early for a Sunday, but I could come and debrief you at nine-thirty or thereabouts, if you like. I've got all morning.*

His reply came back in under five minutes. *Yes! I'll be waiting. Bonnie too, of course.*

Her sense of satisfaction persisted as she gave her kitchen a quick clean and drank her favourite brand of instant coffee – which Christopher still had not got around to providing at his flat. It wouldn't last, she knew. She would be quite happy to start again in a new house with a new husband, making new arrangements for their daily lives. But for the moment, she valued her independence. She wanted to help Ben and Bonnie solve the murder of Jonathan Woolley. More than anything, she wanted that for her fiancé's sake. If he could not summon enough confidence in the youngsters to trust that they could resolve the mystery, then she would have to do it for him. Then everybody would be happy.

Bonnie clearly had to force the smile she gave Simmy. She looked translucently fragile, and Helen Harkness hovered behind her as if ready to catch her when she collapsed. But she did not collapse and spoke out firmly in support of Ben's brainstorming plans. When Simmy asked after Tanya, everyone just shrugged and said she was okay, but a bit droopy.

'You can have the dining room,' said Helen. 'So long as you're gone by half past twelve. We're doing roast pork.' She hesitated before adding, 'You can stay, if you like, Simmy.'

Gone by half-twelve, but invited to lunch? Simmy frowned and stammered, 'Um . . .'

'Oh, sorry.' Helen laughed. 'I mean gone out of that room. I've got Zoe scheduled to lay the table – we do it the old-fashioned way on Sundays. Tablecloth, flowers, silver spoons – the works. Ben's on gravy and custard. That leaves him available to you until almost dinnertime.'

Who knew? Simmy was stunned. When had she last experienced a true domestic Sunday roast? With herself she calculated that would be at least eight people round the table. And who was to say there wouldn't be a stray neighbour or two, invited in as an act of charity? Anything seemed possible. 'Thanks,' she said. 'But I think I'm having lunch with Chris.'

Ben and Bonnie both looked at her, eyebrows raised. 'Think?' said Ben.

'I'll call him in a minute to check. But in any case, I won't stay, thanks Helen. I need to see my parents at some point.'

'So . . . Christopher?' Bonnie nudged.

Simmy sighed. 'If you must know, it all fell apart a bit last night. I've got a lot to tell you.'

Ben bustled the three of them into the room allotted to them, and they sat round the large antique mahogany table. 'I've never been in here before,' said Simmy.

'There's not enough space upstairs to spread everything out,' said Bonnie.

Ben produced several sheets of paper, some with hand-drawn diagrams, others printed. 'It's been great having time to do it all properly,' he said. 'There's a sheet for everyone who could be part of the investigation, a flowchart to connect them all up, spreadsheets with times, places, motives and so forth. But there's still loads of gaps.' He looked at Simmy expectantly.

'Okay,' she said. 'How do you want me to start?'

'Tell me everything since you brought me back here yesterday. Who did you talk to? Has Christopher said any more?'

'And why aren't you there with him now?' wondered Bonnie. 'Did something happen?'

'I'll get to that. The main thing is what Philip told us.

We went to his nursing home, after the auction. He said he's fairly sure that stumpwork belonged to Kathleen Leeson. He saw it in her house, after she died.'

'Wait!' ordered Ben, looking far less excited than expected. 'Is that the first thing that happened, or are you jumping ahead? What did you do between two o'clock and – what? Five?'

'Sorry. Well, I went to the shop first.' She looked at Bonnie. 'I've cleaned up all the mess. The computer's going to be okay, I'm sure. It really wasn't so bad.' She was deliberately avoiding the word *blood*, which seemed to be a wise move.

'A little goes a long way,' said Bonnie, swallowing hard. 'Everyone keeps telling me that.'

'Poor old Bon,' said Ben, giving her shoulder a quick stroke. 'Not the best phobia for a detective to have – eh?'

'I'll get over it. I thought I *was* over it, actually.'

'At least you coped. Most people would have gone wobbly, worse than you did.'

The girl smiled weakly and flapped a hand at Simmy. 'Never mind me,' she said. 'Get on with the debriefing.' They both looked back at Simmy.

'Right. Yes. So, then I drove to Ambleside, and spent half an hour pottering about there. I was too early for Chris, and didn't want to go home, so that seemed a good compromise. I bought a scarf and a shirt in a charity shop.'

Ben waved impatiently. 'Then what?'

'Back to Keswick, where I finally caught up with the Nick chap. Heard him talking to that little man who works there. He was loading up his van. He said the taxman

246

wasn't going to take it any further, and everything was settled, more or less. He'd been afraid that everyone would believe he'd killed Jonathan, but in fact, he hadn't had any bother over it.'

'Exact words?'

'I don't know, Ben. That was the gist of it. I was sitting in my car with the window open, trying not to let them see that I was listening.'

'How did you know it was him?'

'He was loading up that big tin trunk he'd bought. And he had stubble, like the Beverley woman said.'

Ben jotted a few words on a sheet headed 'Nick'. 'Was Christopher there as well?'

'No, he didn't finish up for a few more minutes. Then we dashed right off to see Philip in Grasmere. I don't know how many times I went up and down that damned road yesterday.'

'I make it six,' said Bonnie, effortlessly. 'Early on, with Ben. Then back when I phoned. Then up again via Ambleside. Then to see Philip and back. Then home sometime last night.'

'Six is too many,' said Simmy with feeling.

'Philip,' prompted Ben, pulling the appropriate page towards himself.

'They said he was dying, and he was very weak. But he was sitting up and could talk well enough. He'd read about the murder in the paper, which Chris was upset about. At least, I assumed he was. He didn't actually say so. Nearly all the talk was about the stumpwork – Philip had read about that as well and connected it all up in his mind. He

247

soon guessed it was Jonathan who sold it, and assumed it has to be the reason he was murdered.'

'Sharp for a dying man.'

'He really *cares*. I got the impression he feels almost responsible in some way. Chris promised him that he'd do everything he could to find who'd killed Jonathan. Afterwards, he said to me that he hadn't really meant it.'

'Not very ethical,' said Ben.

'To be fair, I guess he means there isn't anything he can do, anyway. So he's not exactly breaking a promise – just promising the impossible.'

'Not much difference, as far as I can see. Besides, there must be loads he *can* do, if he chooses.'

'Is that why you came home last night?' Bonnie asked. 'Because you were cross with him?'

'In a way,' said Simmy, seeing it in that light for the first time. 'I just felt . . . a bit sick of it all.'

Ben's pen was hovering over the 'Philip' sheet. 'Details,' he insisted. 'We know when the Leeson lady died. What we still haven't clarified is whether Jonathan went to her house while she was alive.'

'He did,' said Simmy. 'And she threw him out because he was mean to her dog.'

'Good.' Ben made a note. 'So did she sell him the stumpwork for far less than its value? If so, why would that matter to anybody? Or was there some kind of competition where Jonathan cheated?'

'No, she can't have done, because Philip says it was there after she died.'

Ben made another note, then located yet another sheet,

headed 'Kathleen Leeson' and stared at it. 'What about this long-lost relative who inherits the house? If there is one, of course. Could that turn out to be somebody local, who resented the way the house clearance chap was much too keen on getting his hands on the spoils?'

'Chris says it'll all be done through solicitors. And most of the bureaucratic stuff has been done now, anyway. Possibly all of it. He is a bit vague about it. I don't think he knows any of the details.'

'Who else would know?' Ben asked.

'Well – Philip, I guess. Nobody else has floated up.'

'Yes, they have. Daphne Schofield,' said Bonnie. 'I told you, remember? Corinne knows her. And she knew Kathleen Leeson, as well as Philip.'

'Oh yes,' said Simmy feebly. 'I forgot about her.'

'We should talk to her,' said Ben decisively. 'Will Corinne tell us how to find her?'

'She might.' Bonnie gave it more thought. 'Daphne's always wanting an audience. She'd probably be thrilled. Might even wonder what took us so long.'

'It's ten o'clock,' Simmy realised. 'I'll have to phone Chris. Valerie Woolley's due at eleven.'

'What? Who?'

'Jonathan's wife. Didn't I tell you? She wants to ask Chris all about finding the body. He's not looking forward to it. Threatened to go out and leave her high and dry.'

'Not very ethical,' muttered Bonnie, echoing Ben's recent comment.

'Stop it, both of you. Nobody's perfect. Chris had a horrible shock, and he's still not over it. Anyway, he's not going to chicken out. He just hopes she won't take long, so we can spend the rest of the day together. Why don't you call Corinne, while I phone Chris, and we can take things from there.'

'We could, but we're not done yet. Nowhere near,' said Ben.

'I'll go and phone Corinne,' said Bonnie. 'I said I would, anyway.'

Ben smiled his thanks, and she went out of the room. He riffled his papers. 'We need to go back to the start and see how it holds together now. I wonder where the police have got to? Moxon hasn't been again, has he?'

Simmy shook her head. 'I'd have told you.'

'The victim's wife,' mused Ben. 'Is she another suspect, then? Wives always have plenty of motives.'

'No idea,' said Simmy automatically. Then she reconsidered. 'Actually, Chris said she is quite big and strong.'

'Why aren't you there as well, so you can meet her? She might have all sorts of useful things to say.'

'We can ask Chris what she said.'

'Can we? Would he talk to us again? I thought it was strictly a one-off on Wednesday.'

'He'll tell *me*,' said Simmy with confidence. 'So, who are your suspects so far?'

Ben looked furtive. 'Well – Nick or someone acting for him. The person inheriting the Leeson estate, assuming there is such a person.'

'Why? What would that person have against Jonathan?'

'Rage at his profiteering from something that ought to be theirs.'

'More likely to be somebody local who thought Kathleen was going to give her things to them, surely? Or somebody whose dog Jonathan once kicked,' she added with a giggle.

'That's probably right – somebody who knew Kathleen. Now we know that the stumpwork could have been hers, that's the best line to take. Have the police factored that in at all? If not, we ought to tell them. Have they even bothered to interview Philip?'

'I think he would have said if they had, when we saw him yesterday.'

'Who else knows, then? Did Christopher seem surprised?'

She tried to think. 'Not really. But I don't think he believes it. He told Philip it couldn't be right.'

Ben sat up straighter. 'Details. That's what we need. Think of Poirot. Jack Reacher . . .'

'Sherlock Holmes?'

'Definitely. The truth always lies in the detail.'

'But they're just stories. Is it the same in real life?'

He treated her to a very stern look. 'It absolutely is,' he told her. 'Connections, links, causal threads. They all come out of the detail. Run some past me.'

'Um . . . Er . . . Mrs Leeson liked dogs and Jonathan didn't. Nick and him both drove blue vans. Mr Pruitt – he must be one of your suspects, isn't he? – lives in Grasmere and probably knows Philip, and a whole lot of other people. The V&A bought the stumpwork. How'm I doing?'

'Not bad. The Pruitt man could well be the main suspect – except why aren't the cops interested in him?

And is there a chance that the two blue vans got muddled somehow? Makes a change from white ones, anyway.'

'Jonathan's has his name on the side,' she remembered. 'Look, I'll have to phone Chris before we go any further. He'll think I don't love him any more.'

'So why can't he call you?'

'Because he thinks I don't love him any more.' She laughed humourlessly. 'Or maybe *he* doesn't love *me*. Although I think he does,' she finished with a little frown.

'Of course he does. Anyone can see that.'

'Good.' Was it significant that she cared very much less about that point than she would have done twenty years ago? Did it just mean that she took Christopher for granted?

'Go on, then. I'll have a bit of a think. Don't be long.'

Christopher answered briskly. 'Had a good night?' he said.

'Fine, thanks. I'm at Ben's now, but I'll be free all afternoon and evening. I'd like to spend it with you.' She silently congratulated herself on the clarity of her assertion. No putting it onto him, no games or tests.

'I'm glad to hear it. I thought I'd come to Troutbeck, as usual. Otherwise we'll be in the same pickle again as we were last night.'

'Good thinking.' A wave of relief, affection, gratitude and other warm emotions flushed through her. 'I do love you, Chris,' she found herself saying. 'You're amazing.'

'Likewise. We're all right, Sim, so long as we stay on the same side.'

'Yeah. So, I'll see you later. I'll be there from one – no, make it two. I ought to do a bit of shopping.'

'When did you last see your parents?'

'Days ago. I can go after work tomorrow. My weekends are yours – you know that.'

'See you soon, then.'

The three of them reconvened in the dining room, Ben glancing anxiously at the time indicator on his phone. 'Still got an hour and a half,' he announced. 'What did Corinne say?'

'She gave me Daphne's number, and I called it. She was a bit weird, but says she's heard about us being involved with the business in Hawkshead – and the thing in Coniston – and sounded pretty keen to talk about Philip and Kathleen. Corinne had primed her, I guess.'

'You called her already?' Ben was plainly unsure of the acceptability of this unilateral action.

'Should I not have?'

'It's okay. Did you fix a time for a talk?'

'She's free this afternoon.'

Simmy felt a stab of panic. She wanted to be there when Daphne Schofield told her story. But she had just lovingly arranged to spend most of the day with Christopher. The clash was a stark illustration of a dilemma that she had begun to understand was likely to be long-term. Although, with Ben's departure to university in the autumn, there might well be no further involvements with crime anyway. These thoughts flew through her mind in microseconds, followed by increased panic at the impossible decision. 'Aargh!' she said.

The youngsters looked at her. 'What?' said Bonnie.

'I can't do this afternoon. But I don't want to miss anything. And you'll need me to take you there. Doesn't she live in Rydal?'

'She said she could get a bus down to Ambleside. She likes going there on a Sunday apparently. So we could easily get a bus as well.'

'Or take the bikes,' said Ben.

'Couldn't Christopher come with us?' said Bonnie.

Ben nibbled his lip. 'Four people would seem pretty heavy,' he concluded. 'It'd feel like an interrogation.'

'He wouldn't want to come,' said Simmy with certainty. 'He's fed up with the whole palaver.'

'Hasn't he ever met her? If he was so chummy with Philip, why hasn't he come across her before now?'

'He's not all that chummy with Philip. He's a distant cousin and they've never been close. His parents put them in touch when Philip wanted someone to look at Kathleen's stuff. I got the impression Chris hardly knew him until then. But now he's got landed with the role of main contact for the nursing home. They call him first if there's a crisis.'

Ben nodded slowly. 'Okay. So, Christopher never met Kathleen Leeson – but Jonathan did. Didn't somebody say that it was Christopher who first sent Jonathan along to do her house clearance before she died?'

Simmy began to chew her own lip. 'Good question. Questions. When I went to Grasmere in March with Chris to see Philip, I assumed they had met before. Chris knew where Philip's house was, and they behaved like old friends. I never actually asked how well they knew each other.'

'We need to know,' Ben persisted.

'I don't see why. What I *am* sure of, is that Chris has seen him a few times since then. He helped him move to the nursing home and got himself noted as a friend who could be called in an emergency. He never once mentioned a woman friend.'

Bonnie interposed, saying, 'Corinne says Daphne probably got the brush-off a while back, but wouldn't take no for an answer. She's like that, apparently.'

'In which case, she wouldn't object to a whole lot of us showing up to talk to her,' said Ben. He frowned at Simmy. 'Are you *sure* Chris wouldn't want to come with us? It would help him fulfil his promise to Philip. If we put it like that to him, he could hardly refuse.'

Simmy started to see glimmers of hope, thanks entirely to Ben Harkness's good sense. 'It's possible,' she agreed. 'First I'll do my shopping, and then I'll call him.'

'So – how about this? We all go to Ambleside after lunch, and you call Christopher to say you're there and can he join you. Don't mention me and Bonnie. We'll get the bus. Just keep it all casual and sort of accidental. Where are we meant to meet this woman?' he asked Bonnie.

'She said Waterhead's her favourite spot, across the road from the bus stop. Sits and watches boats on the lake, with an ice cream. I've got to call her again to fix it for definite.'

'Tell her three o'clock, on the pier. We might find somewhere to sit, with luck. The weather's not brilliant, so it shouldn't be too crowded.'

Simmy's admiration for Ben's encyclopaedic knowledge

255

of the region was once again kindled. 'I've never been on the pier,' she said.

'It's not very impressive, but it makes a good meeting place.'

'Chris might like it,' she said, with considerably less certainty than before.

'Fingers crossed,' said Ben.

# Chapter Twenty

The pier at Waterhead was the point where trippers disembarked from boats after taking cruises on Windermere. It had many of the same attractions as Bowness, at the other end of the lake. Small children ran around chasing ducks; people in colourful summer clothes sat on green benches watching all the activity; ice cream was in plentiful supply. 'How will we find her?' wondered Bonnie, as they got off the bus that had brought them from Bowness. 'We don't know what she looks like.'

'Woman on her own, obviously waiting for someone.

She'll probably be late, so we'll see her hurrying from the bus stop,' said Ben.

'It was sloppy of me not to ask her what she'd be wearing,' Bonnie reproached herself. 'I didn't think.'

'You're still wobbly. It'll be fine. She knows there's two of us.' His kindness was automatic and exemplary. It manifestly made Bonnie feel warm and understood.

'Will Simmy make it, do you think? She's much keener on being involved this time.'

'She wants to clear Christopher's name. All thanks to Moxon – clever old stick that he is. If I've got it right, that was the whole point of his visit to the shop last week.'

'It fits. But why would he want her involved? He mostly seems to want her to keep clear.'

'Probably it was me he wanted,' he said with no false modesty. 'We all come as a package, don't we.'

'We used to. It's all going to be different now, isn't it? With her getting married and you going off to uni, we'll never be a team again.'

'Things change. And it's three months before I go. We've got plenty of time to adapt.'

'Corinne's worried about me coping without you. And she's worried that Christopher isn't right for Simmy.'

'Why? What did she say?'

'Nothing much. It was her face, mainly. She goes all crumpled when she's worried.'

'Is that her?' Ben suddenly darted towards a seat on the short promenade. 'There, look.'

A woman of about seventy was sitting awkwardly, trying to get a good view of the area, her head turning

258

in a jerky arc, scanning every person in sight.

'What's her surname again?' Ben hissed.

'Schofield.'

'Mrs Schofield?' he asked politely, when he reached the woman. 'Am I right?'

She shaded her eyes, as he stood between her and the sun, making his features hard to see. 'Are you Ben, then?' she said.

'I am indeed. And this is Bonnie.'

'Corinne's success story,' the woman smiled. 'Just look at you! What a lovely girl!'

'Your bus was on time, then?' Ben said smoothly.

'I had to choose whether to be twenty minutes early or ten minutes late,' she grumbled. 'Should have thought of that. Sitting here's bad for my knee.'

'Would you rather we walked as we talked, then?' asked Ben with extreme solicitude.

'No, no. I'll just stretch it out.' She followed the words with action, extending her leg into the path of passers-by. 'I've got Corinne to thank for this, then, have I?'

Bonnie smiled, almost simpering. 'She knows everybody, doesn't she? It's a wonder we haven't met before.'

'Well, let's get on with it,' said Daphne, somewhat to the youngsters' surprise. 'I'd like to get the next bus home, if that's all right with you.'

'That suits us very well,' said Ben. Then he gave a little yelp. 'Oh!' His gaze was on two people approaching from a northerly direction. 'There's Simmy and Christopher.' He leant over Daphne. 'Two friends of ours look as if they're going to join us. I hope that's all right?'

The woman gave him a narrow look. 'They just happen to be passing by, do they?'

'I honestly didn't know they'd be here. But they are very much involved in the whole business of the Grasmere murder. If you don't mind, I know they'd be really keen to hear what you can tell us.'

'Where are they going to sit?'

The bench was a good size. Bonnie had already sat on it next to Daphne. 'I think we can all squash in here,' said Ben with a laugh. He waved and beckoned to the newcomers. 'Let me introduce you,' he said, and proceeded to do so.

They made a motley group. Christopher sat at the furthest end from Daphne, leaning back and making no visible effort to hear the conversation. Ben and Bonnie flanked their informant, and Simmy squeezed in next to Bonnie. 'So – you know Philip,' Ben began. 'And you knew Mrs Leeson before she died? Had you ever met Mr Woolley? The man who was killed.'

'Heard a lot about him. Never saw him, though. Kathleen took against him in a big way, all because of her dog. Wouldn't let him in the house. Funny creature it was, anyway, with a nasty temper. Didn't like any men and couldn't abide anyone with a beard. It was a joke, really. Must have been badly treated as a pup by a beardy bloke, we supposed.'

'What happened to it after she died?'

Daphne shrugged. 'It was put down. Too old and unreliable to find a new home. Philip felt bad about it, but what could he do?'

'You weren't tempted to give it a home, then?' asked Ben.

'With my cats! You must be joking. The trouble was, Kathleen believed that those CaniCare people would rescue it for her. She put a bit of money aside for them, to cover their costs and so forth, and then said they could have as much of her stuff as they wanted. But it didn't happen – very dishonest of them, if you ask me. Philip had to get some vet to do the business.'

Christopher finally sat up. 'How is he today?'

'Not good, according to my friend Susan who works there. Can't be long now. Seems peaceful enough.' She sighed. 'Another good man out of the picture. I swear there's twenty women *at least* for every man. And it's getting worse.'

The two couples sitting alongside her made suitably rueful faces at this, apologising for their good fortune. 'Not that I should grumble,' she went on. 'I've had three good husbands, after all.'

'What happened to them?' Bonnie asked, wide-eyed.

'Well, there was Malcolm, when I was just nineteen and he was twenty. He was a dreamer, and no mistake. Fell under a combine harvester and lost both his legs. Lasted another five years, but his heart and lungs failed in the end. Then there was my Mikey. Gorgeous Irish feller. Black curls and brilliant blue eyes. We had two kiddies together. Went off to live in Canada, we did, but never could rightly settle to it. The boys stayed, and Mikey and I came home again. But he took to the drink. Never felt right, somehow, without our lads. He just took himself off one day and I never saw him again. Divorce papers came through in the end.' She shook her head sadly. 'Still miss Mikey, I do. He'd got a lovely singing voice. Dead by now, shouldn't wonder.'

'And your sons? Do they keep in touch?' asked Bonnie.

'Christmas, they phone. Nothing more than that. Shame, really.'

'You said *three* husbands.' It was, to everyone's surprise, Christopher who prompted her.

'That's right, pet. Took on an old boy, name of Dan, when I was gone sixty, and he was pushing eighty. Silly, really. I just got myself into a panic and thought I should have someone to go round with. Never should've married him. Only lasted five years, and when he passed on, his kids went ballistic, 'cause he left me half his money. Said that was the only reason I married him. Nasty, they were.' She scrubbed a tear away. 'And it's not as if it was a fortune, neither.'

'Oh dear,' said Simmy faintly, while the others sat in silence. 'That's a sad story.'

'I'm not complaining. I've done a lot better than most. It's just talking about my boys that sometimes sets me off. They were such darling little kiddies. Over forty now, both of them. Makes you think.' She looked at her outstretched leg with the swollen knee, and everyone plainly read her gloomy thoughts. 'I'm not suited to living on my own, you see. Feels all wrong, it does.'

'But you've got cats,' said Ben bracingly.

'Three of them. It's life, you see – I have to have some life about the place. Typical old girl with her moggies, that's me.'

'So . . .' Ben seemed at a loss, for once. 'All you can tell us about the Grasmere business is that Kathleen didn't like Jonathan and didn't want him in her house.'

'Is that what I said? It wasn't quite like that, you know. She *did* want to get rid of her things. She was getting on with it quite nicely, when her heart gave out. The last time I went to see her, the spare room was more or less empty. I was amazed, to tell you the truth. And she'd got a lot more organised, with boxes in the back room downstairs full of things she didn't want any more. It was really admirable, the way she pulled herself together, in those last weeks. Almost as if she knew she was running out of time and couldn't just leave it all in a great big mess.'

'But she didn't make a will,' Christopher reminded everyone, in a tone that suggested that this point was crucial. 'She didn't put anything in writing.'

'She did too!' Daphne was emphatic. 'She left a note for Philip, saying he was to use his best judgement on where it should all go.'

'Which had absolutely no legal standing,' flashed Christopher. 'It wasn't even properly signed. Anybody could have written it.'

'You saw it, did you?' Simmy asked him.

He shook his head. 'Jonathan told me about it. So did Philip, later on. All it did was complicate matters even more.'

Ben waved this exchange away. 'Did you know about the stumpwork?' he asked Daphne. 'That Jacobean embroidery that sold for such a lot in the auction?'

Everyone heard Christopher's exhalation, expressive of exasperation. Simmy and Ben both glanced at him. Daphne frowned and stared at the lake. They all waited for her to speak. 'I saw it in one of her boxes, when I went there with Philip. That was after she died,' she said. 'Nice bright colours. Funny little people, done in wool. Never dreamt it was anything special.'

'Do you know where Kathleen got it from?'

'Her granny, must have been. Or someone like that.'

'So how did Jonathan get hold of it?' Bonnie demanded. 'That's what nobody seems to know.'

'Must have nicked it,' said Daphne flatly. 'Kathleen would never have let him have it. She didn't let him have anything. He had that key, remember. Could've got in any time and helped himself.'

'No!' Christopher almost shouted. 'He wouldn't do that. For one thing, he'd never have dared.'

'Who'd have caught him, though? He must've hoped nobody even knew it was there. He could make up any story he liked, and no one could prove otherwise. It was his bad luck that Philip and I can both testify to where it came from.'

'It was his bad luck to be killed,' said Christopher sourly.

'Wait!' Ben held up his finger, in a gesture that they all found familiar. 'Did you or Philip tell anybody about it, before Jonathan was killed? If so, who? Because' – he paused for effect – 'that person would be a prime suspect for the murder.'

'No, I didn't. Who would I tell? And Philip never sees anybody.'

'Did Kathleen not have *any* family?' asked Bonnie, who maintained a sentimental attachment to the idea of proper families, lacking such a thing of her own.

'She had a few in-laws, but never kept in touch. The Leeson bloke was dead long before I met her. She told me once she had twins, back in the 1970s. The first one was born alive, but they didn't know there was another one, and it died. Then the first one got meningitis as a little thing and lived a few years with terrible brain damage. Tragic business. She had three brothers, all a lot older, and not one of them had any kids. She used to say there was a curse on the family and she was quite glad it was ending with her. She liked dogs, you know. Liked them better than people. She had five of them when I first knew her. They called her the dog woman in Grasmere, you know.' She looked at Christopher as if he might be aware of this.

'Hmm,' said Ben. Simmy wondered why he wasn't taking notes.

'I should go,' said Daphne. 'I hope I haven't spoken out of turn or broken any confidences. I don't think I have. It's not nice to think of that man dying right there in the middle of a place like Grasmere. It's a disgrace that such a thing could happen. And nobody knowing who could have done it.' She turned her head and looked directly at Christopher. 'Leastways, nobody's saying if they do,' she added meaningfully.

Simmy was between the woman and her fiancé and caught the full impact of the look and the words. 'What do you mean?' she demanded, before Chris could speak.

'Just what I say, no more and no less.' She got awkwardly to her feet, testing the sore knee before requiring it to take any weight. 'No offence intended.'

'Thank you for coming,' said Ben. 'We really appreciate it enormously. It must seem odd, the way we ask all these questions. You see—'

'It doesn't seem odd at all,' said Daphne. 'Not after Corinne explained it all. Says you've got a lot more sense than the police.'

'Ah!' said Ben, as a new thought struck him. 'We should have warned you that we might be telling them some of what you said to us. They might want you to give them a statement. Would that be a problem for you?'

'Not a bit,' she twinkled. 'It would be a very interesting experience, I'm sure. In fact, I was thinking they'd been very slack not to come to me already.'

Ben and Bonnie both laughed, while Simmy and Christopher sat hand in hand, with no trace of amusement on their faces.

Half an hour later, they were all in the middle of Ambleside, having decided that a drink and perhaps a bar snack would go down well. Simmy tried to explain how she and Chris had decided to join the others at Waterhead, but she kept being interrupted. Ben was rehearsing his renewed theories, based on what Daphne had said. Bonnie was chiming in with suggestions and questions. The sky had darkened with thick cloud, and people were disappearing from the streets.

'We have nearly the whole picture,' Ben gloated. 'Just let me write it down and I bet everything will come clear.'

'In your dreams,' snapped Christopher. 'She didn't give a single name that could conceivably be the person who did it. She just rambled on about dead husbands and how lonely she is. Total waste of time, if you ask me. And now she's going to tell everyone she's been helping the famous

Ben Harkness with his clever detective work. That's all she was out for, in the first place.'

'Come on, Chris,' Simmy reproached him. 'That's not fair. You were quite happy to come and hear what she was going to say, after all.'

'Was I? Did I have a choice? It's the same as it's been all week – dragging me into all this game-playing, without telling me what's going on. Did you see the *look* that woman gave me? Made me wish I'd stayed in Keswick, well out of all this.'

'Oh, shut up!'

It was Bonnie who spoke. Like an angry Yorkshire terrier, she placed herself squarely in front of the man and harangued him. 'What's the matter with you, anyway? This is much more your business than any of ours. We're doing everything we can to *help* you, you stupid man. That "look", as you call it, was only what a lot of people are thinking – including the police. Can't you see that? There's nobody else half as suspicious as the person who says he found the body. Especially in this case, where the only other obvious person has a solid alibi. And now Ben's got some leads, something to go on that will very likely get everything sorted – and all you can do is moan. Honestly! There's gratitude for you.'

Simmy and Ben both smiled at this final thrust, more fitting for an adult addressing a child than an angry young woman speaking to a man twenty years her senior. It was Simmy's smile that must have been the final straw for Christopher.

'Okay, that's it. I've had enough. It's like trying to make sense of a bunch of aliens. I can't follow half of what you're all obviously thinking. I'll accept that you think you're doing me some sort of favour – just. But it's obvious that you're all enjoying yourselves at the same time. And it feels as if it's at my expense. The past week has been a total nightmare. And then this morning I had to listen to Jon's wife weeping and wailing, and saying she told him years ago he'd come to a bad end if he mixed with all those shady characters in the antiques business. She blames me, as well.' He directed his rage at his fiancée. 'And you never asked me a single thing about how it went. All you could think about was this Schofield woman and bloody flowcharts.'

'You're right,' said Simmy calmly. 'It has been a horrible week for you. But Bonnie's right as well. We are doing our best to get you through it, even if it seems like a game sometimes. You don't have to be here, obviously. Nobody's forcing you.' She looked round at the almost empty pavements. 'But I think we've all earned a drink first. And I'm hungry. And' – she looked rather sheepish – 'I might have another annoying surprise for you.'

'What does that mean?'

'I texted Flo earlier on – the woman with the baby, and said if she's up for it, we were going to be in Ambleside and she might like to join us for a bit.'

'What? Now? Where's her husband?'

'That's the thing. If he was going to be at home, then that's fine. No problem. But he's been working seven days a week, the pig, leaving her high and dry with a howling baby. She lives just outside Grasmere – she might have picked up some gossip. And I was worried about her,' she finished weakly.

'Good thinking,' Ben approved loudly. 'So, is she coming or not?'

Simmy produced her phone. 'She says – "You saved my life. See you at the Royal Oak 4.30ish." That's just along here, isn't it?'

They all stared at her. 'I'm not happy about this,' Christopher protested. 'It's insane.'

'It's not, though, is it,' said Ben slowly. 'You think she might have some ideas about Jonathan. Gossip, you said. I love gossip. Local knowledge. Clever Simmy, I say.'

Simmy grinned, choosing to ignore Christopher's complaint. Yet again she felt the need to teach him that where Ben and Bonnie were concerned, he was going to have to adapt to a new normal. 'It just felt like a loose end, that's all. But it's not the only one. There's the Pruitt man, as well. He's got to be worth a look, don't you think?'

'Get you!' said Bonnie. 'Move over, Ben Harkness. You've got competition.'

Christopher heaved a noisy sigh and they all laughed at him.

# Chapter Twenty-One

Flo and her baby were not at the Royal Oak. The two couples sat outside, hoping the dark sky would not deposit any rain on them. Christopher was quiet and somewhat embarrassed by his outburst. Simmy was careful with him, doing her best to separate the shaken, suffering discoverer of a dead body from the loving man who wanted to marry her. She reminded herself that it was good to see him in all his aspects, to know the worst before she married him. This marriage, when it happened, would be as different as possible from her first one. She was older now, more experienced and more realistic. She watched him, tracing his features and trying to read his mind. His face was beloved to her. She loved his well-marked eyebrows, his soft-edged nose, the little cleft in his chin. She loved the very fact of his body and the unrestricted access she was permitted to it. However angry, self-pitying, unreasonable or uncomprehending he might be, she could forgive him. She was almost glad that he was revealing his flaws.

'Scott must have come home, after all,' she said. 'We'll have to meet Flo another time. Or maybe her ankle's still sore. She twisted it on Friday evening.'

'Are we getting the bus back to Bowness?' Bonnie asked. 'You two will be wanting to get to Troutbeck, won't you?'

'I'll take you home,' said Simmy. 'Don't I always? It's not far, after all.' The drive to Ben's house would take barely ten minutes. The Troutbeck house was already feeling less like home, as the prospect of selling it became more solid every day. Christopher was right to press for decisions about where they should live, when they should move in together and how they should construct their married life. 'You're coming back to mine, aren't you?' she checked with him now.

'Absolutely.' He smiled at her. 'Sorry I'm such a pain. I'll be okay in a bit.'

'I know you will.'

Then his phone summoned him, from the pocket of his jacket. 'Hmm,' he frowned. 'Who's this?'

They all watched and listened as the conversation took place. 'That's right . . . Oh, God, you mean *now*? I'm in

Ambleside . . . Yes, that would be better . . . I expect you know the house in Troutbeck? I was planning to be there all evening . . . Six-thirty? . . . All right, then.'

None of his listeners could make sense of what they'd heard. Ben looked at Simmy, eyebrows raised. She shrugged. Bonnie mouthed *Who is it?* Christopher ended the call and put the phone back in its pocket. 'Police,' he said. 'They want to ask me some more questions. The man from Windermere's coming to interview me in Troutbeck.'

'Moxon?' said Ben and Simmy together.

'That's not very orthodox, is it?' said Bonnie. 'Although I suppose it won't be the first time. Better than slogging all the way to Penrith.'

Ben threw her one of his looks of admiration. Her grasp of the background details never failed to impress him.

'Was that him? Moxon?' asked Simmy.

'No. But they obviously already intended to send him. I gather he's been quite closely involved in the last day or two.' Christopher's expression was serious, but not unduly alarmed.

'Once he knew Simmy was part of the picture, nothing would have kept him away,' joked Ben. 'He's her number-one fan.'

In spite of herself, Simmy was pleased to be supplying the venue for the interview. If it was Moxon, then she was confident that there was nothing to fear. He would never charge Christopher with murder, never do anything so distressing. 'That's all right, then,' she said airily. 'We'd better get a move on. I'm glad Helen gave me a proper lunch – we won't get any supper for hours yet.'

'I'm starving now,' sighed Christopher. 'All I had was a packet of crisps.' It was several seconds before Simmy realised he was joking. 'No, I didn't. I had a pork pie, as well. And a choc ice.' Simmy gave him a playful slap.

'Simmy . . .' said Ben, ignoring the banter, 'it's not really all right, is it? What do you think they want to ask Christopher? You know how they operate – I wouldn't be too relaxed about it, if I were you.'

'You're not saying you think he's going to *arrest* me, are you?' Christopher obviously didn't know how seriously to take it. 'It didn't sound like that just now.'

'My guess would be that they've come up with some evidence or testimony that pulls you into it. Something they want to check out with you and see how you react. We have no idea what it might be. Wish I could be there,' he finished ruefully.

'Well, you can't. You're going home to draw an algorithm or whatever it is, and make sure you find some cast-iron reason why Christopher can't possibly be a suspect,' said Simmy.

'Right.' Ben laughed uncertainly. 'I'll do my best.'

When Moxon arrived, the door of Simmy's cottage was already standing open and she was waiting for him in the little hallway. 'This has to be a first,' she said brightly. 'Coming to interview a person in his fiancée's house.'

'No, not really. We often see people in whatever place is convenient to them. It suits us pretty well, too, most of the time.' He was wearing a short-sleeved flannel shirt and jeans, perfect for an on-off summer's day in the

273

north of England. She had no doubt there was a jumper of some sort in his car, ready for any further drop in temperature.

'You've never really met Chris before, have you?' she said. 'He's in the sitting room. Be gentle with him,' she added lightly.

'When am I ever anything else?'

'Here you go, then.' She brought the two men together; Christopher standing by the window and the detective hesitating in the doorway. 'Am I allowed to stay?'

'It's your house,' said Moxon. 'I can't insist on you leaving the room.'

'Fine. Do you want a drink? Coffee or something?'

'No, thanks. I don't think I'll be here very long.' He made a sweeping gesture towards the sofa. 'Shall we all sit down?'

Once they were settled, he went on to explain how he had become part of the investigating team, with responsibility for any investigations needed south of Grasmere. 'It won't be the first time,' he said. Then he dived swiftly into the main business. 'The Penrith people had a call this morning from a man called Malcolm Pruitt. I think you know who he is?'

They both nodded.

'You probably won't know that he's a leading light in the Neighbourhood Watch. He likes to keep an eye on everything, and knowing Mrs Leeson's house was empty, he's been giving it his special attention. Okay so far?'

They nodded again.

'So – on Monday last, at twelve noon, he says he observed a man who was very probably Mr Woolley, turning into the cul-de-sac in a blue van with the name of Woolley on the side. He didn't see which house he went to, and it was another half-hour or so before he took it upon himself to walk down to the house for a check. But he was in his own garden for all that time and claims he would certainly have seen anyone else entering or leaving the cul-de-sac, either on foot or in a vehicle. He insists that nobody did so until you, Mr Henderson, came along. That was when he went there himself, five minutes after you, at most. You with me?'

'The killer must have been there already, then. Before Jonathan showed up,' said Simmy, as if that were an obvious point.

'Possibly. But when did he leave, if so? It's a very small quiet road, with only a handful of houses, and no way through at the further end.'

'Of course there's a way through,' snapped Christopher. 'Just because there's a sign telling people not to go any further, isn't going to stop someone who's just committed murder, is it? They could jump over the fence and be off in any direction they liked.'

Moxon sighed. 'That's just about true – and we thought of it already. But there are no indications that any such thing took place. No footprints on either side of the fence, or other evidence. There's an old lady in the end house who spends much of her time looking out of the window, and she'd have noticed someone vaulting the fence. It's rather a flimsy hypothesis.'

'Enough to drill holes through what the Pruitt man's saying, all the same.'

'Why does she look out of the window so much?' asked Simmy. 'What is there to see?'

'Birds. She watches the birds at her bird table. What's more, she says her dog would certainly have barked at anybody passing their gate. It was outside all day on Monday, she says.'

'Oh.' Simmy began to understand that things were not going well. Christopher's ominous silence was as worrying as Moxon's gentle explanations.

'But Pruitt could be lying,' Simmy realised. 'He could be the killer, and everything he's told you is entirely untrue. You can't make a case just on verbal testimony, can you?'

'We have to follow it up and try to find supporting evidence – as you must know.'

'Have you come to arrest me, then?' asked Christopher heavily. 'Is there anything I can say to convince you I didn't touch Jon? I've never done anything remotely violent. I'm a wimp, I promise you.'

Simmy looked at him with fond impatience. 'You don't have to be a wimp to be innocent of murder.' She turned to Moxon. 'Isn't there a CCTV camera somewhere that would help? Hasn't that school got one? What if the killer drove in and out again an hour or more before Chris got there? Pruitt probably wasn't taking much notice of vehicles . . .' She tailed off. 'Oh, no – I see. He saw Jonathan arrive, and whoever killed him got away somehow, right under Mr Pruitt's nose. Even so – if it's been filmed, that would give you another lead.'

'There aren't any cameras directed at the cul-de-sac. One or two show traffic going up and down the main street, but that's really not helpful.'

'Did you ask all the residents if they saw vehicles?'

Moxon sighed. 'Exhaustively. And you could be right about Mr Pruitt not bothering to register ordinary daytime traffic that comes and goes almost invisibly. It's a short list, though. Two delivery vans. A charity collector gathering up stuff for a jumble sale. The postman. And a woman going from door to door asking if anyone had seen her lost budgie. I'm not joking. That was all anyone could remember, between eight in the morning and the time the 999 call was made.'

'Okay. Do you mind if I jot that list down, to show to Ben? He's been very diligent in gathering up every little detail, and this new stuff from Mr Pruitt is going to get him very excited.'

'I can't stop you. Just make sure he doesn't get actively involved – no confronting potential suspects, or even stalking people – is that clear?'

'Don't worry. He's strictly confined to paperwork.'

'That's not true is it,' Christopher put in. 'What about dragging the Schofield woman down to Waterhead this afternoon?'

Moxon sat up. 'Schofield? Who's she?'

'I was going to tell you,' Simmy defended. 'She knew Mrs Leeson and filled in some of the background for us, that's all.'

'Where does she live?'

'Rydal. She'd be happy to talk to you, if you're interested. I think she feels a bit neglected because nobody's been to question her.'

'How would we even know she existed?'

Simmy stared at him, processing this remark. She realised she still harboured a sense of the police as all-knowing, following threads and connections all around a community, knocking on doors and repeating ad nauseam the same list of questions. 'Well . . . didn't anybody mention her? She sounds as if she's quite high profile over there.'

'What's her first name?'

'Daphne. She knows Philip as well.'

'And what did she tell you in Waterhead?'

'Nothing the slightest bit relevant,' Christopher snapped. 'It was a total waste of time.'

'It's a bit soon to say that,' Simmy argued mildly. 'Ben could well come up with some theories, thanks to what she told us. All that background about Kathleen Leeson was interesting, don't you think?' She had found a used envelope and was making notes on the back. 'Vans . . . budgie . . . charity collector. Pruitt. I wonder why he's only telling you now, after nearly a week?'

Moxon ignored her and spoke to Christopher. 'You sound angry. Can I ask why?'

'That boy. Ben. He gets on my nerves. Who does he think he is? What gives him the right to barge in asking all those questions? A grown woman, dragged to a ridiculous meeting, as if it was all just a game. It's ridiculous,' he repeated.

'She went willingly, I presume?'

278

'She knows Bonnie's foster mother – probably didn't want to upset her by refusing.'

'She was tickled pink,' said Simmy. 'And I think there might well have been some clue in what she told us. It just needs sorting out. We all think that stumpwork's the key to the whole thing.'

'It's tempting to think so, I agree. But there are no evidential reasons for doing so. Even if Mr Woolley stole it from Mrs Leeson's house, who would be angry enough about it to kill him? We've talked it round and round, every which way, and nobody can see how it could possibly be a motive. And even if it was, we're no closer to identifying the individual concerned.'

'Hmm.'

Both the men smiled at her note-taking and evident determination to participate. She looked from one to the other. 'What?' she said.

'You're not normally this engaged,' said Moxon.

'She's doing it for me,' Christopher explained. 'Because she wants to save me from the gallows. As Charles Dickens might have said,' he added. 'As it is, I guess it's more like fifteen years, maximum.'

'True love,' Moxon ventured, with another smile.

'Must be,' said Simmy. 'But you seem a bit more cheerful, all of a sudden. Did you think of something?'

'I think we ought to go and speak to Mrs Daphne Schofield, for one thing. And probably put Mr Pruitt under a bit more pressure. There's something not entirely consistent about him.'

'We saw him yesterday, at the auction. He spoke to me

and Ben. He knew exactly who we were, which felt a bit spooky. I think he's a spy.'

Christopher gave a protesting yelp, but Moxon corrected him. 'He practically admitted as much – following you down the cul-de-sac and waiting to nab you when you came out of the house.'

'He thought I was *stealing*?' Christopher was horrified.

'Apparently so. He has rather a low opinion of people in your profession. Quite a few people do, in my experience.'

'They're wrong,' said Simmy forcefully. 'It's all perfectly law-abiding, from what I can see. And it's romantic. Glamorous. All those beautiful things.' She sighed. 'I think it's wonderful.'

'Better than floristry?'

'Probably.'

Christopher reached over to her and laid a hand on her leg. 'Don't go overboard, pet. There've always been plenty of dodgy characters wheeler-dealing in the shadows. I've told you that. They're not the least bit romantic. But they're not murderers.'

'Salt of the earth. Rough diamonds – that sort of thing,' grinned Moxon. 'Most of them are known to us, one way or another. Quite often they're on our side, believe it or not.'

Simmy clasped her fiancé's hand. 'Well, I still think the whole thing's romantic. Don't spoil my illusions.'

Moxon glanced at his watch – an old-fashioned article that perfectly fitted his character. 'I should go and leave you in peace. I know I haven't brought anything like good news, and it could get worse. You'll need to keep yourself available for further questioning, I'm afraid. There is still a strong feeling that you're holding something back,' he told Christopher. 'And I admit I'm still not entirely confident that the feeling is misguided.'

'I've told you everything I can think of, that could possibly have any bearing on the subject. I've answered every question put to me. We'll just have to trust that justice will be done, that's all,' said Christopher. 'I dare say it's my own fault. I should have realised it was stupid to go meeting Jon as I did.' He looked from one face to another. 'That's why I can't give a sensible explanation, you see. There really *isn't* one. We'd all been getting excited about what there might be in that house, and what would come to us for auction. And we were all a bit worried about losing out.'

'We still don't know who the long-lost heir is,' said Simmy. 'Do we?'

'I can answer that, as of two days ago,' said Moxon, consulting his notebook. 'It's a Miss Jemima Hapgood. She lives in County Cork. Now, listen to this. Her grandfather, born in 1876, was the brother of Mrs Leeson's grandmother, born in 1865. So, she's a third cousin. There's a researcher somewhere paid to figure out these things. The report that came back said there appeared to be no other blood relatives now alive. What about that?'

'How old is she?'

'Seventy-nine. She made a statement to the effect that she

281

simply wishes all the property to be disposed of in whatever way is usual, and the proceeds despatched to her in due course. Washes her hands of it, in other words.'

'So she's not the killer,' said Simmy.

'I think we can safely say she is not.'

# Chapter Twenty-Two

'We could go to the pub for a couple of beers,' Christopher suggested, as they contemplated the evening ahead of them. 'Otherwise we'll drive each other mad.'

'Will we? Are we that useless at being a couple?'

'We won't be, when this is all sorted out. But now we're jangled and scared, and don't know where we are with each other.'

'How will it be better at the pub? People might be there who know about the murder and make the connection with us. Wouldn't that be embarrassing!'

'Unlikely. Who knows me in Troutbeck?'

'No. I don't want to go out again. It's raining, look. And I've hardly been here all week. I just want to slump in front of the telly. We could watch *Antiques Roadshow*.'

She had hoped to make him laugh. Several months ago, he had broken it to her that everybody in the antiques business loathed the programme with a vengeance. 'The last thing we want is for Joe Public to recognise a piece of Rosenthal at a car boot sale, or an eighteenth-century Turkish rug in a junk shop,' he had explained. 'And it gives them an inflated idea of whatever old rubbish they own is worth. It's taken a lot of the fun out of the business, according to Oliver. He can remember a time when nobody knew anything.'

And now there were programmes about antiques on TV every day of the week, and everyone in the land could spot a piece of Moorcroft at a hundred paces – though Rosenthal was still pleasingly obscure. As was Jacobean stumpwork, she reminded herself.

'Must we?' he whined. 'When are you going to get Netflix, so we can access practically any film we fancy?'

'We'll have it in our new house,' she promised. 'First thing we do, okay?'

He got up and roamed restlessly around the room. It was not large enough for any serious pacing, so he began to fiddle with her few books, and then the ornaments on her mantelpiece. She watched him helplessly. When a knock came on the front door, she was startled at how relieved she felt.

Before she could fully open the door, Moxon had pushed in. 'Can you come?' he panted.

'What? Why? Oh God – is it my father? Has he had another stroke?'

'No, no. Listen – it's complicated. There's an incident ongoing in Grasmere, which involves people you know. Your name has been mentioned. There's a baby . . .'

'You mean Flo? And Lucy May. But what's happened? She was supposed to come to meet me in Ambleside earlier on. I meant to phone her, to see if she was all right.' She put a hand to her cheek. 'You can't really want me to go with you now. I hardly know the woman.'

Christopher was standing right behind her, but she ignored him. Moxon's demand was still being processed, with no discernible implications penetrating her brain. 'You don't have to go,' said Christopher. 'Not without a proper explanation.'

'She says she tried to call you.' Moxon's air of desperation had subsided slightly. 'Is it on your voicemail?'

Simmy located her phone and turned it on. There were three voicemails, to which she listened while still standing in the hall. The first was from her father. 'Here is your peevish old dad, wondering when he's likely to see you again,' he dictated. 'It seems that being engaged to be married is already taking you away from your fond parents. Perhaps you could call in after work tomorrow? That would be Monday.' Simmy smiled at the excessive formality, which Russell often employed when leaving phone messages.

'My dad's okay,' she reported.

The second recording was from Ben. 'Waiting for an

update on what Moxo had to say. Why is your phone turned off? I'm leaving you a text as well.'

The third was, as Moxon had predicted, from Flo, who spoke in a whisper. 'Oh Simmy – I couldn't make it after all. Scott came home just as I was leaving. He's in a vile mood. I've no idea what's wrong with him, but no way can I go out. To be honest, it's a bit scary. I know it's an awful cheek, but if you could get up here and drop in, that would be brilliant. A visitor would probably calm him down.'

She stared at the detective. 'She wants me to go there,' she said. 'But that was an hour ago or more.'

'And things have escalated since then. You know they live in a remote cottage at Banerigg, don't you? No neighbours close enough to hear anything. But there were people walking in the woods, and they heard shouts and screams and called the police. The door's locked, and Mr Penrose won't allow his wife to leave the house.'

'But—' Simmy had a hundred questions. Her reluctance to go out had not abated, and somewhere she felt a lurking suspicion that there was a subtext that she was missing. Something wasn't right. Police detectives did not scoop up peripheral witnesses and drive them to scenes of violence – did they? Had Scott taken his wife and child hostage? 'Has he got a gun?' she asked, with a sudden chill.

'Not that we know of. It's not like that. Everything's very low key at the moment.'

Simmy's visions of loud hailers, police vehicles strewn across the little lane, summer visitors gawping from a safe

286

distance – all receded. 'So . . . ?' She still didn't understand. 'Why me? I've never even met the husband – unless he was the man I saw at the charity shop, which I think he probably was. All I did was take some flowers to the baby.' This final wail of protest was one she had made before, on other occasions.

Christopher, still behind her, with a hand on her shoulder, gave a snort. 'Seems as if that's enough,' he muttered.

Then Moxon's phone summoned him and he automatically took a step away to answer it. He had remained just inside the open front door, rain providing a blurry curtain behind him. 'Yes? . . . Are you sure? . . . Well, that's a relief. Thanks for letting me know. Keep me in the loop, will you? Thanks again.' He killed the call and met Simmy's enquiring gaze. 'It's all over. You can relax. Mrs Penrose has left the house with her baby, saying she intends to go down to Bristol to stay with a relative. Her husband has been located and has expressed profound regret for creating a disturbance and claims to be under great stress at work, exacerbated by sleepless nights at home, thanks to the baby. In other words, he's backed off, and she's had the sense to get away from him while she can.'

'She's gone to Great-Granny Sarah,' nodded Simmy. 'That's a long drive at this time of night.'

Moxon shrugged. Christopher let go of her shoulder. Apparently both men felt the whole thing was adequately resolved. 'Sorry to alarm you,' said the detective. 'I'll be off again, then.'

Simmy lost no time in closing the door behind

him. Then she almost ran into the sitting room and started keying her phone. 'Hey, Flo, it's me, Simmy. I hope you'll hear this before you get too far down the motorway. I've just had the police here. Listen – don't go to Bristol tonight. Come here instead. Troutbeck. Phone me when you get this.' Then she texted a briefer version of the same message. She looked at Christopher. 'She can't drive all that way, can she? She won't have packed properly. Great-Granny Sarah won't have any baby equipment. Neither have I, I know, but Flo can pop back home for essentials from here.' She frowned at all the implications running through her head. 'Flo's got a twisted ankle. She must be absolutely *desperate*. And the police have lost all interest in her, just because that bloody man said he was sorry.'

'They never like a domestic,' said Christopher feebly. 'So, we're to have company, then, are we?'

'If I can get hold her in time. I have a feeling she'll see my text before long. She'll have to stop to feed the baby, or just catch her breath. Poor woman! Maybe I'll try again, so she realises somebody's trying to speak to her.' She thumbed the phone again and left a shorter message to the same effect as the first.

'Are you sure you want to do this? What if you get lumbered with her indefinitely? If the husband's calmed down, and she's got some relative to go to, why not leave it at that?'

'Because the relative is too far away, and that won't solve anything. It must be sheer desperation that's sent her rushing down there.'

'But, Sim, you don't *know* her. She might be a total leech. A real pain in the backside.'

'She's neither of those things, and she's got a very small baby. It would be better to go to a refuge than drive all the way to Bristol.'

'I give up,' he said. 'I should be pleased that I'm marrying someone with such a good heart. I *am* pleased. Bring them here if you want to. I can change nappies if need be.'

'Anybody can change nappies, and I wasn't actually asking your permission.' She spoke softly but did not mince her words. It was something that had to be said. There were moments when Simmy Brown did her mother proud. Angie Straw would have welcomed Flo and Lucy May in without a second thought.

'You're right. And I didn't mean to sound dictatorial. Perish the thought. I still wish we could go for a beer, all the same. I'm even willing to ask your permission.'

'I can't, Chris. I need to phone Ben and my parents. And I need to be here if Flo calls me. I don't want to talk about all this stuff in a pub, where people can hear. I wouldn't enjoy it at all. I'm sorry. It's all going to be over in a few days, and then we can get back to normal.'

'Whatever that might be.' He had sunk into a sudden gloom. 'Why do I feel so bad about everything, while you seem to be thriving on it?'

'I know how you feel – honestly. That's how I've been for most of these investigations, with Ben and Bonnie driving me mad. But somehow this one's different. The business with Flo is nothing to do with the murder, anyway. It feels like a sort of respite, as well as something I might actually be able to help with. Right from the first moment I saw her, she's seemed like someone needing to be rescued. She more or less said as much when she phoned me on Friday night.'

'I thought you wanted to rescue *me*,' he sulked.

'From the gallows – right. I will if I can, but you've got to believe that Ben's a far better bet when it comes to that. He's going to have one of his brainwaves any time now. I can almost feel it. His mind works like a computer – you feed in all the information and out pops the answer.'

'Really?'

'Well, sometimes. Actually, it's never quite as straightforward as that. And last time, I think it was more me than him, in the end. Because he was so busy with his revision for the exams.'

'And the time before that – when it was my father – *my father* – who was killed. Didn't you wade right in and tackle your suspect, like a total lunatic?'

'It wasn't like that at all. I knew nothing was going to happen to me.'

'Too dumb to live – isn't that what they say about you?'

'And haven't I proved them wrong – whoever they are? It's just a phrase people use, anyway. It doesn't mean anything, especially when I'm definitely not dumb.'

'So, nobody thinks I might be rescuing *you* by marrying you? That's a shame. I'd like to be a rescuer.'

'You are. In a whole lot of ways.' She gave him a squeeze, somewhat awkwardly, as they sat side by side on her sofa. 'This must be real life, as most people know it. Interruptions, panics, misunderstandings. And look at us – we're coping brilliantly.'

'You might be. I don't feel as if I'm coping at all. All I can think about is a pint of Sally Birkett's in the pub garden as the sun goes down. I know I'm whining, but that really would make me happy.'

'Chris, it's eight o'clock. Quarter past, actually. And it's raining, you idiot.'

'So what? Isn't this the perfect time? And we can sit in the bar just as happily. I don't see what's stopping us. Your phone calls can wait an hour, surely? I bet Ben will be on the doorstep of the shop first thing tomorrow, anyway. You can update him then. And your parents aren't expecting you to phone tonight, are they? You're just making excuses.' He lapsed into another sulk.

'And what about Flo?'

'It's half an hour at least since you left those messages. She'll be well out of Cumbria by now.'

'All this fuss about a pint of beer,' she tutted. 'Anyone would think you were addicted to the stuff.'

'It's a craving, not an addiction. Humour me, *please*.'

She knew she'd lost. His little-boy act was barely masking a more adult anxiety and stress. He wanted to be among people, with laughter and good cheer all around him. The beer was incidental. He wanted to avoid any more intense emotional discussions between the two of them, not because he was afraid of what might be said that could damage their relationship, but because he felt it had all been said already. She could feel his weariness with it all, his desire for normality. 'All right, then,' she said.

* * *

It was much as expected. The rain had turned to a half-hearted drizzle, which had not deterred a committed number of drinkers. The three bars were all occupied, but there was space for more. The Sally Birkett's Ale was readily available, and there were packets of Christopher's favourite pork scratchings. At his insistence, Simmy had left her phone behind, with the promise that they would only be out for an hour.

'But what if Flo calls?' she protested.

'She'll leave a message. There's no more you can do for her tonight.'

The image of the distraught new mother driving blindly southwards in the darkening evening remained with her. The roads would be full of weekenders going home. The baby would be tightly strapped into a car seat, probably wailing with hunger or discomfort. 'I wish I could believe she'll be all right,' she said wretchedly. 'How could the police just let her go like that?'

'How could they stop her? She's probably been defending her husband and saying there's really no problem. Isn't that what wives usually do?'

They were still talking about Flo as they arrived at the pub. Christopher had given up trying to reassure Simmy and attempted one or two unhelpful suggestions as to what might be done – but not until the following day. 'She'll have stopped at a Premier Inn or somewhere,' he insisted.

'It sounds like such a *mess*,' Simmy said, more than once.

But finally, they moved onto happier themes. 'I'll go and talk to an estate agent tomorrow, in the lunch hour,' said Simmy. 'See if I can get the house valued, and then put on the market. It seems silly to rent it out. Indecisive. Having my cake and eating it.'

He reached for her hand. 'You're sure, aren't you? It'll be a wrench, selling it so soon. You might lose out financially, as well. And we still haven't decided where we want to set up home together.'

'I'm sure,' she said. 'I want to get on with it quickly. We're just treading water like this. I feel so lucky that we got together again – it's our destiny. It has been for nearly forty years, if you listen to my mother. I'm so sorry that your parents aren't here to see it, though. They'll be horribly missed at the wedding.'

'We're not having an actual *wedding*, are we?'

'What do you want to call it? Ceremony? What other words are there for it?'

'Your father could probably think of something. What I meant was – can we keep it really simple? Just your parents and my sisters and brothers? And a meal in a pub somewhere afterwards?'

'I'd want Ben and Bonnie,' she warned him. 'And probably Melanie.'

'And I'll have to ask some people from work.'

It cheered them both to be contemplating the future, holding hands and swigging local ale. Simmy had an image of a stony foreshore, representing the immediate complications of a murder enquiry and fleeing wife, leading to a sunnier, smoother beach, which was married life with Christopher. All they had to do was traverse the sharp stones as quickly as they could, before reaching the happy land ahead.

Then the pub landlord approached their table. 'Are you Chris and Simmy?' he asked.

They looked up in bewilderment and nodded.

'There's a phone call for you. A girl called Bonnie wants to speak to you urgently.' He cocked his head in puzzlement. 'Haven't you got mobiles, either of you?'

But Simmy was already on her feet.

## Chapter Twenty-Three

'Simmy! Thank goodness! Can you come to Ben's place right away? There's a man here. He's really angry and he won't go away until he's seen you and Christopher. It's all Ben's fault, really. Oh, Simmy, please come.'

'But who *is* he?'

'His name's Scott Penrose. He runs that charity shop in Ambleside. The dog one. The police have been at his house. He thinks Ben sent them. His wife knows you. There's a baby . . .'

'Scott Penrose! I know about what happened this evening. Ben didn't send the police. It was some walkers who heard shouting. Why should he think it was *Ben*?'

'He says if it wasn't Ben it must have been you. He says you've turned his wife against him. He wants to talk to you.'

'But where's Helen, and Ben's dad? Are they just letting all this happen?'

'They've gone off somewhere with Zoe. They're due back any minute. We were hoping we could get this sorted before they turn up. And Tanya's here. She's not feeling very well. Her cut's throbbing. Natalie's out with some boy.'

'So where's the Penrose man? Can he hear you?'

'No, but he can see me. He's not scary, exactly. Just won't go away. We can't work out what we should *do*.' She sounded very young and helpless, and Simmy badly wanted to help. But she was still deeply confused. Bonnie went on, 'If you and Christopher both come, then he'd *have* to leave, wouldn't he? We'd have the strength of numbers.'

Simmy didn't relish the prospect of watching Christopher and Ben manhandle an angry man out of the house. 'I think I should call Moxon about it,' she said.

'Not yet,' Bonnie said urgently. 'Later, maybe. First you should talk to Scott.'

There were many things that Simmy did not understand. The man's anger. The very fact that he and Ben were somehow connected. The odd contrast between the underlying threat of violence and the relative calm in Bonnie's tone. The subliminal alert caused by mention of the charity shop. It was all coalescing, very slowly, but definitely excitingly. 'We'll be there in fifteen minutes,' she promised.

\* \* \*

Christopher's bemusement was almost funny. 'But what *happened*?' he kept asking. Simmy would only say, 'I'll tell you in the car. Come on, we should run.'

And run they did. It was exhilarating, in the soft rain, the sky almost dark, the urgency increased by a youthful sense of adventure. Either the beer or the reassuring intimacy with Simmy had changed Christopher's mood to one of relatively willing cooperation. Simmy grabbed her bag, car keys and phone and almost pushed Chris into her car. 'Why not take mine?' he protested.

'I drive faster than you,' she said. 'And you had more beer than me.' Never before had she cast any aspersions on his driving, but privately she had often wished he would speed up. A streak of innate caution was something to be valued, she had told herself, while chafing at the way he crept around bends in country lanes, in contrast to his tendency to go rather too fast on bigger roads. *It must be me*, she thought, *never satisfied. Just a nagging female.*

'But won't you want to be on the phone?' he asked, as she turned the little car round.

'No – why would I? If it rings, you can answer it for me, anyway.'

'Am I going in the capacity of bodyguard? Will I have to punch somebody?'

'No. Listen. I'm going to talk all the way to Bowness. It would be better if you don't interrupt, even if it doesn't make sense. Is that okay?'

'Try me.'

'Somehow there's a link between Flo and Jonathan

being killed. It's about dogs. Jonathan was brutal to Kathleen Leeson's dog. She loved dogs, enough to give things – and probably money – to CaniCare. I think she gave that stumpwork to them. I think Jonathan found it, paid three quid for it, and when it sold for thousands, the man in charge of the charity shop was so furious, he killed him. And the man in charge of CaniCare in this area is Scott Penrose. That's what I think Ben must have worked out, and somehow approached the man, hoping to trick him into confessing. Or something. But the thing is, I forgot to tell him that I went to that shop in Ambleside and met the man himself. At least, I'm assuming it was him. I didn't make the connection at the time, except a vague awareness that Flo's husband was with them somehow. So now he's furious again, because Ben's tracked him down somehow. The name and address are on my work computer, because I took flowers there on Monday. Bonnie must have found it and given it to him. Are you with me?'

Christopher was sitting upright in the passenger seat, watching her face as she spoke. His hand was over his mouth as if holding back a flood of questions or arguments. He gave an ambivalent wag of his head, to indicate yes and no.

'You can speak now,' she told him.

'He would have paid more than three quid for it,' was the first thing he said. 'And it's not credible that the charity people would hold such a grudge that they'd kill him over it. It happens all the time. It's part of the whole deal. If everyone paid the real value of everything

298

at the start, we'd all starve. There'd never be any profit for any of us.'

'I see that. But there's something more going on here. Probably to do with dogs.'

'I can't believe the same man would be causing trouble in two different places on one evening. It's a rampage. Didn't he learn his lesson when his wife ran off? Does he blame Ben for that as well?'

'Me,' said Simmy. 'He blames me. That's why he wants me there now.'

'So I *am* going to be your bodyguard, after all.'

'Let's hope not.'

They parked in Helm Road, three houses away from the Harkness residence and went to the door. Bonnie threw it open, with a wan smile. 'That was quick,' she said. 'Come on in.'

In the big family living room, a man was sitting on the edge of an armchair, intently watching the door. He had dark hair, a trim little beard and moustache. Simmy stopped dead, staring at him. 'That's not him, is it?' she said.

The man got to his feet. 'Whoever you expected, I can assure you that I'm Scott Penrose, and Florence is my wife.'

Ben was on the sofa, a big white jotter pad on his lap. He gave Simmy a thoughtful look. 'Have you ever seen him before?' he asked.

'No.'

'But you thought you had? Is that right?'

She paused. 'It's pretty silly of me, I suppose. I just

thought I'd worked it out. The shop in Ambleside . . . Jonathan and dogs, and the stumpwork.'

Ben nodded and waved his pen over the notepad. 'Me too,' he said. 'Mr Penrose is very cross with us.'

'What did you say to him?' She was entirely engaged in the present moment, desperate to understand all the interactions and implications.

Again, Ben indicated his notepad. 'I pulled everything together. Daphne provided most of the final pieces. Kathleen Leeson didn't like or trust Jonathan. He ended up with the stumpwork somehow, and we can safely assume she would never have willingly let him have it. So, she donated it to CaniCare, because she was so obsessed with dogs. Which can only mean that Jonathan got it from the charity shop, paying some derisory sum for it. Again, we have to assume he knew exactly what it was and exploited the ignorance of the people at the shop. So, when it was in the papers, with pictures, saying how much it sold for, the CaniCare people would have felt terribly cheated.'

'Yes!' Simmy was thrilled at the almost identical scenario to the one she had spelt out to Christopher in the car. 'I came to exactly the same conclusion.'

They all looked at Scott Penrose, who spoke calmly. 'So he phoned me at home and started asking extremely intrusive questions.'

'Was Flo there at that point?' Simmy asked.

'She was. I'm afraid she took a lot of the fallout.'

'Unfairly,' Simmy accused. 'You've been a pretty poor husband to her lately, haven't you?'

'Um . . .' Ben interrupted. 'That's another issue, Simmy. Can we stick with the main point?'

'Sorry. The thing is, I forgot to tell you and Bonnie that I went to the CaniCare charity shop yesterday. There was a man there. I assumed – stupidly – that he was Mr Penrose. Of course, there must be loads of volunteers, working to a rota. It's just that you don't often see men doing it. Not men of working age, as that one was. I don't suppose it makes any difference,' she finished slowly. Somewhere a thought had gone astray.

'You didn't accuse him of murder, did you?' Christopher asked Ben. 'He can sue you for slander, if so.'

'I've got more sense than that,' said the youth with dignity. 'And you obviously don't know the law concerning slander.'

Scott Penrose was beginning to look agitated. Simmy's criticism had struck a nerve, it seemed. 'We've had a major crisis over that stumpwork. It's turned everything upside down. The problem is, we've been victims of our own success. Mountains of stuff keep coming in from old ladies. We can't keep up with it. We all spend hours in that back room, trying to sort it all out. We take bags of it home with us and wash the clothes, and write the labels, and try to get an idea of value.'

'Not you, surely?' Simmy faced him. 'Flo would have told me if you'd been doing that. She'd probably have enjoyed helping you with it.'

'She's been very strange since the baby was born. Paranoid about germs. Clinging to me and crying all the time. I did my best,' he finished fiercely, glaring at

Simmy. 'But I've got responsibilities to my employers as well. There are only two of us who are actually paid to be there. All the others can come and go as they please. And that week when it rained every day was the final straw. Florence wouldn't go out in case the baby got wet. She just sat there by the window, with the baby on her lap, both of them in tears.'

'Why didn't you get some help? That sounds like puerperal psychosis to me,' said Ben. 'It's a serious matter.'

'And now she's out there somewhere,' Simmy remembered. 'She must be at risk, surely. And the baby even more so.'

'So, who killed Jonathan?' Christopher burst out. 'Eh? Ben? Bonnie? Haven't you solved the mystery yet? Well – after my talk with his wife yesterday, I can tell you who I'm pretty sure it was. Must have been.' He stopped and waited for a reaction.

'Valerie!' Simmy remembered. 'You haven't said a single word about what happened between you and her. I forgot all about it. What did she say?' His silence on the subject felt sneaky to her. As if he'd been withholding something important. 'Why didn't you tell Moxon you'd seen her? Come on, damn it – you can't just drop a bombshell like that and then go quiet.'

'We were talking about Flo,' said Bonnie in a quiet voice. 'And Christopher stopped us. Was that deliberate, I wonder? A diversion, for some reason?'

Ben gave her one of his admiring glances. 'Good work, Bon,' he murmured. He addressed Christopher. 'How about it? What's the sense in muddying the waters now?'

'You're being ridiculous,' said the auctioneer. 'All I was trying to do was get Simmy to stop agonising over that woman and her infant. She's got it into her head that she's somehow responsible and should offer them a home for the indefinite future. All I was doing was try to bring us back to the matter in hand.'

'For heaven's sake!' Simmy was manifesting a rare flash of anger. 'Is Valerie relevant, or isn't she?'

'She's sure it was Nick who did it,' said Christopher. 'She thinks he could have wangled the alibi, calling in favours and so forth. She's never liked him and thinks he's quite capable of violence. There was no need for me to say anything to Moxon about it, because she'd already gone to the Penrith lot.'

'Oh.' There was a silence, as each person digested this. A hint of disappointment hovered in the room.

'So does that let me off the hook?' Scott Penrose asked, with a slight smirk. 'Because if so, I really need to go and find my wife and daughter.'

'You haven't seemed very worried about her up to now,' Bonnie observed.

'And you haven't mentioned that the police were called to your house, either,' said Simmy. 'She phoned and texted me, sounding frightened and desperate. You were heard shouting at her and threatening to keep her locked in the house.'

'Who the hell told you that? How could you possibly know what went on between me and my wife?'

'I don't know exactly, of course. But what I do know contradicts quite a bit of what you've just said. There's a lot more going on than we think, Ben.' She pointed at his notepad. 'There's another connection somewhere. Maybe more than one. Something we've been missing all along.'

'Dogs? Stumpwork? Something that happened a year ago? The auction house?' Ben was going down a list on his pad, item by item. 'I've got all that. I've got that Nick had a grudge against Jonathan, as did Mrs Leeson, because he might have kicked her dog.' He looked up. 'And CaniCare went back on their promise, according to Daphne.'

Scott Penrose scowled. 'The animal was on its last legs. It would never have been rehomed. Sometimes the kindest thing is to put them down.'

'You remember it, then?' Ben gave the man a probing look. 'A year after the event with all the old ladies and dogs you must have dealt with since then – and still you remember Mrs Leeson.'

Penrose said nothing.

Ben turned to Christopher. 'You were involved, weren't you – right back at the start? When the old lady died?'

'Haven't I already said so? My parents knew Philip. They suggested I could help with the old lady's things.'

'You told me you didn't meet him until a few months ago. You did it all on the phone,' said Simmy.

'That's right. So?'

Yet again, Ben scrutinised his notes. 'The van,' he said. 'A charity van was in the cul-de-sac on Monday morning. Collecting stuff for a jumble sale. Was it somebody from CaniCare?'

304

'We think it might have been the murderer,' said Bonnie. 'It does seem to connect, you see. Doesn't it?'

'It could have been any one of a dozen charities, on perfectly innocent business,' said Scott carelessly. 'So what?' The echo of Christopher's challenging *So?* was impossible to miss.

'Come on, mate,' Christopher interrupted. 'You can't just dismiss it like that. If your charity is implicated, then the van's a vital part of the picture. The police will know from the witness which charity it was that was holding the jumble sale, then you could be in for a grilling.'

'Christopher's right,' Ben endorsed.

Simmy had lapsed into thought. 'Why did you demand to talk to me?' she asked Penrose. 'When you should be out there trying to find your wife and child.'

'I needed you to convince this boy – and his little friend – that I did not kill the Woolley man. I wanted an adult who would hear me out and realise what nonsense the whole thing is. And no way am I going "out there" looking for Florence. I haven't got a tracker on her car, you know. She'll be all right. She'll come home tomorrow, you see.'

'You've got two cars, then?' said Ben, as if this in itself was cause for suspicion.

'Yes,' said Scott shortly.

'Your parents are back,' said Bonnie, lifting her head. 'I heard the car. And we should see if Tanya's okay.'

'Tanya!' Simmy was horrified at her own neglectfulness. She should have enquired for the girl at the very start. 'Is she all right?'

'She says the wound is throbbing, and she felt a bit warm,' said Ben. 'But they slathered it with antiseptic cream, so she'll be fine.'

'I should go and see her. Where is she?' Simmy got out of the armchair. 'Upstairs?'

'She went to bed. You're too late, if Bonnie's right that my parents are back. They can take over now.'

Bonnie was right. The front door closed loudly, and voices were heard in the hall. 'We should go,' said Simmy to Christopher. 'It's half past ten.' She found herself feeling nervous about facing the Harkness parents. Her reason for being there was flimsy, and she had done nothing useful regarding the injured Tanya. Helen had not been particularly friendly when they had spoken the day before.

Christopher followed her out of the room, where they found Ben's father in the hallway. Helen was just visible at the top of the stairs. 'Hello?' said the man, raising his eyebrows. 'You're Simmy Brown, aren't you? Is something the matter? What time is it?' He looked tired and slightly confused. 'Must be late. I'm knackered. School again tomorrow.' He sighed. 'Is Tanya all right?' he added.

'I'm afraid I haven't seen her. Ben asked me to come round and talk to a man who turned up here this evening. We got carried away talking and didn't give Tanya a thought. I'm sure she's fine – she'd have come down otherwise.'

'A man? What man? Is this part of Ben's latest venture into solving a murder?'

'I'm afraid so,' said Simmy, suddenly seeing the whole business through the somewhat jaded eyes of a schoolteacher nearing retirement. 'And I'm afraid we haven't got very far, after an hour of talking.'

Then Helen Harkness came to the top of the stairs. 'David – call an ambulance. Tanya's unconscious. I think it might be septicaemia.'

# *Chapter Twenty-Four*

It was almost midnight when Simmy and Christopher got back to Troutbeck. Self-reproach had reduced Simmy to a quivering wreck. Septicaemia had been a growing terror in recent times. Renamed sepsis, much to Angie Straw's disgust, it had killed a soap opera character, as well as one or two high-profile local figures. 'Why didn't we *think*?' she moaned. 'We just sat downstairs talking to that man and forgot all about the poor girl. What if she dies, Chris? Did you see that ambulance woman's face? I'm sure she thought it was touch and go.'

'She won't die,' said Christopher. 'She wasn't really unconscious. Just a bit out of it.'

'Delirious. Terrified. Hardly able to breathe,' Simmy corrected him. 'And Helen's going to blame me – quite rightly.'

'She'll blame herself more. She should never have gone out. She's the mother, after all.'

'It makes all that talk about Jonathan seem so silly now. Childish. We didn't even get anywhere, did we? I can't remember it all now, but I don't think we made any headway at all.'

'I guess not. It wasn't a very focused discussion. We never even told them what Moxon had said. We were all over the place. Everyone kept interrupting and changing the subject.'

'That was mostly you,' she reminded him.

'I never was very good at sticking to a logical thread,' he admitted. 'I'm hopeless in an argument.'

'Oh, I hope Tanya's going to be all right,' she moaned. 'It's so scary, thinking of what could happen. There's all this talk about sepsis these days, you'd think Ben would have realised the risk. He must be feeling awful.'

'It'll all be better in the morning,' Christopher said, with little conviction.

'Hmm. Well, whatever happens I'm going to see my mum and dad after work tomorrow. I've been a very neglectful daughter. They might want to talk about our wedding. Knowing my dad, he's probably found us a house to buy by now.'

'Are they going to think they've gained a son?'

'They always did think you were a sort of son, anyway. My mother's always been possessive about you, having known you since you were about two hours old.'

'My head hurts,' he complained. 'We didn't have a proper supper, and there's been far too much talk. And I can feel that policeman hovering over me, trying to decide whether or not I'm a murderer.'

'I'll make us a milky drink and we can go straight to bed,' she consoled him.

But they both slept badly. At three in the morning, Simmy suddenly said, 'We never once mentioned the Pruitt man, did we? Ben's sure to have him on his flowchart somewhere. He's just as likely to have had some sort of grudge against Jonathan as anybody else.'

'Erghh?' said Christopher.

'And what about that wife of his? Beverley? She seemed to know everybody and everything that was going on. And you know what – she must have deliberately tried to fob us off about the stumpwork, on Saturday. She told us all sorts of nonsense about it, and Jonathan.'

Christopher came more widely awake. 'Beverley Pruitt? She's an amazing woman. Didn't I tell you? She does a lot of work for the National Trust, repairing ancient tapestries and so forth. Oliver was furious with himself, and me, when we never thought to ask for her opinion on Jonathan's stumpwork.'

'What?' Simmy sat up. 'But isn't that crucially important?' There were blurry threads inside her head, struggling to connect into a proper sequence. 'She must have known Mrs Leeson – they lived so close to each other. She probably knew all about the embroidery. Good

310

God, Chris! The woman told outright *lies* to me and Ben, in that case.'

'Lie down,' he ordered. 'Lie down and go to sleep. It'll all seem clearer in the morning.'

She did her best and finally drifted off shortly before four. When the alarm went off at seven, they were both in the deepest of sleeps.

'Jonathan's been dead a week,' said Christopher lugubriously, when he finally stirred into wakefulness. 'And I still don't believe it really happened.'

'I'll have to phone Ben. Or maybe Bonnie. Or should I wait to see if she comes to work as usual?' The dithering struck her as a bad omen for the day, and possibly the week.

'Why wouldn't she?' He was walking round the kitchen with a mug of coffee, waiting for the toast to pop up.

'She can't have got much sleep. Did she go home, I wonder?'

'Doesn't she sleep in Ben's room these days?'

'I'm not sure. I rather think not, actually. As far as I'm aware, they don't have sex. That might have changed, of course.'

He shook his head in bewilderment. 'Is there something wrong with one of them? Or both?'

'No, of course not. They absolutely adore each other – you can see that. But when I mentioned it to Ben, he said he didn't think Bonnie was ready. Something like that. I knew exactly what he meant. And they seem to have a different take on all that than we did. It's a different generation.'

'No comment,' said Christopher warily.

'You should go. You need to go home for a clean shirt and pants. What happened to your packing? You usually plan better than you did this time.'

'I was distracted. I still am. Did I dream it, or did you wake me up in the small hours to talk about Beverley Pruitt?'

She laughed. 'I think it was real – but I'd forgotten all about it. I still feel half-asleep. We only had about four hours, didn't we?'

'At most. There was a lot of tossing and turning between two and three, I seem to remember.'

'And I've got to go and see my parents this evening,' she reminded herself. 'I won't be staying long. Bed by nine tonight.'

'I got the impression you thought Bev might be significant. When did you talk to her anyway?'

'In your cafe on Saturday. She told us quite a lot about the stumpwork and how the V&A bought it, and Oliver had no idea what it was actually worth. Because if she had, she'd have told Kathleen, and they'd have got a proper price for it, a year or more ago. Wouldn't they?'

'Mm,' mumbled Christopher.

Simmy went on, 'You think Beverley saw it back then, do you? So, what would she feel when she knew Jonathan had got it and sold it for all that money?'

'I assume she never saw it. She can't have done. Why would she?' He looked away from her, out of the window. 'I've gotta go. I'll eat the toast in the car. I'm starving.'

'Right.' Already she was speaking to Ben in her head,

adding to his notes, drawing new connections. The urgency and eagerness behind it were new to her, and she was still unsure of the reasons. 'I'll phone you – or you phone me. When will I see you?' This last question pulled her up. They had no plans whatsoever for the coming week. It was still June, and there was still a promise of summer weather and glorious evenings. 'We should go somewhere nice,' she added vaguely.

'Where?'

'What about Patterdale?' The name came to her unbidden, apropos of nothing. She had seen the place barely twice, but remembered the fabulous scenery, the unpretentious pubs, forcing visitors to take whatever came their way, with few concessions. 'The first nice evening, we should go there.'

He was altogether bemused. 'Why? Are you thinking we might buy a house there or something?'

'I wasn't thinking that, but—' The idea took root instantly. 'Wouldn't it be amazing if we could? It's sort of midway between Keswick and Windermere, isn't it?'

'No. It's on a road that goes nowhere, narrow and winding and slow. When the road was blocked between me and Grasmere with that landslide, everybody had to go that way, and it nearly drove them mad. The only time I've heard anyone mention Patterdale, it's been to curse the small roads and impossible traffic.'

'But it won't be like that now the road's open again, will it?'

'I can't talk about it now. I'll be late as it is.' He was pulling the front door open, juggling his toast, phone and

313

car keys. 'We'll talk later today.' He almost ran to his car, with a brief wave before getting in and driving off.

Simmy couldn't blame him. The whole weekend had kept him rushing from point to point at other people's urging. The hours spent auctioning antiques from the relative peace of his rostrum must seem like an interlude of blessed serenity in retrospect. For Simmy herself, those same hours devoted to watching and admiring him felt very much like that. Whatever scams and deceptions might have been going on amongst the bidders – and she had seen no sign of anything like that – did not affect her delight in the whole process. The days of *Lovejoy* when every item was a fake, and dealers crept around at night trying to kill each other, had seemed pure fantasy as she sat there with Ben.

But a dealer had been killed, here and now. In Grasmere a week ago, he had been viciously strangled by a person unknown. It was an awful truth that made her angry and afraid. And it was very probably down to Ben and Bonnie to rectify the situation by identifying the perpetrator. Which they might well still believe was Scott Penrose, if she had properly understood their drift the previous evening.

As she prepared to leave the house, she did her best to focus on her business. Monday morning in the shop was traditionally quiet. Simmy and Bonnie would review the events of Saturday and Sunday and plan the coming week. The income she derived from the shop was modest but adequate. She knew she ought to be introducing new lines, diversifying into baskets, small garden features, imaginative indoor displays. Every now and then she would have a creative burst, generally impelled by Bonnie, and then lapse back into familiar routine again.

Flowers could represent such a huge variety of human emotions, integrally woven into all the major emotional landmarks. They brought her into contact with people at pivotal moments in their lives, with high drama often not far away. Which fleeting musings quickly brought her back to the unfinished business with Flo Penrose and her baby. There had been no phone calls during the night, and no texts were waiting to be read. Had Scott found them, then, with everything readily reconciled?

The contents of her mind felt like a crazy conveyor belt of urgent topics, each one coming into focus for a few minutes, to be pushed aside by the next in line. After Flo came Tanya. Then Beverley Pruitt, followed by Daphne Schofield. They all came insistently to the forefront, their roles in Ben's investigations still not clarified. There was poor dying Philip, as well. And chief suspect Nick. Valerie Woolley, too – who Christopher so oddly seemed to set aside until she was almost forgotten, only to reintroduce her as a diversion when it suited him. There was Malcolm Pruitt, and the CaniCare charity.

And there was the dead Jonathan and the highly valuable piece of stumpwork.

What hope could there be for any kind of work-based concentration, with all this going on? Any one of these claims on her attention was enough to drive all thought of floristry from her mind.

She saw nothing of the mild June morning over Windermere as she drove to work. The fells dotted with sheep and enthusiastic walkers were an unnoticed backdrop to her thoughts. There was one big notion waiting behind all the others – the one that had prevented her from sleeping peacefully that night. Doggedly, she kept it away, encouraging the parade of names and faces, motives and mendacities to obscure it.

But Bonnie Lawson was made of stronger stuff, and within five minutes of arriving at the shop, having conveyed reassuring news about Tanya, she was giving it voice.

'Simmy,' she said, in a tone that could not be ignored. 'Ben says, have you thought that an awful lot of the evidence points to Christopher not being altogether honest with us, or the police? He says it's obviously not definite, and he knows you won't want to admit it, but when it's all there on paper, it really looks a bit bad.'

Standing beside a collection of buckets containing cut flowers, Simmy froze. Several instincts fought within her. Defensive anger, scornful dismissal, pained argument were all quite acceptable options. Instead, she said, 'I have, yes. It's what Moxon came to say again yesterday. It's been hanging over us all along, really – but we wouldn't admit it at first.'

'So – what if it's true? You have to face every possibility, however horrible it might be. People never entirely know each other, do they? You can't say "So-and-so would never do such a thing in a million years" because they would. They *do*, sometimes. I mean – every murderer probably has a wife or sister or somebody who refuses to believe they did it.'

'For heaven's sake – surely nobody's accusing him of *murder*. It's nowhere near as bad as that. And anyway, what am I meant to do about it? I'm going to marry the man. I love him, and he loves me. We fit perfectly together. But I do understand that I don't know what he's thinking much of the time. I'd even agree that he's been rather odd over the past week and has said one or two things that I don't believe can be true. I think he might well be hiding something about Jonathan. But I am as sure as I can possibly be that he didn't kill him. And I'm also fairly sure that he doesn't know who did. Not for certain, anyway.'

'You think he has an idea?'

'I think he does. And it must be somebody he likes, or relies on, or has some shady link with, that he doesn't want made public.'

'Ben's coming in later. His mother's in a real state about Tanya, and she's blaming him. The hospital said another hour and she might have died. They spent hours keeping all her organs going, right through the night. But she's all right again now. The infection's almost gone already.'

'So, it was septicaemia, then?'

'So they say. All because of that cut. It happens really fast, you see. She was fine yesterday afternoon, and then just went all droopy after that.'

'Her parents shouldn't have left her. They must know that Ben's not terribly good at practical stuff.'

'Helen's pretty hopeless when it comes to anything medical, as well. So is David. The whole family's awfully airy-fairy in some ways. And I'm just as bad. I still keep seeing all that blood . . .' She looked at the floor where Tanya had bled. 'You've cleaned it all up, I see.'

'It was nowhere near as bad as you said. Gosh – it seems *days* ago now. Such a lot keeps happening.'

'What about the woman and the baby?' Bonnie asked. 'Wasn't that weird, the way the man didn't seem to care what happened to them? All he could think about was what Ben said to him, and how he had to prove he wasn't the killer?'

'Is that what he was doing?' Simmy thought about it. 'I suppose it was. He seemed desperate to defend himself – and I still think he's been horrible to Flo in some way. You should have seen her texts yesterday.'

'I expect she'll be okay,' said Bonnie vaguely.

'Let's hope so. I worry about that poor little baby.'

'Babies are very tough, according to Corinne.'

Simmy put both hands to her head. 'I keep going over everything, again and again. In the middle of the night, I was quite certain that it must have been Beverley Pruitt. But Christopher doesn't agree with me.'

'Why did you think that?'

'I don't remember now. She was so upfront with me and Ben on Saturday, it wouldn't really make much sense. Unless she was bluffing or lying. Did we tell you about that?'

'Not in any detail. So tell me now. No – wait till Ben gets here, although that might not be for a while. I think they've all gone back to bed for a couple of hours. Except David, of course. He's got to go and take Year Eleven on an outing to Barrow or somewhere.'

'Poor man. Couldn't he get out of it, on compassionate grounds?'

Bonnie shrugged. 'I doubt it.'

'What about you? Aren't you shattered as well?'

The girl grinned. 'Actually, I fell asleep on the sofa, about two minutes after you and Christopher left. I missed the ambulance coming. Just crashed out like a dead thing. Woke up at seven with a blanket over me, and desperate for the loo.' She looked down at herself. 'These are the same clothes I had on yesterday. Do they look really, really crumpled?'

'Not at all. Christopher's got the same problem. He forgot to pack a bag before coming to mine yesterday.'

A customer diverted them for the next ten minutes, followed by two orders on the computer and a list of upcoming funerals, with times by which flowers had to be delivered. The normal weekly processes were underway, and it was eleven o'clock before there was another lull. 'I've got to go down to Newby Bridge this afternoon,' Simmy said. 'I'd better get cracking on the order. They want a large spray in purples and pink.'

'I know,' said Bonnie. 'It's somebody's fortieth birthday.'

'Life goes on,' said Simmy, for no good reason. Again, she was reminded of Flo and baby Lucy May, and wondered with fresh concern where they might have found a bed for the night.

When a text announced itself, she hoped it would be the missing woman, with news that all was well, but instead it was Christopher. 'Summoned to Penrith. Will phone when it's finished.'

'Good God!' cried Simmy.

Bonnie looked up from the flower buckets. 'What?'

'He says he's got to go to Penrith. He must mean the police want to ask yet more questions. That's ridiculous after seeing Moxon yesterday.'

Before Bonnie could speak, the door pinged and Ben Harkness appeared. 'Hey, Ben,' the girl greeted him. 'Christopher has been taken off to Penrith again. It's all happening.'

'Tell me about it.' His face was pale and downward-drooping. He sighed and dropped into the chair in front of Simmy's computer. 'I think I've cracked it, though.' He extracted a folder from his ever-present bag and opened it. 'The Pruitts. If Penrose didn't do it, then it's got to be one of them – or both. The woman's an expert needlewoman, and she must have known Mrs Leeson. It's all fallen into place, knowing that.'

The uncanny echo of Simmy's night-time inspirations made her yelp. 'That's what I thought. I woke Chris in the middle of the night to tell him. But how did you know?'

'The Internet,' said Ben wearily. 'She restores antique textiles, including stumpwork. She must have known what it was worth and decided to get it for herself somehow. Then when Jonathan beat her to it, she went mad with rage and killed him. She's big and strong enough – and could probably have taken Jonathan by surprise. I mean – whoever did it managed to get his belt off him, before using it to throttle him. How would they manage that, unless he trusted them and thought they wanted the belt for some harmless purpose?'

320

'They could have knocked him out first,' said Bonnie.

'We never mentioned the Pruitts last night,' said Simmy.

'We were stupid not to.'

'It looks as if Moxon was right to warn me and Chris, though,' Simmy concluded. 'They must think they've got more reason than ever to believe it was him.'

'What exactly did he say yesterday?' Ben asked. 'You haven't told us.'

She gave a rapid summary, the gist of which was that Malcolm Pruitt had done his best to incriminate Christopher, and the police seemed to be taking it seriously.

'We should call Moxo and show him what I've worked out,' said Ben. 'Then he can call the Penrith people and get them to release Christopher. I did think he looked a bit dodgy, I must admit.' He hesitated, giving Simmy an uncertain glance.

'It's okay,' said Bonnie. 'I already told her there's a lot that points at Christopher. She took it really well.'

'Well done,' approved her swain.

'She also thinks there must be something Christopher isn't telling us. Something about the auction business, probably. Something he knows about the stumpwork.'

'Hey – I am here, you know,' Simmy protested. 'I can speak for myself – and I didn't say any of that last part.'

'Any news of the runaway wife?' asked Ben, with a meaningful expression. 'If she really has run away, that is.'

'What does that mean?' Simmy was feeling very much as she had the previous evening, perhaps more so. Names were once again flying around, with hints of conspiracies

321

and concealments. 'You're not accusing *her* of murder, are you?'

'It did cross my mind,' he smiled. 'I promise you, I've gone through absolutely everybody, including Daphne Schofield and Valerie Woolley.'

'But not poor old Philip, I hope,' said Simmy impatiently.

'No, not Philip. But he very probably knows a lot more than he's told you, as well.'

The conversation took place in bursts of high intensity, between customers and phone calls and a big delivery of fresh flowers. Bonnie carried the new blooms into the back room and set about sorting them, bringing batches through to the shop to be displayed. Ben ran through his findings in exhaustive detail. The Pruitts were causing some difficulty, with much more speculation than hard evidence informing his theories. The behaviour of Scott Penrose, when looked at from a degree of distance and detachment, struck them all as bizarre. Ben repeated his suspicion that some kind of smokescreen was in operation. 'He should have been more worried about his wife and baby,' he kept saying.

Simmy's attention was painfully split between Christopher and Tanya, with Flo also nagging at her. 'How long will they take to question Chris?' she wondered. 'I can't bear not knowing what they're saying to him.'

'It probably depends on how forthcoming he is,' said Ben. 'If they think he's holding something back, they'll keep at him for quite a while.'

'I could phone Moxon and see if he knows what's happening.'

'You could, but it won't do any good.'

'You should go home,' Bonnie told him, shortly before one o'clock. 'See how Tanya is, and patch things up with your mum. You're too tired to think straight, anyway. You've said the same things about eight times already, and it makes less sense each time.'

He laughed in rueful agreement. 'Okay, then. Can you tell me if you hear anything from Christopher? Or anybody else. It's all going to kick off today, I can feel it. There'll be an arrest by sundown, I bet you anything.'

Simmy delivered the pink-and-purple flowers to Newby Bridge, and drove back through Bowness, as heedless of her surroundings as she had been earlier in the day. *What if it was Christopher?* The question kept running through her mind and churning through her guts. Would she still marry him, and wait for his release from prison? Of course not. If he had committed murder, that would make him an entirely different person from the one she thought she knew. How could she even be giving the thought space in her head? However tricksy the antique business might be, with labyrinthine transactions going on behind the scenes, she could not believe it ever ended in cold-blooded murder. But it *was* tricksy. And Christopher had gone to Grasmere to find the man who cleared houses and did dark deals, giving an explanation that had felt weak from the start. Had he, along with a number of others, been so enraged, even humiliated, by the startlingly large sales figure for the piece of Jacobean embroidery that it made him want to kill the man responsible? Had there been some kind of horrible conspiracy, involving both the Pruitts, and possibly even Nick the tax avoider?

And where was Florence Penrose?

# Chapter Twenty-Five

'The police did a re-enactment,' said Christopher, at five o'clock that afternoon. 'It was remarkably thorough. They reconstructed the exact times, with all the neighbours where they were last Monday. They had me and Malcolm Pruitt doing exactly what we did then.'

'So, they didn't take you to Penrith, after all?' said Ben. He had been invited to the debriefing by Simmy, the street door firmly closed, and the four of them drinking tea and talking intently at the back of the shop.

'They did, actually. They explained what was going to happen and then we all trooped down to Grasmere.'

'Was Moxon there?' asked Simmy.

Christopher shook his head. 'Didn't see him all day.'

'So – let me get this straight. They knew from the start that it wasn't you who killed Jonathan – right? They took you into their confidence and got you to play the part of the man who found the body.' Ben was tapping his teeth with his pen, having yet again brought all his notes and flowcharts and spreadsheets.

'Not at all. Right to the end I thought it was some sort of trap. They watched me like hawks, waiting for some contradiction or inconsistency. They made me go over and over my reason for being in Grasmere in the first place, and when I last spoke to Jonathan and what I knew about the stumpwork.'

'That came into it, then?'

'Very much so.' Christopher flushed and glanced uneasily at Simmy. 'There's quite a lot I haven't told you, I'm sorry to say.'

'Does that mean you knew all along who killed Jonathan?' asked Ben.

'No. Absolutely not. I still can't see exactly how it must have happened. At least . . . I suppose I can, if I think about it.'

'So, they've made an arrest? Did you see that happen? When did they let you go? Come *on*, man. Tell us everything.' Ben's impatience was reflected by Bonnie and echoed by Simmy.

'All right, don't bully me. It's complicated, okay? And it's not finished yet.'

All three stared at him hungrily, wanting the whole

story, while also desperate to hear the name of the killer. They stood around him, where he sat on the only chair on the premises, the very picture of a reluctant witness having the truth dragged out of him. 'They had everything noted down, like the script of a play. Vehicle movements, actual words spoken – as close as they could get to what happened. Malcolm Pruitt got a real grilling, the same as me. There was a woman detective constable, recording it all. They got local shopkeepers to try and do the same as they did last week, as well.'

'Vehicles,' Bonnie repeated slowly. 'That charity van, collecting for a jumble sale, as well?'

Christopher nodded, with a smile of approval. 'You're getting warm,' he said.

'CaniCare! I knew it!' yelped Simmy. 'I was right all along.'

'You very nearly were,' said her fiancé. 'Apparently. As I keep saying, I don't know the final details. All that happened afterwards, while I was sitting in a police car at the other end of Grasmere.'

'Was it a fake? The stumpwork? Did Beverley Pruitt forge it, or whatever the word is for needlework?' Bonnie had pushed forward, claiming this new theory as her very own.

'No, of course it wasn't a fake. The V&A person would soon have spotted it if it was. But it was never Kathleen Leeson's. When Jonathan brought it to us to sell, he had to explain where he got it, and he just said he'd spotted it in the CaniCare shop a while back. I went along with it, like a fool, and let it go at that.'

'But – didn't Daphne Schofield say she'd seen it in Mrs Leeson's house?' said Simmy.

'She did, because Jon had put it there, with all her other junk, as a way of hiding it. After the old lady died, Jonathan already had it in his possession, and knew it was worth a fair bit. And he couldn't tell the true story of where he'd got it from.'

'Which was *where*?' Bonnie and Simmy asked simultaneously.

'I don't know, but I'm guessing it was some poor innocent car boot seller, who might well cut up rough if he or she spotted it when it was sold. So, he had the crackpot idea of letting it go to charity, with a lot of other stuff from the Leeson house, then buying it back for a few quid, all fair and square. That would give it a proper provenance, and the car boot person would never make the connection.'

'What a risk, though!' Ben blew out his cheeks. 'What if someone else got to it first? Or if the charity people recognised what it was worth? Didn't Scott say they have experts to come and value things they're given, before they put it up for sale?'

'Yes, they do. And Jonathan was one of those experts. The trouble was, there were people involved in CaniCare who knew Jon's attitude towards dogs and objected to him on those grounds. Sounds bonkers, I know, but everybody's heard the way he kicked Mrs Leeson's dog, which set her against him. She made enough fuss for most people in Grasmere to know about it. It made him a hated figure amongst the old ladies who volunteer for CaniCare, and he was blacklisted.'

'So – what happened?'

'He sent Beverley Pruitt to do it for him. She could at least go through the textiles, with her special knowledge. She bought the stumpwork on his behalf.'

'But she knew how valuable it was and demanded a share of the proceeds,' Ben interrupted. 'And when he didn't pay up, she throttled him.'

'No, she didn't. Don't jump ahead. She gave the charity twenty-five quid for it, saying it was exactly what she needed for a little collection she was making, and that it was probably only worth twenty or less. She took two or three other things at the same time, to muddy the water.'

'Hang on,' said Bonnie. 'How do you know about that?'

'Jon told me,' said Christopher simply. 'It's what I've just told you. He said he couldn't give the full facts, and how would it be if we fudged it a bit. I didn't take much persuading, I must admit. I was new and wanted to keep in everybody's good books. We decided to sit on it for a year or so, then say it was originally Mrs Leeson's, if anybody queried it, because she was dead by then and no relatives existed to contradict us.'

Simmy stared at him as she processed the implications of Christopher's confession. 'That makes you an accessory to a crime,' she realised. 'Good, God, Chris!'

'I know it does,' he said softly. 'But it's not such a terrible one, is it? Not like murder.'

'Hardly a crime at all,' said Ben. 'Not if Jonathan really did buy the thing in the first place. Which it sounds as if he did.'

'He never said for sure, one way or the other,' Christopher admitted. 'But wherever it came from, he needed to keep it covered up for a while. That's what started the whole ludicrous business in the first place.'

'So, who else knew the truth?' asked Ben.

'One of the volunteers at the Ambleside shop soon put two and two together and told Scott Penrose. Then things got very nasty.'

Simmy wanted to crawl away and analyse her feelings in private. But first there were still more questions to be settled. With an effort, she asked, 'Have they found Flo yet? She's still not answering her phone. I tried just after lunch today.'

'I don't think she's in any danger,' said Christopher calmly. 'I was just coming to her, in fact.'

'Good,' said Bonnie, who was beginning to look worried. 'Simmy's very concerned about that poor little baby.'

'This is where I have to start guessing,' said Christopher. 'I overheard some comments from a couple of police people, which sounded as if the drama at Banerigg yesterday was mostly staged. I got the impression they'd worked it out and weren't at all bothered about the safety of the woman. All that kerfuffle last night with Penrose was carefully planned.'

'What?' Simmy was floundering. 'Why?'

'Think about it. He knew his wife had been seeing you and didn't know for sure what she'd told you. He might have heard that you were pally with Moxon, as well. So, he needed to quell any suspicions you might have.'

All three of his listeners fell quiet at the implication. 'So – are you saying the killer was Scott Penrose?' asked Ben slowly. 'Just like that?'

'I'm saying I think it must be. It's not Nick, or the Pruitts, or Valerie. Process of elimination.'

'Hmm,' said Ben. 'I wonder.'

'You left yourself out of the list,' said Bonnie.

Christopher flinched, and then leant forward to glare at her. 'I told you – they've got nothing on me.'

'Except collusion to sell a valuable artwork of very doubtful provenance,' said Ben. 'And being in possession of knowledge of a grudge against Jonathan as a result. You would have known that the CaniCare people would have realised their loss as soon as the sale results were announced. And I don't see that Beverley Pruitt is altogether in the clear, either. There was a scam going on, however you look at it.'

'Lots of people had grudges against Jon. It goes with the territory.'

'And Scott Penrose's must be rather recent,' said Simmy. 'Only since the sale two weeks ago.'

'Unless it's been happening regularly, of course,' said Ben. 'What if Jonathan had been systematically ripping off the charity shops around the whole area? It's easy enough, from the looks of it.'

Simmy was still fighting to stay focused. 'I went to the Ambleside shop,' she said suddenly. 'The man there was complaining at the huge job of sorting donated stuff fast enough. There was a great stack of it in the back room. I suggested a jumble sale.' She frowned. 'Do charities run jumble sales? He didn't seem very taken with the idea.'

'Useful,' nodded Ben with a patronising air. 'Seeing it for yourself, I mean.'

Bonnie was watching Christopher. 'That's right, isn't it, about the scam?' she challenged him. 'And you knew all about it.'

He attempted a flippant reply. 'You might think that. I couldn't possibly comment.'

Simmy sighed. 'I've got to go,' she said. 'I promised to go and see my parents.'

'And my mum told me to say she wants to see you this evening,' said Ben. 'I guess it's about Tanya.'

'And I should go home and check in with Corinne,' said Bonnie. 'I need fresh clothes, as well.'

Again, they all looked at Christopher. 'Well, I don't have to be anywhere,' he said. 'They'll have got on without me at work, and my flat can look after itself.' He faced Simmy, with an expression of defiance. 'I guess we need to talk.'

'Tomorrow,' she said. 'It can wait until tomorrow.'

Then his phone warbled, and he answered it with an obvious feeling of dread. 'Right . . . Thank you . . . Yes, I'll get back to you tomorrow. Thank you again.' He looked up at Simmy. 'It's Philip. He died at three o'clock this afternoon,' he said. 'And I'll have to arrange his funeral.'

Simmy fulfilled her promise to her parents and was there before six-thirty. The summer season had meant that every room in their B&B had been full for many weeks, with relentless washing, cooking, cleaning and organising as a result. 'We double-booked the big room last week,' said Angie, with an angry look at her husband. 'He took the message and never told me about it. It was enormously embarrassing.'

'You should let an agent handle all that for you,' said Simmy.

'It sounds sensible but would be hugely irritating in practice. As it is, I can weed out the obvious troublemakers. And it would all be done by Internet robots who wouldn't understand the nuances. To them a dog is a dog – but I like to know the size of the thing before I let it into one of my bedrooms.'

'Can I stay for supper? I've hardly had anything all day.'

'You look as if you haven't slept for a week, either. What's the matter with you?'

'Well . . .' She had no wish to try to explain the complexities of the past day, let alone week. 'It's been a bit chaotic lately. I went to Christopher's auction on Saturday, and I don't seem to have taken a breath since then.'

'It'll be that murder, I suppose. The man who was killed because he stole some antique embroidery. Did they catch who did it yet?'

'What makes you think it was because of the embroidery?'

Angie eyed her daughter with an expression that said, *Don't play games with me*. 'It just seems obvious, I suppose.'

'Does it? I don't think the police are finding it very obvious. They've been doing one of those crime reconstructions in Grasmere today. Chris had to go and do everything all over again.'

'Poor chap. That must have been upsetting.'

Simmy paused. For the first time, she considered how it must have been for him to go back into the house, and – what? Handle a dummy that was standing in for the murder victim? Did it reawaken the original trauma? Or was he too busy trying to remember his exact movements for any emotion to intrude? 'I don't think it was, actually,' she said. 'He's been rather odd, one way and another. And he has told me rather a lot of fibs. I've got a terrible lot to think about.'

Angie took this a lot more seriously than expected. 'Sit down,' she ordered. They were in the big room set aside for guests to use on rainy days. It contained games, spare clothes for children, books, old towels and much more. The chairs were saggy and soft and indestructible. 'You're not thinking Christopher has something to do with the crime, are you?' demanded Simmy's mother. 'Is that why you look so ravaged? Now listen to me. You're going to marry the man. That means you have to know you can trust him completely. There's obviously an issue there, thanks to Tony going off the rails as he did—'

'That's nothing to do with it. Absolutely *nothing*,' Simmy interrupted.

'All right. Good. So, what's the matter, then? You've known Christopher literally all your life. If anything, you know each other too well. There's very little mystery between you. So, what's going on here?'

'You're overreacting,' Simmy protested. 'What sparked this off?'

'We've been talking about you,' came her father's voice from the doorway. 'We think it's most unfortunate that there's been this business in Grasmere, just at the very moment you've decided to marry. The two things are going to get entangled, in a bad way. And the way you've kept us in the dark has been a worry, as well.'

'I was just terribly *busy*. There were no secrets or anything like that.'

'So why hasn't he come here with you now? Why isn't he eating with us? You realise we haven't seen him since you got engaged? Is this the way it's going to be from now on – sidelining your parents?' It was Angie speaking. 'We've been rather hurt, I can tell you.'

Simmy recalled her father's phone message, referring to himself as 'Your peevish old dad'. Its significance had passed her by at the time. Now it hinted at self-pity, reproach, wounded feelings.

'I'm sorry,' she said. 'I know it's your busy time. But I'm here now, and it has only been a week.'

'Here on your own,' said Angie again. 'Why is that?'

'No special reason. We just . . . went our separate ways. I think he needed to get back to work, or phone them, at least. He spent most of the day helping the police.'

'So where will he eat?'

'I don't know. A pub, I suppose.'

'Not good enough,' said Russell. 'Anyone would think you don't care.'

'I just . . .' She tailed off helplessly, unable to explain

335

herself. She hadn't been aware of a need to get away from her fiancé until now. And he had made it easy for her, slipping off to his car with hardly a word. They had phones; they could make arrangements at a moment's notice. Either he would spend another night with her in Troutbeck, or he would go home to Keswick, keeping her informed of his movements. His movements had slipped quite a way down her list of urgent preoccupations. 'I'm supposed to go to see Helen Harkness after I leave here,' she said. 'So, I'll just stay an hour or so.'

'What does that have to do with anything?' demanded Angie. Then she softened. 'Look, love, I can see that it's all been a bit too much. I heard that young Tanya hurt herself on Saturday. But the main thing is how you and Christopher get through all this. And I can tell you, as someone who's been like a second mother to him at times, he is much too *normal* to be a murderer. It might sound daft, but it simply isn't in him. He hasn't got the imagination, or even the courage. He'd never be able to hide it afterwards, either. He's just a pleasant, affectionate, uncomplicated soul, with little in the way of hidden depths. What you choose to see as suspicious behaviour is nothing more than bewilderment, and probably sheer terror at being so close to such a terrible event. Don't forget his own father was killed not long ago. That must have shaken his world more than you realise. Now this as well – he doesn't know where he can go to be safe. That's your job. Don't push him away because that boy Ben thinks he fits the profile of a murderer. Trust works both ways, you know. How does he know *he* can trust *you*, if you behave like that?'

It was a remarkably long speech for Angie Straw, and even more remarkable in its subject matter – even if she'd jumped to a few inaccurate conclusions. Angie tended to the brisk and the practical. She was seldom given to insightful analyses of human behaviour. The deviation from usual only gave it more impact. Simmy bowed her head and wept.

An hour or so later, she was restored to something more like normality, and had spoken to Christopher on the phone. 'My mother says I'm neglecting you,' she said, with a watery laugh.

'She's right. But I forgive you. What are we going to do about it?'

'I don't know.'

'Let's start again tomorrow. I've had a sandwich and a pint in the Elleray and now I'm going home. Is that okay?'

'That's fine. I love you, Chris. I absolutely do, you know. But I wish you'd told me everything about Jonathan from the start.'

'I know, and I'll always be sorry about it. But I can't see that I had much choice. You'd have splurged it all to Ben – you know you would.'

'Perhaps you're right,' she said, and ended the call feeling considerably better.

Then she drove down to the Harkness house, with a fresh feeling of apprehension. Was Helen going to chastise her for neglecting her suffering daughter? Or would she try to blame Simmy for Ben's latest obsession with violent crime? It was, after all, Simmy who had brought it to his attention, and given him a way into part of the investigation. She could, with some effort, have excluded him completely.

As she walked up the little path to the front door, she met a man coming out. A man she had definitely not expected to see. 'Good Lord, what are you doing here?' she gasped.

'I'm sure you don't really need to ask that question,' said Detective Inspector Moxon. 'Do you?'

'Is it done, then? Have you arrested somebody? Has Ben come up with the answer?'

'Go in and ask him,' smiled the detective. 'It's rather a long story, and I have places I need to be.'

Ben, Bonnie, Natalie and Helen were all in the front room when Simmy went in. Moxon had held the door open for her, so she had no need to knock. Natalie, Tanya's twin sister, looked tear-stained. Bonnie, if Simmy remembered rightly, was not supposed to be there. Helen stood up as Simmy entered the room.

'Thank you for coming,' she said, with a friendly smile. 'Not that I can hope to get a word in until Ben's brought you up to date. I'll give him half an hour, and then you can come and have a coffee with me in the kitchen. Not a minute longer, okay?' She addressed her son, with her usual mixture of admiration and exasperation. 'He's been very clever, I must admit,' she added, as she left the room.

'So? What's happened?'

'It was a conspiracy,' said Bonnie. 'They were all in on it.'

'Even Christopher,' Ben said cautiously. 'Which is why Jonathan phoned him that Sunday. Christopher was the only person he could trust.'

Simmy heard her mother's voice again, prompted by the word *trust*. 'Explain,' she begged. 'You don't mean four or five people all attacked Jonathan and killed him, surely?'

'No. Only one. But they all had reasons to want him dead. They all had grudges against him.'

'But they won't all be arrested for murder,' said Bonnie. 'Not Flo, or Beverley, or Daphne or Valerie.'

'They're all women,' Simmy noticed. 'Probably not strong enough to throttle a fully grown man.'

'Moxon's wildly impressed, you know,' said Ben boastfully. 'They'd never have worked it out without me. Us.' He threw a loving look at Bonnie. 'And Christopher helped a bit as well.'

'Please explain,' Simmy begged. 'Start at the beginning and I promise not to interrupt.'

'The charity. It starts with the charity, okay? They were the victims of their own success, tapping into a rich vein of sentimental old ladies who saw them as deserving recipients of all their accumulated junk. From Carlisle to Lancaster, and all the way over to places like Durham, they advertised as being willing and able – and terribly grateful – depositories of house contents. I found their website, it's sheer genius. They paint a picture of these houses full of a lifetime's collection of *stuff*. And their owner can't cope with it all, has no idea what to do with it. Wants every single item to go to a good home, but however can you manage that? So, they promise to take it, sort it, and sell it to people who'll take good care of it, and the proceeds will all go to rescuing and rehoming unhappy dogs. Simple. Straightforward and a huge relief. The old people don't really want money for their things – they just want the house to stop being so cluttered. They might want to sell it and move to a bungalow or residential home. They think they'll never be able to move if the place is packed full of possessions.'

'Okay. She gets it,' said Bonnie. 'Let's get to the chase.'

'*Cut* to the chase,' Ben corrected her. 'So – CaniCare end up with a warehouse full of all these donations. They deliver it by the vanful to all their shops, which all do remarkably well, because they pile it high and sell it cheap. Everybody pitches in, including Florence Penrose, when she has a moment.'

Simmy's head went up at this. 'How do you know that?'

'Moxon told us just now.'

'Does he know where she is? Is she all right?'

'She didn't go far last night. Stopped at a B&B in Kendal, and then came back here and presented herself at the police station. That's all part of the story, but it might take too long to tell it now. Moxon said to tell you she's sorry she got you worried and she'll phone you tomorrow.'

'So – Jonathan swindled the charity. Have we established that?'

'Not quite. It goes further than that. The charity swindled itself, in effect. Or rather, it swindled the trusting old ladies who gave them all their valuables. The dogs didn't do nearly so well out of it as they ought to have done.'

340

'So?' Simmy's patience was rapidly running out.

'So, Jonathan became a threat to them. He saw what was going on. He probably made use of the stumpwork as a good way of exposing what was going on. He put it on the market to see what happened. It was his way of alerting people to what was going on.'

'And who killed him?' Simmy almost shouted.

'Who do you think?' Ben teased her. 'Isn't it obvious? Hasn't it been obvious since Saturday?'

'Stop it, Ben,' Bonnie chastised him. 'Don't be such a beast.'

'All right,' he conceded. 'You were right. We were all right. It was Scott Penrose. He's had a grudge against Jonathan for a year or more, fuming about needing his expertise, but not trusting him to be honest. He's the area manager – the buck stops with him. But it was all slipping out of his control. Half the volunteers were ripping him – or his charity – off and he was scared everything would unravel. His wife was just as bad. She never liked dogs and hated to see lovely things being sold for a tenth of their value just so some old mutt could have another few months of life. And it was taking Scott away from her when she needed him at home with the baby.'

'She's an artist,' Simmy remembered. 'She'd know the value of a lot of the things.'

'Precisely. But she never connected Scott with the murder – until yesterday.'

'I still think it was very odd for Scott to turn up here the way he did and demand to see me.'

'He wanted to prevent you from getting together with

341

Flo. It worked, didn't it. Now he'll be off somewhere, with twenty-four hours' start on the police. But they'll catch him easily enough.'

'And how much of all this did Christopher know?' Simmy asked the question in a shaky voice, not really wanting to hear the answer.

'All he really did was turn a blind eye to the chain of provenance for some of the things he sold. Jonathan was the main dealer involved, but not the only one. That Rosenthal, for example – it came from an old lady in Kirkby Steven, originally. She gave it to CaniCare, in all innocence, and our friend Nick bagged it. Nick's as bad as Jonathan was – worse, if anything. But they both played by the rules, such as they are. Hardly any of it was actually illegal.'

'But what about the charity? The scandal – the outrage. The loss of reputation.' Simmy's head filled with some of these same emotions. 'Such a terrible betrayal of trust. When people find out, Scott Penrose is going to be lynched.'

'Precisely,' said Ben. 'So, when he thought Jonathan was going to be the cause of all that happening, it's not so surprising that he killed him. He had to keep him quiet. There's nothing so guaranteed to incense old ladies than a charity that doesn't do what it claims.'

'Five minutes,' Bonnie suddenly announced. 'You've got five minutes before Helen wants Simmy.'

'That's it then, is it?' Simmy said. 'Scott Penrose drove into the cul-de-sac in a van, pretending to collect jumble. He knew – but *how*? – that Jonathan would be at the house, went in and strangled him, drove out and left Christopher to find him. But Mr Pruitt? Why was he there as well? I still don't get all of it.'

'Scott simply made an arrangement with Jonathan to meet him at the house. But he didn't expect Jon to call Christopher and ask him to be there as well. And Pruitt – well, he's a nosy parker, possibly suspicious that his wife was up to something with Jonathan and wanting to keep track of what was happening to the Leeson house.'

'Did Moxon tell you all this?'

'Not at all. I told *him* most of it. It's all a matter of following all the evidence and making a coherent picture out of it. Moxon's job is to check all the facts and assemble a case.'

'Hmm,' said Simmy. 'I suppose it will all come clear if I sit down and think about it.'

'It will,' said Ben with a confident grin.

Helen was sitting at the kitchen table with two mugs of coffee in front her. She pushed one at Simmy. 'All done?' she asked.

'I think so. My head's in an awful jumble, but it seems as if the police can take it from here. Ben's remarkably clever, you know.' She sighed. 'He makes me feel hopelessly thick, most of the time.'

'Join the club. Now – Tanya. I just wanted to assure you that I'm not blaming you at all for what happened. She was a fool to cut herself in the first place, and David and I were irresponsible to leave her last night. I'm still shaking at what almost happened. This sepsis business is terrifying – and there's so much of it happening at the moment. She'll be all right, though. The hospital people were fantastic. And when she comes home, she wants to do more work for you. I really just wanted to say, I won't try to stop her. It'd be a nice Saturday job for her, and I'm hoping she'll have learnt how to handle sharp things, from now on.'

'Thanks,' said Simmy, taking a large swig of coffee. Something about the taste made her wince. 'Ugh,' she said, automatically.

'What? Is it too strong?'

'I don't know. It just seems *sickly*. Really odd.'

'Uh-oh,' said Helen, at the same moment as Simmy recalled that same weird sensation, a few years ago when married to Tony Brown. 'Is it what I think it is?'

'It might be,' said Simmy.

When she got home she was delightedly surprised to find the lights on and Christopher's car outside. She ran in, abandoning all thought of questions or debriefings. She found him in the sitting room with a glass of cheap red wine in his hand. 'I couldn't just go back to Keswick without seeing you,' he said.

'You'll have to drink the whole bottle yourself,' she told him. 'I won't be touching alcohol for quite a while.'

'Just as I thought,' he laughed knowingly. 'I think I keep better track of your cycles than you do yourself. So, I bought you this, as a congratulations present.' He bent down and brought a poorly wrapped parcel from beside the sofa.

She tore off the bubble wrap, to reveal the beautiful, delicate piece of antique Rosenthal porcelain.

'It was Ben's idea,' said Christopher.

'It would be,' said Simmy, wiping away a happy tear.

REBECCA TOPE is the author of three bestselling crime series, set in the stunning Cotswolds, Lake District and West Country. She lives on a smallholding in rural Herefordshire, where she enjoys the silence and plants a lot of trees, but also manages to travel the world and enjoy civilisation from time to time. Most of her varied experiences and activities find their way into her books, sooner or later.

*rebeccatope.com*

DON'T MISS SIMMY'S NEXT MYSTERY

# *The Patterdale Plot*

Persimmon 'Simmy' Brown had hoped that her autumn would be less frantic than usual to give her a chance to enjoy her pregnancy, her upcoming nuptials, and some time looking for a new house in the Patterdale area of the Lake District. But it is not to be …

Simmy's ideas of a quiet run-up to Christmas are cruelly dashed when one of the lodgers at her parents' B&B dies in her arms after seemingly being poisoned. It is clear the victim had some connection to a controversial new building project near Patterdale, and Simmy soon becomes embroiled in a complex investigation, headed up by her friend DI Moxon, as the nights grow darker and a killer roams free.

To discover more great books and to
place an order visit our website at
**allisonandbusby.com**

Don't forget to sign up to our free newsletter at
**allisonandbusby.com/newsletter**
for latest releases, events and exclusive offers

**Allison & Busby Books**
**@AllisonandBusby**

You can also call us on
**020 3950 7834**
for orders, queries
and reading recommendations